THE GOURMET
DETECTIVE

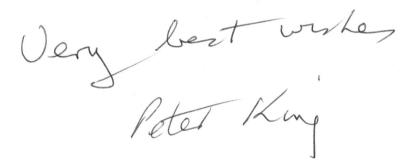

Very best wishes

Peter King

Peter King

THE GOURMET DETECTIVE

a novel

BREESE
BOOKS
LONDON

First published in Great Britain by
Breese Books Ltd
164 Kensington Park Road, London W11 2ER, England

ISBN: 0 947 533 206
First edition 1994

Typeset in 10½/12½pt Bembo
by Ann Buchan (Typesetters), Middlesex.
Printed and bound in Great Britain by
Itchen Printers Ltd., Southampton.

CHAPTER ONE

H e shuffled into my office, his outsize suit hanging loosely on his oversize frame. I recognised the face like a St Bernard with all the troubles of the world on its back, the lugubrious expression, the large sad eyes and the drooping lips. A strange figure but then I see a lot of them in my business.

"You're the one they call 'The Gourmet Detective?' " he asked. His voice was deep with melancholy.

"Says so on the door."

He nodded. "We have an appointment."

We did indeed. He had called the day before and said he wanted to consult me. He had refused to give his name but I knew him the second he walked in the door. I waved him to a chair. He eased his 23 stones or so into it cautiously and with good reason. It creaked in protest, never having been subjected to such a strain.

"You specialise in culinary investigations," he said flatly.

"For some detectives, it's divorce, for others it's missing daughters. Some chase statues of birds while —"

"Birds?" he asked, puzzled.

It was clear he was not a private detective aficionado and I let it pass. "Specialisation is the name of the game today," I told him. "So for me, it's smoked salmon, salsify and Sauterne."

"You come well recommended," he said, looking at me as if he thought it strange that anyone would recommend me.

"By whom?" I asked but it was his turn to let one pass.

"This commission I have for you is —"

"I haven't said I'll accept it yet," I reminded him.

"I think you will," he said, obviously a man used to having his own way. "What are your rates?"

"The latest job offered a thousand pounds on acceptance, a hundred pounds a day plus expenses and a further thousand pounds on completion."

"Who was your client?"

"I can't tell you that."

He moved his bulk fractionally and the chair groaned in agony.

"It would be worth it for Tattersall's to locate a substitute for tamarind in their Tangy Sauce. They sell four and a half million bottles year — nearly 40 per cent of the market for bottled sauces other than ketchup. Your fee would be negligible to maintain such a market share."

"Confidentiality is, of course, something all my clients insist on," I said in that lofty tone employed so effectively by lawyers and abortionists. Inwardly, I was seething. How on earth had he found out about the Tattersall offer? He was right too. The fee would have been negligible — and the truth was that it had been only half of that.

"And it wasn't a substitute for tamarind they wanted." I had to keep talking to take my mind off the painful reality of only getting 50 per cent of what I should have had. "It was an alternate. There are half a dozen different kinds of tamarind but they have been using only one —"

"The wild tamarind from East Africa."

"— which is now being affected by drought so an alternate is vital."

"You did well to find one — but then that is your principal business, I believe."

"Whoever found it did well," I conceded, determined to play out this part of the charade to the bitter end. "But yes, my main business consists of locating rare and exotic foods, advising on substitutes for scarce products, finding alternate sources of ingredients which are difficult — sometimes nearly impossible — to obtain. I help people with unusual foods to find outlets for them."

We eyed each other for a long moment. I couldn't tell from his mournful expression whether he was thinking about ethics, food or money. Perhaps all three, he certainly took long enough.

Then he said, "It must have been you who tracked down those six bottles of Château Yquem, Premier Cru Superieur. I heard the client wanted them forty years old."

"Not an easy assignment. Somebody did well again — that

man really knew his business."

He nodded his massive head. "Phillipe at the Grand crowed about that for days. He considered it quite a coup."

So he should have. It was quite a coup for him — less so for me. I didn't make much money out of that job. Those confounded bottles were much harder to find than I had expected.

He considered me carefully. "You know who I am, I suppose?" He didn't say it with any condescension. He just wanted to clarify the point.

"Yes. You're Raymond Lefebvre. Your restaurant, Raymond's, is one of the top ten in London —"

That brought the first real reaction I had had from him. He leaned forward and the chair screeched. He wagged a finger like a banana at me.

"Top three!"

"And maybe one of the top twenty in Europe."

"Top six! And no maybe!"

This man's reputation was considerable. I had seen his face in magazines and on television though he did not court publicity as avidly as did so many in his profession. He had been known to say that he preferred to let his food speak for itself. Bocuse and Guerard might do it differently but Raymond was a respected figure among his peers despite his rather aloof and isolated attitude.

I knew also of his earlier days — long, hard years in Paris learning the trade, turning his hand to everything that now contributed to his status. His accent was almost unnoticeable for he had been in Britain many years. Now here he was in my tiny office — what could he possibly want me to do for him? He was a top-flight restaurateur and I was a second-rate private eye (top half dozen though — well, among the specialists anyway).

His next question took me completely unawares.

"Do you carry a gun?"

"A gun!" I yelped. It probably came out as a yelp anyway and it must have ended at a note approaching high C. I coughed to conceal it but couldn't help blurting it out again. "A gun!"

The faintest twinkle of amusement flickered across his face.

"Not an unusual question to ask a private detective surely?"

I struggled to regain my voice. "I have already explained my activities — although you seem to know plenty about them. So why would I need a gun to help find a European equivalent of Birds' Nest Soup or help the Australians to market kangaroo livers."

He looked appalled. "Kangaroo livers! You're not serious!"

I was pleased to learn I knew something he didn't. "Why should ducks and geese have the only tasty livers?"

He studied me, not sure what to make of this. Was I pulling his leg? he was wondering. I wasn't but I let him wonder.

"We can talk about this some other time," he said dismissively.

I wasn't going to hold my breath. The day a French chef contemplates serving kangaroo livers in his restaurant will be the day Colonel Sanders studs his chickens with truffles.

"Very well," I agreed. "What shall we talk about today?"

"This is confidential —" he began.

"I thought I had already made it clear that —"

"I know you did but my business could be severely affected if one word of this leaks out."

"So could mine."

Still he hesitated then he plunged in.

"You know Le Trouquet d'Or?"

"Of course," I nodded.

Who didn't? If Raymond said his restaurant was one of the top three in London then Le Trouquet d'Or was one of the other two. It was run by another displaced Frenchman, François Duquesne who had earned three Michelin stars before he was 30 years old and was renowned for his elegance and originality.

Another thing came into my mind. There was bitter rivalry between Raymond and François. Not quite as desperate as between the Hatfields and the McCoys or between Robin Hood and the Sheriff of Nottingham but certainly more intense than that between Maceys and Gimbels. Of course, all top chefs are wary of each other, all striving to outdo, out-think and out-cook the others but there was more to it as far as Raymond and François were concerned.

Some said it was an old feud, dating perhaps to teenage days although comparisons of their biographies did not suggest that this was likely. The romantics said that there had been a quarrel over a woman but then romantics always said that. No one knew for sure and speculation was rife — but what did all this mean now? Like a simmering sauce, the plot was beginning to thicken. I tried not to look too eager but I was hanging on every word.

"At Le Trouquet d'Or, they serve a dish called Oiseau Royal," said Raymond.

"I've heard of it," I admitted. "It's the speciality of the restaurant. When Prime Minister Kom was here from Singapore, it was the one dish he wanted to eat. A well-known Australian critic was reported as saying that it was the best meal he had in London during his recent trip and —"

"Yes, yes," said Raymond testily. "That's the one. I want you to find out exactly how it's prepared."

So that was why he was here. I was surprised. With his reputation as a chef, why did he want to know how a rival prepared a dish? Perhaps the breach between them was reason enough in itself. Or was there more? He saw the uncertainty cross my face.

"Oiseau Royal isn't just another meal. It's a classic of cuisine — oh, yes, I admit it. I must know exactly how it's prepared."

I said cautiously, "As long as we agree that's what I'm doing. If I accept this job, what I give you will be a distillation of observation, investigation and deduction. There will be nothing illegal or underhanded. I want to make it clear that I am not a thief or a spy."

"Of course."

Did he acquiesce just a little too readily?

"I wouldn't want it any other way," he assured me.

I wanted to believe him and I thought I did but then I had been wrong on previous occasions when I had believed people. In any case, it was a good opportunity to put on a little pressure.

"It has been said that Oiseau Royal is more of a secret than Coca Cola," I told him.

"Pfft . . ." he puffed out in a typically Gallic dismissal, packed with scorn. "How long will it take you?"

The clever so-and-so. If I said too long a time, I would

sound inefficient. If I said too short a time, I would be cutting down on my fee. I had no choice but to be honest.

"Not more than a week."

He nodded. "I'll write you a cheque for a thousand pounds. Another thousand on completion. A hundred pounds a day fee plus expenses."

How could I say no? "I'll have a contract made out and —"

"No," he said quickly. "Nothing in writing." He pulled out his cheque book and scribbled, handing me a very handsome piece of paper.

I reached for it then stopped. "Just one thing . . ."

"What is it?"

"When you say 'completion' . . . let's decide what that means precisely."

"I mean that you will tell me everything I need to know in order that I am able to produce the same dish."

"Who's to decide if it's the same?"

"It must appear and taste the same to any discerning diner."

Still I hesitated. He eased back in his chair and shrugged. The chair shrugged too in its own creaky way. "After all," he continued, "you are a gourmet detective and I am a gourmet restaurateur. Surely two such men can agree on such a point?"

It sounded reasonable and it was evidently the only assurance I was going to get.

"All right. How do I get in touch with you?"

He took out a card. "Here is the restaurant number."

"What if you're not there?"

He looked at me in astonishment. "I'm always there."

I should have known. Then another thought occurred to me.

"I'll need to eat at Le Trouquet d'Or and I'll have to taste Oiseau Royal." I hadn't fully decided whether I had to or not but it was not an opportunity I intended to forego. "The last I heard, the place was booked up a month in advance. How am I going to get a table?"

He "pfft'd" again, derisively this time. "When they say a month, they probably mean ten days. Still . . ." he pondered a moment then he said, "There's a New York man, a millionaire who has a lot of people visiting London for his business. He always advises these people to eat at either my restaurant or at

Le Trouquet d'Or. Just say that Mr Winchester told you to ask for a table — they'll fit you in."

"Winchester? *THE* Harold Winchester?"

"This too will be kept confidential," he admonished. He began manoeuvring himself out of the chair which sighed in woody relief. "I'll expect to hear from you in a week," he said.

"You will."

I escorted him to the door, watched him out and went back to my desk where I took another look at the cheque. It looked just fine.

As it was now late afternoon, the banks would be closed. Depositing the cheque would have to wait until tomorrow. Even as I fingered the cheque, enjoying its nice valuable feel, a few niggling doubts lingered.

Why had Raymond come in person? Wasn't this the kind of mission he would delegate to a subordinate? A chef of his reputation would surely not want to have his name associated with the lifting of a recipe from a rival restaurant — even if it was done without any illegal or unethical actions. He had checked me out carefully — there was no question of that. Only someone with a lot of excellent contacts in the trade could have found out about Tattersall's and the Château Yquem that had gone to the Ritz. Still, he was taking a risk and an unnecessary one at that.

Aside from that — could I do it? Could I learn the closely kept secret of Oiseau Royal and enable Raymond to duplicate it? I was less concerned about that. It was a challenge but I was sure I could do it. The time was not a problem either. If the secret could be learned at all, it could be learned within a week.

As for the money — well, that would be extremely welcome. Business hadn't been overactive lately. I had had a period when things were fairly brisk but clients aren't notoriously swift in paying bills for the kind of services I provide. I had been preparing for a lean month or two — this fee would tide me over very handsomely.

It was the final thought that was disturbing and it wasn't one I wanted to dwell on . . . but why had Raymond asked me if I carried a gun?

CHAPTER TWO

The next day was Wednesday. I was in the office early after a light breakfast of fresh-squeezed Martinique grapefruit juice, curried eggs with Virginia ham, toasted rye bread and Cuban coffee. Arriving at the office early is no problem for me. The office is near Hammersmith Bridge and I have only a five minute walk from my flat in Shepherd's Bush. I detest cars and refuse to own one. I find them virtually useless in today's London with its streams of barely moving traffic, its agonies and aggravations, the high cost of petrol and the even higher cost of parking. The Tube gets me around most of the time and when I am on a case, expenses cover taxis. Getting to the office is my first exercise of the day.

I worked until 9.30 then walked up to King Street to deposit Raymond's cheque in the bank. I returned feeling reasonably affluent. About the case itself I was still mildly uneasy but couldn't think of anything I could do about it.

My office is small — some would describe it as miniscule. A desk and a swivel chair plus another chair for visitors (I had examined it and there seemed to be no permanent damage resulting from Raymond's brief if punishing occupancy), a wall of file cabinets (each in a different style and none matching) — and nothing else. Certainly nothing personal — I'm a private person as well as a private eye. In my flat, I have a silhouette drawing of Sherlock Holmes' profile, a lithograph of Allan Pinkerton and a photograph of Auguste Escoffier and have contemplated putting them on the wall of the office. But I've never done so — keep clients guessing, I'd decided.

The day's work was clear-cut. Take care of as much of the correspondence as possible then review all of the jobs in hand and establish which I could wrap up quickly and which could be put on hold. I intended to spend as much of every day as I could on Raymond's assignment so that I could meet the week's deadline I had set.

The first letter I opened had been a beauty. I get a lot of correspondence now that I am becoming known as a gourmet detective. Some of it is crazy, some even bizarre. A few requests are preposterous while others are impossible. There are still the few that are intriguing and this first letter was one of those.

"We are a U.K. company," it began, "small but ambitious. We have had modest success in bringing to the British market such products as mangoes, saffron, girolles and wakame.

"We are now embarking on a programme to put snails on to restaurant menus and wish to start with some in London.

"Can you help us? We would welcome a proposal from you and an outline of your terms and conditions."

The letter touched on a subject that was dear to my heart because I had often pondered over the mystery of why the French should eat snails when the British don't. I know the French eat some foods that are strange to the British palate but in defence of our island race, we are much less prejudiced against foreign foods than was the case just a few decades ago. Frogs' legs are no longer considered to be unusual on a British menu. Salami, pasta, olives, garlic, sweetbreads, bamboo shoots . . . The list of the foods we now accept was lengthy and growing.

So why not snails? We used to eat them. The Romans introduced the edible snail on to the South Downs and the Cornish coast where they thrived. Working people ate them and loved them right up to the turn of the last century.

The French, on the other hand, haven't always liked them. In the 14th century, snails were only for the very rich but in Rabelais' day, everybody consumed them. In the 18th century, they were regarded as food for the peasants only but they came back into favour when the Czar of Russia was served snails at a banquet held in his honour at Versailles. During the famine that followed Napoleon's downfall, snails were greatly prized as of course was anything eatable but in the case of snails, being reasonably available, they regained their popularity and it has not waned in France to this day.

Snails are not difficult to raise and they live as long as five years. They lay a hundred eggs at a time and these hatch out in four weeks. Plenty of opportunity here for raising them and I could see why my correspondents were enthusiastic about the business possibilities.

Could I help them? It would require a great deal of careful thought but it was certainly a project I would enjoy. Besides, an amount of tasting would be essential. I put the letter under the red paperweight — meaning highest priority.

Next was a letter from the Wine Advisory Panel of which I am a member. It gave the date of the next meeting and stated that the subject would be "Sparkling Wine — its Future".

This was a meeting I would have to attend. Some of the burning questions in the wine business would be at the heart of the debate. Questions such as "How can sparkling wines take more of the champagne market?" and "Are there sparkling wines as good as champagne?" and "Can sparkling wines be made as good as champagne?"

Champagne producers are adamant in affirming that sparkling wines don't taste like champagne and never will but the issue gets complicated after that. Most of the champagne houses have huge financial investments in areas producing sparkling wines. Could they therefore not make sparkling wines close to champagne quality if they wished? Or do they want to suppress the quality level of sparkling wines and thus protect their primary market of champagne?

It would be a great meeting with all kinds of accusations and criticisms being hurled around. Invective and insult would fill the air, personal feelings and professional reputations would be bruised and a wonderful time would be had by all. The atmosphere of bonhomie, camaraderie and knives in the back would be greatly aided by a liberal flow of wine supplied by the more generous (or cunning) vineyards. Would it be champagne or sparkling wine on this occasion? Certainly not both — neither party would want to allow direct comparisons to be made. What a terrific evening!

The next letter was from a metallurgist who said he was writing a book on cobalt. He knew all about its use as an alloying element and in cutting tools but he wanted his book to be complete. Did cobalt have any effect on the human body?

What foods was it in? Should we avoid it or eat more of it?

Much is known about many metals and their significance in food. Aluminium, magnesium, selenium, lead, copper, zinc, manganese, sodium, potassium and the notorious mercury have been documented in recent years and research continues. Cobalt was a new one to me and one I should have to investigate. In my line of work, it is just as necessary to know which food ingredients are dangerous or even harmful and I made a note to start checking on cobalt.

Would I endorse a new health food diet? asked the next one. That was easy — no, I wouldn't. Another was a plaintive request from a hotel in the Lake District. A guest was suing them for inefficient service during a stay. Did they have any defence? Probably not, was my immediate answer but it was a matter for a lawyer, not a private eye. I made a note.

I plodded on, wading my way through the reasonable and the ridiculous. At 10.45, I took a folder up to the next floor of the building where the Shearer Secretarial Agency is located. They type all my letters and I brought them some to be working on. The truth is that I have a refrigerator and a cupboard — but they are both in Mrs Shearer's premises — my theory being that if they were in mine, I might be tempted too often. So I keep them up there and make a schedule of taking up a folder of work twice a day, mid-morning and mid-afternoon. At the same time, I permit myself a refresher or a pick-me-up or whatever euphemism seems appropriate at the time.

Mrs Shearer, short, beaming, bustling — runs her place like a cross between a convent and a sweat-shop. She looks after her girls but she makes them work. I looked at them now, about thirty of them, fingers flashing over keyboards, the only sounds the rustle of paper and the whirr of electronic equipment. Mrs Shearer told me that Theresa, who usually does my typing, was out with the flu but a new girl, Mary Chen would do it. Mrs Shearer pointed across the big room to an attractive Oriental girl with lustrous black hair.

I said I would have another batch of work this afternoon and then got myself a half bottle of Asti Spumante from the fridge. I drank it looking down on the hordes of traffic battling for position to go around Hammersmith Broadway so that they could gain a few seconds before entering the next traffic jam. It was a bit like a Roman chariot race but at greatly reduced speed and no prizes except survival.

The remainder of the morning was notable only for a phone call from Norman, an old friend who now ran an Italian restaurant. Norman is from Barnsley and has been having a love affair with Italy and all things Italian since he was a boy. When the growing-up process encompassed food, Norman became so passionately fond of Italian cooking that he set as his life's ambition the establishment of the best Italian restaurant in Britain. He hasn't reached that peak yet but he is making good progress despite the fact that his chef and all his waiters are English. There is, in fact, nothing at all Italian about Norman's restaurant except its name and the food. It is Norman's chutzpah which is carrying it through on a wave of boundless enthusiasm and determination.

Norman said he had some Italian customers who had been asking for Orzo e Fagioli, a hearty bean-and-barley soup, popular in the north of Italy. They had enjoyed it but told him that it wasn't exactly the way they remembered it. He had tried various ways but just couldn't get it right — at least not the way it presumably tasted in Bologna. We discussed it for a while then I put my finger on it. "A prosciutto bone," I told him. "You have to cook the soup with a prosciutto bone to develop the full flavour." He thanked me and promised me the best Italian meal in Britain. I asked where he wanted to take me but hung up before he could summon any Northern vituperation.

At 11.30, I phoned Le Trouquet d'Or. A French accent was already informing me politely that I was wasting my time asking for a reservation when I dropped the magic name of Winchester. Raymond was right. The voice immediately became subservient and I was informed that they would look forward to seeing me tomorrow evening. I had made the reservation for two people, not wishing to give any cause for suspicion. Who would I take? I occasionally take Theresa when I need a companion for professional purposes. A man alone could arouse some suspicion. I had forgotten she had the flu . . . well, it was nearly lunch-time and I would have to tackle the problem later.

The question of where to go for lunch is always made simpler when I know what I am going to do in the evening. Today I knew so I caught a number 391 bus to Kew where I had a modest but very satisfying lunch at a bistro near the railway station.

I don't doubt that there is a school of thought which preaches a) never eat in Kew, b) never eat near a railway station and c) avoid any restaurant called a bistro. All of this proves that schools of thought can be wrong and generalisations should be avoided. There are many excellent small and unsung establishments which may never get into any of the guides but serve delicious, well-cooked and inexpensive lunches. I had mussel soup and then rack of lamb with roast potatoes and haricots verts. Andrew and Paula don't sound — or look — like chefs but they produce a superb meal. I usually skip dessert at lunch-time so after a cup of coffee and a complimentary cognac which I couldn't turn down, I went back to work.

The afternoon was much the same as the morning, ploughing through invitations to events I didn't want to attend, foods I didn't want to sponsor, wine tastings promoted by vineyards who made wine I wouldn't brush my teeth with and people asking me questions when I knew I wouldn't get paid for the answers.

Taking the afternoon folder up to Mrs Shearer reminded me that I didn't have a companion for the dinner at Le Trouquet d'Or. Would Theresa be recovered from her flu? I asked. No, not a chance was the reply. Mary Chen was proving to be very efficient though — was there something she could do? I decided not. The meal tomorrow must be low profile and Mary Chen was too noticeable.

I phoned Lucy who works in the cheese department at Fortnum and Mason's. No, they told me, Lucy was in Savoie. It was a good place to buy cheese but of no help to me. I was tempted to try Margaret at the British Tour Centre but the last time I had invited her to dine had been when I was on a case too. (I give out invitations more often when an expense account is operative.) Margaret had declined on that occasion, giving as her reason that it was her yoga night. I recovered my speech in due course and reminded her that this was dinner at a good restaurant and not at the corner hamburger place. Again she declined and I have still not determined whether I should strike her off my list permanently. A girl with no sense of priority is highly suspect.

Still pondering the problem, I walked home. My flat consists essentially of a very well-equipped kitchen, a large storage area (part of it refrigerated) and a room full of books. There's a bedroom, a bathroom and so on tucked away there somewhere.

I drank a leisurely Pisco Sour while assembling the ingredients for dinner. Then I cooked a langoustine soufflé with some fresh asparagus and ate it along with a bottle of Berncastler Doktor. I sliced some Packham pears, heated them and poured malvasia over them. A cup of Paraguayan maté completed the repast and after thirty minutes to fully digest, I set off for a meeting.

P.I.E. meet twice a month in a room off Horseferry Road. It used to belong to the Ministry of the Environment and one of our members got it for us at a very low fee. When the Ministry moved out to Haywards Heath (to a better environment presumably), some bureaucratic oversight left it available for us to use. Consequently we haven't paid anything for about a year. One day I expect we will get a bill which we will refuse to pay.

The initials P.I.E. confuse everybody and those who know me as a gourmet detective automatically assume that at the P.I.E. we make good culinary use of apples, rhubarb, blackcurrants and probably steaks and kidneys. They are quite mistaken.

Private Investigators Etc is a club which was originally established as a sort of union where private eyes could protect their rights, put together rules for their profession and get together periodically for some socialising and shop talk. Eventually membership declined, not because there were less private eyes, there were in fact more, but because the newcomers were not individuals but organisations which felt they didn't need the umbrella of P.I.E.

To keep our group active, we opened membership to non-detectives as long as they had some connection. As a result, we now had two book editors, both specialising in crime fiction; a historical novelist who had been trying for a year to write a private eye novel; an engineer who worked for an electronics company making sophisticated gear for surveillance, eavesdropping and such; a girl who worked in a forensic laboratory, was a private eye devotee and had, a few weeks ago, shown a video of a Quincy episode from television and had accompanied it with some well-informed comments on TV versus reality in forensic medicine. Most of the others had some tenuous connection but were basically PI fans.

I said hello to Tom Davidson. He is a marine insurance investigator who lost his job because of excessive drinking, joined AA and recovered both his self-respect and his job.

"How's business?" I asked him.

"Ships keep sinking," he told me.

"Enough of them under suspicious circumstances to keep the wolf from the door?"

"Just enough. How about you? Still finding the impossible spice, the missing flavour?"

"Always on the trail of the lonesome vine," I assured him but further conversation was curtailed as we were joined by Miss Wellworthy, a prim, elderly spinster who fancies herself as a Miss Marple and drops repeated hints about a conspiracy at her local town hall which she is determined to uncover.

"Any progress in the investigation, Miss Wellworthy?" Tom asked mischievously.

"They're very clever, you know." Her steel-rimmed glasses glinted and it was woe betide any conspirators. "There's nothing in the files. Oh yes, they're clever. The annual reports don't show anything either."

"It's understandable they wouldn't want anything to appear in one or the other," Tom agreed. "What's your next move?"

"I shall have to interview that girl who resigned last August," said Miss Wellworthy grimly. "Trouble is, I think she went to Cornwall."

"Knows something, does she?"

"Why else would she resign?" demanded Miss Wellworthy but Tom and I were saved from having to answer by the rapping of Ben Beaumont's gavel summoning us to take our places.

One of the reasons I had stayed on as a member of P.I.E. after it had thrown open its membership to non-detectives was that it gave an equal amount of time to the private eyes of fiction — one of my weaknesses. I had over three hundred novels featuring all the great eyes of fiction and I loved discussing them. Tonight, I could see from the blackboard that we were going to have a talk on "The Female Eye". With some surprise, I noted that it was to be given by Francine Drew. Francine was in her thirties and personal assistant to a famous crime novelist. Francine was not unattractive and could be a dazzler if she would wear make-up, dress properly and have her hair fixed. She was her usual mousy self tonight though as she stepped up on to the platform. I awaited the outcome with curiosity as public speaking didn't seem to be one of her attributes.

Ben Beaumont introduced her. Ben is our genial president — at least he would have enjoyed hearing himself described that way. He had served thirty years in the regular police force, retired and then conducted a successful private investigation service before retiring again.

Red-faced, beaming, Ben completed his introduction and waved to Francine to take over. We gave her a polite handclap of welcome and she looked as if she needed encouragement for she was a little nervous and flustered at first. She got herself under control though and launched into her subject.

"Private eye novels have been dominated by men for too long. The expression 'private eye' means to most readers Sam Spade or Philip Marlowe, Lew Archer or Mike Hammer.

"The balance is now being adjusted and we are seeing female private eyes. Tonight, I want to talk about two of them — and both created by women writers."

I leaned forward eagerly, anxious to hear who she would choose.

She continued, still slightly breathless but enjoying herself.

She chose Kinsey Millhone, a double divorcee from California who drives a VW, carries an automatic and lives in a converted garage. The creation of Sue Grafton, the daughter of two China missionaries, Kinsey Millhone was tough, female and believable. Her other choice was V.I. Warshawski, a former insurance investigator who now has an office in Chicago's Loop, is skilled with a variety of weapons and is an expert at unarmed combat. Her creator, Sara Paretsky, is a Ph.D.

Francine talked for about fifteen minutes, got a nice round of applause and a couple of complimentary comments. I followed her over to the drinks dispenser where she was sipping thirstily at a lemon tea.

"That was great, Francine," I told her.

Her face lit up. "Did you really think so?"

"I did. If I'd had to guess who you were going to talk about though — I think I'd have said Sharon McCone."

"Yes, she was one of the first, wasn't she? Did you know she's part Indian?"

"Shoshone, I think."

She made a wry face. "I might have known you'd know that. But then you're a surprising person."

This was the first time we'd talked and I raised an eyebrow. "Surprising?"

"Well, yes. I mean, you're a real private eye and yet you know all the fictional detectives."

I basked a little. After all, a detector of rare spices and a hunter for exotic foods doesn't always get the credit he deserves.

"One's a business and the other's a hobby."

"Yes," she said, "but it's unusual when they are both on the same lines."

"You ought to give another one of these talks," I suggested. "This time, tell us about the sexy female private eyes."

"Such as?" she asked, open-mouthed.

"How about Honey West, Angela Harpe and Alison B. Gordon?"

She didn't answer.

"Have you read them?" I asked her.

She nodded.

"So how about a talk on them?"

She sipped reflectively at her tea.

"I suppose because they're too much sex and not enough detective."

"A good enough reason."

"What do you like about Sharon McCone?" she asked.

"Marcia Muller is one of my favourite writers. She has created a very credible female eye in Sharon McCone. She stays on the right side of the law and co-operates with the police."

Francine smiled. It did a lot for her.

"That's the way you operate, isn't it?"

She must have been listening to club gossip. Her mention of operating gave me a sudden flash of inspiration.

"Are you doing anything tomorrow night?"

The change of subject took her unawares. She stared at me then she coloured slightly. You don't see many girls do that these days.

"Nothing special." She could hardly have said she was having her hair done.

"How about having dinner with me?"

Her eyes widened.

"I'm on a case," I told her. "I have to do some investigating. It involves having dinner at a restaurant — two people." I watched the expressions cross her face and wasn't sure whether my approach was too personal or not personal enough. I plunged on, regardless of perhaps making it worse.

"I need a female opinion. I think you could provide it."

She looked pleased. "You mean I could help with your investigation?"

I put on my best Jim Rockford look (which nobody recognises).

"Nothing dangerous," I assured her.

"All right." She nodded eagerly. "It sounds exciting."

We made arrangements for me to pick her up at her flat in Chiswick and then Ben Beaumont was calling us back to our seats as we were about to hear a review of a new book by Max Byrd. His first novel *California Thriller* was set in San Francisco and won an award as the best PI book of the year. The review was to be given by Ray Anderson who had retired last year as a PI himself. Some thought he had done so just in time for Ray was apt to cut corners and take risks. If he had been caught, it could have been bad for our profession . . .

Was I becoming too prissy? I wondered. Ray hadn't been caught and now he was likely to be our next president. While I was being introspective, I might as well reflect on whether I should have invited Francine to Le Trouquet d'Or. She sounded like a bit of a women's libber. There had been that opening sentence, "Private eye novels have been dominated by men for too long . . ." Why pick on private eyes? Where were the female Hopalong Cassidies and Shanes? Then there was her reaction to my comment about the sexy female eyes . . .

That lead to thoughts of Le Trouquet d'Or. Surely she wouldn't show up looking like this? I'd probably put my foot in it if I made any suggestions . . . how diplomatic could I be, I wondered.

As we walked back to our chairs, I asked, "Are you sure eight o'clock isn't too early to pick you up tomorrow?"

"Oh, no, it's fine."

I didn't like the sound of that.

"It's a fairly fancy restaurant so I'm sure you'll need plenty of time to get ready."

When it was out, it sounded untactful but she didn't react as if it were.

"No, that's plenty of time, really."

I hoped she meant she was going to leave work early.

CHAPTER THREE

My investigation began in earnest the next morning even as the first rosy fingers of dawn began to creep across the sky. At least, I suppose dawn's rosy fingers were creeping — there was certainly no way of knowing what might be happening above the heavy grey clouds which were tipping down periodic showers of cold and very wet rain.

Good weather for an investigation though — people are more occupied trying to keep warm and dry to notice anything out of the ordinary. Not that I expected much suspicion. I looked the part — I wore my second shabbiest suit, a sort of faded off-blue serge and a greasy peaked cap from which the identifying badge had long since been removed.

I might have been anything from a water board inspector to a taxi rank starter as I took the tube to Covent Garden Station then walked down James Street, turned and walked until I came to Le Trouquet d'Or. It was silent in the still early hours. I went on past till I came to the alley that passed along the back of the restaurant. From there, I picked out a coffee shop on a corner which gave a perfect view of the restaurant's rear exit.

I took a table by the window and ordered a cup of coffee from a big amiable girl with "Amy" embroidered in black on her white blouse. She would normally have been wearing a wide smile but what could you expect this early in the morning on a cold wet London day?

Across the room, two students were deep in a discussion of a music score and a bus driver was drinking tea and eating a jam doughnut. It was evidently too early for serious breakfast customers. I settled in for a long vigil.

Soon after nine o'clock, a van stopped at the back door of Le Trouquet d'Or. I had already slipped the plastic sheath off my clip board and I began making notes. Two more vans came within the hour and I kept scribbling. There were deliveries of bottles of milk and cream, boxes of butter and cheese, cases of eggs . . . I wrote down all the identification on the vans and noted every little thing I saw. Then an unmarked green van turned into the alley. I waved to Amy, put the right coins on the table and hurried out.

I timed it so that I was walking by when the driver pulled open the van door and it almost hit me. He apologised, I examined myself for non-existent injuries and we chatted for a minute or two. I offered to help but he declined and I stood by the van while he carried in his first load. I had plenty of opportunity to examine the consignment notes on the other crates.

After half an hour in the alley and by the street corner, I went back into the coffee shop. It was a little busier and the smell of bacon filled the unventilated interior.

"Our coffee must be good, huh?" asked Amy. "You back for more."

"Best I ever tasted," I told her and she laughed till she quivered.

An hour went by. It was boring but as Dashiell Hammett must once have said, most detective work is spade work. Amy came over with more coffee. She eyed my clip board as she poured.

"You one of these health food inspectors?" she asked.

"Don't worry," I told her. "The secrets of your kitchen are safe with me."

She looked curiously at my clip board again. I went on, "As a matter of fact, I'm with the Sewage Board."

She took an involuntary half step back.

"No need for concern. I haven't been down today," I said, "there's a blockage somewhere in this district and we're trying to trace it. When our equipment shows us where it is, we'll have to go and open it up but we can't seem to find it. So I just have to wait."

It satisfied her. "Hope it ain't on this street," she said and her nose wrinkled in unpleasant anticipation.

"I don't think so. Probably nearer to the Opera House."

"Hope it don't turn their singing sour," Amy giggled and I went on with my watch, my credentials established.

By noon, there had been no more deliveries. Le Trouquet

d'Or would be opening for lunch and there would be no accepting of goods so I could get out of here and get something to eat.

"The lamb chops is good today," Amy called out as she saw me head for the door.

"My favourite lunch but unfortunately I have to call regional headquarters," I said.

Inside the complex of shops, stalls and boutiques that make up the new Covent Garden is a health food shop run by an old friend, Tony Livesey. The term "health food" puts a lot of people off. They think that in order to be healthy, food must be boring and Tony has devoted the recent years of his life to disproving this. Natural materials only are used, the cooking is imaginative and original and the place is self-sufficient, baking its own bread, savouries and cakes and making every dish daily from fresh ingredients.

Tony brought me his Armenian Soup which has the unlikely combination of lentils, apricots and potatoes and then moussaka made from soya protein instead of minced meat. The elderflower wine which Tony's wife makes was a perfect accompaniment and I walked back to my beat refreshed.

I hung around in the street and the alley for a while. The rain had stopped and there was an occasional glimpse of clear sky but the clouds hastily covered each one over as quickly as it appeared.

Amy had finished her shift and her place had been taken by a skinny Scottish girl with long, bright red hair who slopped some of the coffee into my saucer as she poured. Still, I didn't have to explain what I was doing there. I sat in tedium through the rest of the afternoon, broken by only one delivery which I duly noted down. Then I rode the tube back to Shepherd's Bush, reading my notes and starting to piece things together.

CHAPTER FOUR

It was close to nine o'clock that evening when our taxi pulled up in front of the restaurant that had been the subject of my attention all day. This time, however, I was at the front door.

Maiden Lane had been blocked by an accident involving a car and a motor-cycle which had forced our driver to make a detour. Then opening night at the Theatre Royal, Drury Lane was evidently coinciding and the street was filled with pop-eyed fans, popping flash-bulbs and pop-stars so that our cursing driver had to inch his way through the crowd. A thinner-skinned breed would have perished from the looks he received and the names he was called.

The name of Winchester worked like a charm and we entered the Aladdin's Cave of cuisine. It was elegant but discreet. The subdued lighting sparkled on the silver cutlery, the gleaming white and blue dishes and the pristine white table cloths. The panelled walls were mellow and the atmosphere refined yet welcoming. The hum of conversation was polite without being restrained and the waiters moved smoothly and competently between the tables.

I had breathed a sigh of relief on seeing Francine. Whether deliberate or note, she had erred on the side of underdressing rather than overdressing and wore a light beige two-piece suit. Her hair was piled neatly and she even wore a hint of make-up.

"Thank you," she said demurely when I congratulated her on her appearance. After glancing at the menu she said, "I think I'll let you order for me."

I was still studying the menu when I heard her gasp. I looked up to see her eyes widening as she stared over my shoulder.

She was looking at all the tables in turn, celebrity spotting.

"I think that's somebody in the government," she said finally, "but I don't know his name."

"In that case, he isn't very important."

"This is a very nice restaurant, isn't it?" she commented. "Do you come here often?"

"No, not often."

"You said you were on a case."

"That's right, I am."

"You aren't body-guarding one of these people, are you?"

"Nothing like that," I told her. She waited for more but I didn't give her any more. She resumed celebrity spotting and I went back to the menu.

I chose the cucumber and sorrel soup to start. It would leave my palate unsullied. That way, I would be able to analyse the taste of the main course more fully — the main course being, naturally, Oiseau Royal. The name came off my tongue as if I had just decided on it and the waiter wrote it down without the flicker of an eye. Why shouldn't he? There was no reason for suspicion and people ordered the speciality every day.

The sommelier suggested two or three possibilities as the most appropriate wine to accompany the bird and I selected a Coche-Dury Montrachet. I preferred to stay with the same wine throughout the meal — again for reasons of being able to taste the oiseau better.

"You have a nice job — to be able to come to places like this," Francine said.

"Doesn't happen too often unfortunately."

"It must be exciting though," she went on, still fishing. "I mean, being a real private eye."

"Some of the time," I admitted. "A lot of it is just plain dull."

I was scanning the room while I was talking, looking for all the doors and establishing where they led. I counted the waiters and estimated the times of their movements in and out of the room.

"You said this case isn't dangerous," Francine said abruptly.

"What? Oh, no, it isn't."

"You look nervous."

"Of course not. Just tense. Always am when I'm on a case."

I hoped she wasn't going to ask me if I carried a gun. I still hadn't recovered from Raymond asking that. The difference was that Francine's question would be casual whereas I couldn't get rid of the thought that Raymond hadn't told me everything.

She didn't ask that — instead she said, "You're shadowing somebody, aren't you?"

Perhaps it had been a mistake to bring her after all. Surely I could have found a girl who wasn't a private-eye fan and wouldn't keep asking these questions.

"Nothing like that. Just a matter of observation" I said and she was assembling another query when the soup arrived.

It was superb, light and yet full of flavour. I gave it my full attention then as the plates were removed, I could see Francine shaping up for more inquisition so I moved in to circumvent it.

"You're probably a Travis McGee fan."

"I do like him, yes."

"Nearly everybody does. My theory is that it's partly envy of him living on a boat."

"He's a good detective too."

"He is."

"Although he's not really a private eye — he's a marine salvage expert."

"Very good. Not every reader of detective fiction realises that."

"He's also one of the few current detectives they haven't made films about — I'm glad too — it's often disappointing when they do. I mean, I don't think Paul Newman looks like Lew Archer, do you?"

"I think writers are smarter when they hardly describe their heroes at all. Let the reader imagine them, I say . . ."

The diversionary ploy worked and we discussed private eyes until the main course arrived. Then all conversation stopped and I concentrated every sense I had on Oiseau Royal. It was so delicious I kept forgetting I was on a case and found that I was enjoying myself to a degree that I had not experienced for a long time. When Raymond had described it as "a classic of cuisine", he had not been exaggerating and it was no surprise that every food writer and gourmet who came to London wanted to taste it.

"Good, isn't it?" said Francine. I nodded.

The flesh was moist and delicate yet bursting with flavour.

The sauce was tangy but did not mask the taste of the bird. It was one of those sauces which brings several flavourings to mind but they are so cunningly blended that the mind rejects each one of them as contributive.

"What is it?" Francine asked. "It's a bit like turkey."

I hid a shudder. "They call it 'Oiseau Royal', " I told her. "It's the speciality of the house."

"It's nice — you say it's not turkey?"

I shook my head, trying not to let her question affect the succulent mouthful I was relishing.

"What is it then?" she persisted.

"They don't say. Just call it 'Oiseau Royal'."

"But you're the Gourmet Detective," she said accusingly. "You must know."

"Not yet," I told her. "I'm trying to figure it out though."

We finished — I, with great reluctance and only because there was not even a morsel left. We sipped the wine for a few minutes and I scanned the room again. I knew exactly where all the doors led and I had the movements of all the waiters in my head. It was now or never. I excused myself to Francine and headed for a doorway. I pushed through it and down a short corridor. There was no doubt as to which way to go — my nose led me.

I pushed open the swing doors and stepped into the kitchen. It was a heady atmosphere of aromas and spices, of bubbling pots and spirals of steam. Dishes clattered, pans rattled and voices echoed sharply. Cleavers thudded on to chopping boards, carving knives slithered on metal. All was action, excitement and motion yet all was controlled and directed in the search for perfection.

No one seemed to have noticed my entry and my eyes roamed like laser beams while my brain clicked notes and impressions, numbers and weights, storing them all away as fast as more flooded in.

Things were beginning to add up. I turned to look across the kitchen when a head swivelled in my direction. There was a frozen moment. Denouncing tones whipped out words I didn't catch and then out of the corner of my eye, I spotted a blur of movement and an upraised arm. I tried to step away but too late. Something crashed into the back of my head and reality went swimming away down a river of darkness.

I came to as if I was clawing my way out of a jacuzzi full of plain yoghurt. Faces looked down at me in condemnation. They were all in white uniforms and I was seized in a paroxysm of terror.

I knew exactly where I was because I had encountered the same situation in dozens of private eye novels. All of them had found themselves in this same frightful predicament at some time in their careers — Philip Marlowe, Mike Hammer, Lew Archer, Tony Rome. I was in a private sanitorium where I had been injected with scopolamine, the truth serum.

Would I tell them the truth? Of course I would.

Could I tell them the truth? Did I know the truth? What if Raymond hadn't told me the truth? Would these people believe me?

If the truth serum didn't work, what would they do then? Would they torture me? Or worse — feed me food with preservatives and artificial colouring and MSG?

The fiendish faces staring down at me looked capable of anything. Then, the whitish haze began to clear . . . Those weren't doctors' caps, they were chefs' hats. Those weren't medical uniforms, they were kitchen wear. Pots still simmered and grills still sizzled. I smelled onions, garlic, lemon . . . I was lying on the floor of the kitchen at Le Trouquet d'Or.

"You must not blame Marcel, M'sieu," said a moustachioed face, helping me to my feet. "He came through the door with a full tray — he could not know that you were standing there behind it." His tone was commiserating but did I detect a hint of suspicion in it?

"I must have taken a wrong turn. I was looking for the —"

"It is in the opposite direction. Still, I hope you are not hurt?"

"I — I'm fine," I said. I saw the shattered dishes and the mess on the floor. "I'm sorry about the —"

"T'cha — it is nothing. Charles will escort you back to your table."

Francine glanced up as I returned to my seat then did a double take.

"Did something happen? You look pale."

"I'm okay."

"It's not the food, is it?"

I just shook my head.

When the waiter came around again, I persuaded Francine to have the chocolate cake with almonds and chocolate butter cream. I watched her eat it while I drank a cup of coffee. She looked surprised when the waiter brought two liqueurs and said, "Compliments of the restaurant."

"They must know me," I said quickly in order to forestall more questions.

The taxi ride back was quiet. My head stopped aching but I was in no mood to satisfy Francine's curiosity although she was clearly bursting with it. She however was determined not to ask and so, at her door, I gave her a kiss on the cheek, thanked her for her company and said we must do it again sometime. She smiled automatically and thanked me for a nice evening.

A PI's lot is not always a happy one.

Back on the beat again next morning, Amy greeted me like an old friend.

"Not found that blockage yet? Hey, you gonna be so healthy from all this good coffee of ours you drinking, you ain't gonna notice smells down there."

"Takes days to find blockages sometimes," I told her. "How's the tea today?"

Amy tittered. "Take my advice. Stick to the coffee."

The day was a wearisome repeat but I listed three more delivery vans and doggedly stuck it out till after six o'clock. That made me just in time for rush hour on the tube. I could have put it on Raymond's expense account and taken a taxi but that would take longer.

At home, I poured a glass of champagne and put on a CD of Vivaldi's Four Seasons. It was the version by the Academy of St Martin-in-the-Fields, an orchestra which surely interprets the work of "the red priest" better than any other.

I am a firm believer in the coupling of food and wine with music. Every food and every drink goes perfectly with some piece of music — at least, that's my contention. I keep a continual list of the "compatibles" and am constantly experimenting so that I can add to it. It's not easy to find ideal matches but even the failures yield something satisfying. A complete lack of success is rare and Vivaldi and champagne rated high marks, I thought, making a suitable note.

Whether this was entitled to be called champagne was a matter for the language purists rather than the wine-drinkers in my opinion. The latter tend to be a stuffy lot on some issues. This beverage was a Brut Cuvée Royale from the Gloria Ferrer Caves in California. It is produced by the méthode champenoise and the vineyard is now owned by the Freixenet house in Spain. I had done a job for them recently and they had sent me a case as a bonus.

As a stimulant after a tiring day, a morale booster after a depressing day or a pick-me-up when the mind is stagnating — champagne has no equal. Dom Perignon and the widow Clicquot deserve all the homage we can pay them and I can't accept that either of them would have been so petty as to criticise this excellent libation just because it didn't come from the Marne valley. Certainly, their eyebrows would have been raised by the revelation that this one came from the New World but both must have been far-sighted enough to recognise that wine (in their future) would expand its horizons around the globe.

I poured another glass — clearly the spell was working. The orchestra swept into Opus 3 of the Concerto for Four Violins and I made a note to determine if the categories of champagne and Vivaldi could be further sub-divided. The bassoon, flute and trumpet passages might be better with a fuller, richer brand . . . clearly, there was a lot of research to be done.

I put together a Caesar Salad and ate it to the accompaniment of an Oscar Peterson track. There were some lamb's kidneys in my larder and I first tossed them in baking soda to tenderise them and neutralise their acidity, then rinsed them off and tossed them in vinegar and salt. This would give them a clean, fresh taste before stir-frying them in garlic, chilli, soya sauce and rice wine. With a garnish of spring onions, I chose as a musical balance Smetana's "Die Moldau" played by the Berlin Philharmonic. Chinese food is always difficult to accompany and I am always trying different possibilities.

After a cup of Colombian coffee, I was ready to go to work.

"Ready" is perhaps an over-statement as I wasn't looking forward at all to this part of the investigation but it was essential and at about midnight, I walked to the tube station.

When I reached the vicinity of Le Trouquet d'Or, I strolled round for a while. Some of the streets still had late-nighters but the alley behind the restaurant was already quiet. None the less, I waited till nearly three o'clock when it was dark and deserted. I pulled on a pair of rubber gloves. Adjacent to the back door was an alcove with about a dozen trash barrels. I went to work on them, one by one.

You can learn a lot from trash barrels. After all, that's how Watergate started and the CIA have a training course in how to draw conclusions from the things you find in them. Part-way through the third barrel, I heard footsteps coming down the alley. I slipped into the shadows and listened. The footsteps sounded erratic — a drunk, most likely. I waited until his irregular clip-clop passed and then continued.

I don't know what was in the next barrel but it was a horrific combination and had been in there too long. The smell would have bowled over a full-grown water-buffalo. I breathed as shallow as was concordant with survival and kept going, stopping only to scribble on a note pad with a pencil flashlight.

A sudden hissing noise froze my blood then, after a few paralysing seconds, a cat stalked across the alley, barely visible in the darkness. I was on the last barrel when the back door of Le Trouquet d'Or slammed open and light poured out in a flood.

A figure was silhouetted in the doorway, massive shoulders, bullet head, long arms. He could crush me like an empty cigarette packet. My hand crept inside my jacket pocket — I had come prepared for such emergencies. I didn't think he could see me but I stayed still, hardly breathing. He spat, yawned, stretched. The seconds were eternal, time didn't exist.

Then he turned back inside and the door banged shut. The darkness was intense by contrast. I waited a few more moments then slowly let go of the wallet in my pocket, thankful I hadn't been forced to use it. I completed my inventory of the last barrel and hurried off, a bath for once higher on my priority list than food or drink.

When Raymond came into my office, it was exactly one week after his first visit. I had looked the chair over and it seemed capable of its task. It groaned only gently as Raymond sank into it.

"You say you have the answers for me," he stated without formality.

I handed him several hand-written sheets. "I assumed you wouldn't want a typist to see these."

He grunted, reading quickly. When he had finished, he grunted again. "Let's go through this."

"All right."

"First, you say François uses ortolans."

"Yes. I thought it was ortolan from the Landes when I tasted it. But his are from Piedmont — they're plumper even than quail."

"How do you know where they're from?"

"I saw the airway bill when they were delivered."

"You say he marinates in vinegar, lemon grass and saffron . . ."

"I smelled the marinade and I saw the jars in the kitchen."

I thought a brief look of surprise flitted across his face when he heard me mention being in the kitchen but then it was gone. He looked at the sheets again.

"He glazes with honey before roasting?"

"Not ordinary old honey though. It's from Crete — has that extraordinary amber colour."

"You saw that in the kitchen too?"

I had seen the jars in the garbage barrel but I wasn't going to tell Raymond that. PI's have to have some secrets. I moved my head in a motion which he was free to interpret as a nod.

"Garlic?" He frowned. "Surely not with the lemon grass?"

"Rocambole, the Spanish garlic. It's milder, as you know. He gets this from Valencia." I had seen the labels in the garbage barrel too.

He read again in silence, his mind re-creating each step in the preparation and the cooking. I could see him searching for errors in judgement or mistakes in identification.

"They roast at 230 degrees, you say?"

"Yes and if you look at the menu list there, you'll see that this is logical," I said. "Take the chicken dishes first. The Demi-Deuil and the Fedora are both poached while the Anette, Bordelaise and Perigourdine are all sautéed."

He nodded and I continued. "The Paupiettes de Veau are braised, the veal chops and the lamb are casseroled. The Andouillettes and the Pig's Leg Zampino are boiled. The fish dishes are all grilled or meuniered.

"There are three ovens in the kitchen. One was cold, two were operating. There are only three beef dishes on the menu and all would require temperatures well below 200 degrees. That means that the third oven — which was set at 230 degrees — must be used for the ortolans. Besides, as it is the house speciality and such a delicacy, François would use one oven for that dish alone so as not to pick up any aromas or flavours."

Raymond said nothing. He read through all the sheets again. He tapped all the sheets neatly together, handed them to me and reached into his pocket and took out his cheque book.

"Expenses?" he asked.

I had the list on my desk. I handed it over. He paused at the item showing the meal at Le Trouquet d'Or.

"Is that what he charges?"

"It is."

"H'm," he commented. He opened the cheque book and wrote out another fine-looking piece of paper for the full amount — the thousand pound balance, seven days' work plus expenses.

"You did a good job," he said. Coming from a man who clearly didn't pass out many compliments, that was quite an admission.

"Good enough to earn a bonus?" I asked.

He looked at me, questioning.

"A meal at your restaurant when you cook Oiseau Royal," I said.

His look turned to one of mild astonishment.

"But that will never be on the menu at my restaurant."

"Well, you'll change the name, of course —"

"I will never cook it."

It was my turn to be astonished. "But after all this — the work, the money —"

Raymond's large, sad face showed a hint of contempt. "A creative cook doesn't copy, he originates."

"Then why?" I asked perplexed. "Why did you hire me?"

He looked at me, almost pitying. "He —" he said and I knew he meant François — "originates too. I wanted to know how original he is."

I felt deflated. I had done a good job — and for what? The cheque helped to take the edge off the disappointment but I found myself a little baffled by the convolutions of the creative culinary mind.

We shook hands and I let him out. I went back to my desk and picked up the sheets that marked the end of a case. I wrote "Raymond" on a folder, made a few notes on another sheet and filed the whole thing.

Now I could get back to routine. The first item in the morning mail had been an invitation to a blind tasting of eight vintages of Mouton Rothschild from 1971 to 1983. How could I say "no" to that! I wrote an acceptance for Mary Chen to type.

Then there was a letter from the Aluminium Producers' Association. Would I be willing to be a member of a panel to make an impartial examination of the evidence relating to aluminium in food? This looked like a tricky one. How impartial did they want me to be?

Aluminium is a potentially lethal metal which is leached out of the soil by acid rain. In high acid-rain fall-out areas, aluminium exists in high concentrations in both surface and ground water. Fish are affected first naturally but the alarming news for humans is that aluminium is implicated in most neurological disorders — particularly Parkinson's Disease and Alzheimer's Disease. People still cook with aluminium pots and pans, use aluminium foil and cans and other sources of aluminium include baking powder, spices, food additives, antacids . . . What would the aluminium producers expect me to say? No prizes for the answer to that — maybe I should stay clear of the whole thing.

On the other hand, I was on a couple of committees which

watched out for any elements which could be present in food and might be considered harmful. If I did my duty to these committees, I had a duty to speak out. Joining this panel would furnish a lot of useful data — would it be considered treacherous to obtain such information in such a way when I knew I would use it against aluminium? Another dilemma to ponder over.

I was still working my way through the pile of correspondence when the outside door bell rang. I glanced at my desk calendar. It confirmed what I was already sure of — I had no appointments. I pushed the button to release the door and went to open the door to my office.

A man was standing there. He looked like he might once have been a boxer. His nose was slightly awry, his face was scarred. His eyes though were piercing and alert and his voice was clipped and strong.

"You're the Gourmet Detective?"

"Right. Do we have an appointment?"

"No," he said and pushed past me. I barely had time to wave him to the chair when he was sitting in it. He moved with an agile stride and he eased an athletic body into the chair as he said:

"I want to talk to you about a very serious matter," and my mouth went as dry as if I had just ingested a box of croutons and a sack of salted peanuts.

I was trying to gather my thoughts so as to explain everything. I had no doubt that some very good explanations were going to be necessary — some very good explanations indeed because I recognised my unannounced visitor as François Duquesne, the owner and proprietor of Le Trouquet d'Or.

CHAPTER FIVE

I had done nothing illegal. That was the thought that kept racing through my brain. I just hoped I could convince François of that. Had I done anything unethical? Well, I had unveiled a secret recipe but I had done it by ingenuity, experience and intelligence, not by stealth or lying. I hoped I could convince François of that too.

Recollections of a magazine interview came flooding back. François not only looked like he might have been a boxer — he had been a boxer. Struggling to accumulate enough money to open his first restaurant, he had done some prizefighting among other things. I couldn't remember what those other things were and it might be better if I didn't try. Prizefighting was bad enough — the others might be even more terrifying.

The alert eyes had me transfixed. He had still said nothing so I decided to take the initiative — whatever it might be. It turned out to be a pretty feeble initiative.

"This — er, serious matter . . ." was the best I could summon and even then I had to clear my throat to continue. "Perhaps, well perhaps it's not that serious . . ."

François moved his position slightly. The chair made no protest. "Oh but it is," he said softly. "Very serious indeed."

I would have groaned but my parched throat wouldn't have allowed it. I swallowed so that I could speak.

"But you're a great chef — you have conceived so many great dishes —"

"You know who I am?" He sounded more pleased than surprised. I was relieved — even the most important people respond to a little flattery and I needed all the help I could get.

"Of course," I assured him. "Everyone knows you." I was laying it on a little thick but the exaggeration was pardonable under the circumstances. He nodded, not with pride but rather with the confidence that comes from the recognition that one's talents are known and appreciated.

"I have been told that you are the man I should talk to," he said and even those chilling words didn't prevent me from noting that his English was without accent. Nevertheless, my body temperature dropped several degrees because I had another irrelevant thought. I had just remembered the other job he had had besides prizefighting. He had been a butcher.

"My business has been a little slow lately," I pleaded. "When a good assignment comes up, I take it. I mean, I have to, I can't afford to say no."

"I hope you're not going to say no to me." His slightly gravelly voice was softer yet. Was it with menace? I tried not to shiver.

"Things are picking up now though," I told him hurriedly. "I'm getting quite busy. Anyway, you're not concerned about the past, it's over and done with. It doesn't matter who or what —"

He cut in smoothly. "Let me tell you why I am here and then you can judge whether you really want to say no to me."

I was getting desperate. His cool calm manner was infinitely more terrifying than any threats.

"Some activities of a detective — well, any kind of detective really — are not always evident to the outsider," I rushed to explain. "What may seem like trickery and deception may be merely observation and deduction. No puzzle can be devised but that someone can't find the answer. No code can be invented that can't be broken —" I broke off. He was looking at me strangely. I plunged on anyway, "— and no recipe has ever been created that can't be re-created."

"Re-created?" he said as though baffled. He went on in a firmer tone. "Someone is trying to put me out of business."

"Surely you're mistaken!" It was fatuous but it simply blurted out. How could one recipe put him out of business?

He shook his head again, very firmly. His eyes were grim and his mouth was tight and determined. That pugnacious chin jutted out as he said, "No. I'm not mistaken. Someone is trying to put me out of business."

I was really in trouble and I knew it. Worse, I didn't have a clue on how I was going to get out of it. But how had he found out? Had one of the staff recognised me? A customer even?

Perhaps Raymond had been seen leaving my office? Otherwise, how . . .

François was speaking again. "Let me tell you what has happened at Le Trouquet d'Or during the past few weeks. Shipments of food items have been diverted — always vital ingredients for certain popular dishes. Mice were found in the kitchen the morning of a visit by a food inspector. VAT records disappeared and were never found." His voice was bitter and I found I was holding my breath. We looked at each other. Neither spoke. Then I asked in a croaky voice "Anything else?"

His eyes widened. "Isn't that enough?"

I let out a sigh of relief that rustled the unpaid bills on my desk. At the same time, I coughed to hide the sigh of relief and the combination wasn't pleasant. I didn't care. He didn't know! He didn't know about Raymond or about Oiseau Royal! I felt ten years younger and was so pleased that I said genially, "And what do you want me to do?"

François smiled for the first time since he had been in my office. "I knew you'd accept the assignment. Only a man with your detailed knowledge of food and restaurants could take it on. I want you to find out who is trying to put me out of business and why."

I had put my foot in the trifle and no mistake. I tried to backtrack hastily. "Ordinarily I would be delighted to help you but as I said I'm very busy right now —"

He went on as if he had not heard me. "The first question you're going to ask me is if I have any ideas on who might be behind this — well, I don't. I have competitors naturally —"

I was so elated at being off the hook that I went boldly where I might not otherwise have gone. "Raymond in particular?"

He said nothing for a moment. He looked at his knuckles. They looked scarred and formidable from where I was sitting and I was glad he was here as a restaurateur looking for help rather than as an ex-prizefighter disgruntled at having his pet recipe taken from under his nose.

"It's no secret that Raymond and I are competitors."

"Rivals, would you say?"

"Rivals certainly."

"Enemies?"

He hesitated. He sighed and then said, "Many years ago, there was an incident between us . . . since that time a gulf has divided us —" he broke off. He seemed to be considering whether to say more but when I couldn't wait any longer I asked:

"Enough of a gulf that he might want to put you out of business?"

He spread his hands in a Gallic gesture that meant he wasn't going to answer this one at all.

"Especially after so many years?"

He looked at his knuckles again. Perhaps he wanted to punch somebody with them. Was it Raymond or was it me?

"If I could tell you anything helpful, I would. But I can tell you nothing useful at all, I'm afraid." His manner seemed sincere enough. "That incident I referred to with Raymond — well, there's really nothing there either — I mean nothing with any relevance to this affair."

The tough private eye always growled, "Best let me be the judge of that" but I didn't think that would work with François. Besides, now that I knew François wasn't there to pin me to the wall for unmasking the secrets of Oiseau Royal, I was breathing a little easier although I still wasn't sure I wanted this job.

"Actually I'm not that kind of detective," I told him. "What I do is —"

"Oh, I know what you do," François said. "And you do it very well. You're the man who found a new source of lotus leaves for Johnny Chang."

I wasn't too worried about him knowing that. It was good publicity when the occasional commission was leaked.

"Yes, I am. So you can see that I'm not really the kind of detective you want." I said it in my most persuasive voice. It was as ineffective as recommending a Ploughman's Lunch with pickles to a ploughman.

"I told you I need a man who is well-informed about food and restaurant procedures."

"If it's an investigator you want, try Knightsbridge Inquiry Agency," I suggested. "They're very reliable, their reputation is —"

"What do they know about food?"

"Everybody knows something about it —"

"Do they know as much as you?"

Honesty was pushing me towards saying "no" whereas self-preservation was yelling "yes, yes". I was still trying to reconcile the two when François was saying:

"I won't take no for an answer. I love my work as a chef, I love my restaurant. No one can take them away from me — I'll do whatever I must to protect them." He eyed me almost accusingly. "You must feel the same way. You can't want to see a place like mine forced out of business."

"Of course I don't but —"

"Or a restaurateur of my calibre being humiliated."

"It would be unfair —"

"Who knows if the same underhanded tactics might be used on another restaurant — and another — and another? It could affect the whole culinary scene!"

So I wasn't as tough as Mike Hammer. I was weakening and François knew it. With masterly timing, he reached into his pocket and pulled out his cheque book. Grabbing at any straw, I asked feebly: "You've received no threatening notes? Ransom to be paid — anything like that?"

"Nothing. No." He pulled out a pen. "What are your fees?"

From wondering how I was going to get through the rest of the month financially, suddenly money was pouring in, first Raymond and now François. I had run out of ways of saying that this wasn't my kind of detection. Anyway, I had already deviated a little from usual operations in accepting the task of uncovering Oiseau Royal. Now François wanted me to deviate a little further. It was how people became alcoholics and embezzlers — a little more every time. Well, just this once and no more. They probably said that too.

With more time to think about it, I would have been able to come up with a really nice figure. After all, if I wasn't that enthusiastic about taking the job, I could set my demand high. Then it wouldn't matter if François backed down. But was I that sure I didn't want the job? Any private eye would have wanted it. It would probably have appealed to Nero Wolfe most of all — eating was how he got to weigh a seventh of a ton.

"A thousand pounds down and a thousand pounds on completion," I said promptly. Too promptly and I knew it as soon as the words were out of my mouth. Fortunately I had the presence of mind to add, "— and a hundred pounds a day plus expenses."

François already had the cheque written before I could think of anything else to add. I took it with a sinking feeling that I was making a mistake.

"Come around tomorrow morning about nine-thirty," said François. "I'll introduce you to the staff and you can get all the information you want." He stood and shook my hand in a hard grip. His athletic stride took him to the door and he was gone. I was still a little dazed. I looked at the cheque for comfort. It looked fine.

I left the office early after collecting my mail from Mrs Shearer. I felt I was entitled to do so after all that excitement. I walked through the Hammersmith mall and bought a few items, for once not bothering to look at the prices. It's amazing the security one can feel from the comforting crackle of a piece of paper with numbers on it.

What's the best music for relaxing? Vivaldi is high on the list though some people say they find his melodies lively and stimulating. This is more true of his violin concertos but his chamber music is more soothing. I put on Mendelssohn's String Octet, Opus 20. It can be criticised as being slightly repetitive but it is simple and charming.

The Octet tinkled through the apartment as I read the day's letters. It wasn't much of a haul today. Would I like to take advantage of a special offer on dog-food? No, I wouldn't, I seldom touch the stuff. There was an invitation to a cook-book signing which I put aside to consider.

There was one really interesting letter though and it read:

"Dunsingham Castle is about to re-open after 200 years as a ruin and 20 years of intermittent restoration.

"It will be a luxury hotel of unequalled excellence with no efforts spared to raise it to the category of the very finest hosteleries of the Western World.

"As part of this re-development programme, we intend to

offer mediaeval food in keeping with the period when the castle was at the peak of its importance.

"We have sampled mediaeval meals at several places and found them to be unsatisfactory. We seek your recommendations on suitable menus, balancing as far as possible authenticity of food and style with availability of raw materials.

"Please advise us if you will undertake this project and advise us of your fee."

Now that was something I could get my teeth into. I had eaten a couple of so-called mediaeval banquets myself and found them to be pale and unconvincing replicas. Could I do better? It would be great fun to try and I began to scribble some notes.

Monchelet, for instance. It is a 14th century dish and unaccountably absent from modern menus. Pieces of neck of lamb are cooked in stock, mint, thyme, marjoram, onion and wine. Then ginger, saffron and cinnamon are added and it is cooked further. Egg yolks and lemon juice are blended with some of the broth and returned to the pot. The sauce resulting from thickening is aromatic and spicy and of a delicious golden colour. It is a superb dish and one I have cooked several times. It is fully deserving of revival and as all the ingredients are readily available today, no dish could be more authentic.

Goose should certainly be considered. It was a popular dish in the Middle Ages and is still eaten on feast days in Germany and Eastern Europe. It is a shame it is rarely encountered on menus today and hardly ever in the shops.

Potatoes were unknown so vegetable accompaniments should be the floury or starchy type to make up for them. Small tarts of fruit stewed with honey would be a simple and appropriate dessert. Several British restaurants offer syllabub today but it is usually pleasant yet uninteresting. I could hardly recommend making it by the original method — milking a cow directly into a bowl containing ale or cider but I could look into tastier variations. I had a dim recollection of an orange pudding I had once eaten but couldn't recall the details. I made notes to research these points and offer any other mediaeval suggestions.

Did Dunsingham plan blazing torches and low-cut wenches? I wondered. This would be where decision-making became tricky — steering a course between historical accuracy, reality and the images that we all have in our minds which are difficult to translate without appearing tawdry and cheap.

The soft, gentle music of Mendelssohn continued to roll around the room. I put down the notes and François' unexpected request came to the forefront of my mind. Some request — he had had me on the ropes from the moment I breathed that sigh of relief on finding out that he was not aware of losing his prized recipe.

The idea of putting a restaurant out of business was a terrifying one. Extortion and bribery were not unknown in the restaurant trade but this sounded different. What would be the point? Jealousy perhaps? Of the restaurant itself? Or the owner? Seemed a bit extreme but I supposed it was possible. Large amounts of money were involved when the establishment was as prestigious as Le Trouquet d'Or.

So maybe the job wasn't as far out of my field as I had insisted. François was most likely right when he asserted that his beleaguered position could best be resolved by someone with an appropriate background and experience. It appealed to me though, I had to admit. Now that I had been more or less forced into it, I almost liked the thought — me, a private eye, a real one!

I had bought a bottle of tequila at the market, Sauza Blanco being a brand I particularly like. I poured some into the mixer then squeezed in the juice of three limes and added a few drops of Curaçao. I poured in a generous splash of tonic water to give it balance and a few bubbles. Somewhat removed from a classic margarita but I like it.

When the mixer motor finished buzzing, I put Ravel's *Bolero* on the CD player. Ravel described it as "a lewd piece" and marked it in very slow tempo. He was furious when Toscanini played it quite fast. So Ravel was wrong and every conductor has played it at the Toscanini tempo ever since. Played at a pulsating pace, its insistent beat makes it an exhilarating composition even if outraged Spanish musicians declared it alien to traditional folk dances.

Good cooking requires planning but you can't always plan meals. It can be a challenge to come up with a good meal at short notice and with little work. I had bought some shelled shrimp and I tossed them in a pan of clarified butter, added a fair amount of fresh ground pepper and some lemon juice. I cut a tomato in two, hollowed out each half and spooned the hot shrimp/butter mix into them. A generous sprinkle of chopped chives over them and into the refrigerator to chill.

One of my other purchases had been a filleted Dover sole. This is the name given to real sole to distinguish it from the other and inferior varieties. Its flesh is firm and tasty and it has the merit of being ideal for simple frying or grilling although on this occasion, I wanted to make it a little fancier. I buttered an oven dish, put in the fillet, covered it with a mixture of white wine and fish stock and added seasonings and a bouquet garni. I put it into the oven to bake and set the timer for fifteen minutes.

I finished the margarita then ate the shrimp and tomato. When the oven timer sounded, I took out the fillet, put the liquid in a pan with more white wine and some beurre manié then boiled it until the sauce thickened. I added my other purchase — some stoned green grapes and cooked until they were hot. Like the margarita, it was a departure from the original, in this case Sole Véronique. I had put on a few small potatoes to steam, they don't detract from the subtle taste of the sole.

A bottle of Bourgogne Hautes Côtes de Beaune 1988 was the wine I selected from the rack. I had been wanting to try it and a white Burgundy seldom disappoints. This one came through fresh and clean with a stronger finish than expected.

Bolero lasted from the shrimp to the sole and with the last of the wine, I put on an Errol Garner disc for a complete change of pace. Searching the refrigerator, I found some crème brûlée that I had made a few days ago. That topped off the meal.

Meditating while Errol Garner's fingers slid over the keys was pleasant. What would tomorrow bring? A second visit to Le Trouquet d'Or was a prospect to enjoy especially under the present circumstances. I had only the most niggling of worries that I would be recognised as the dummy who had walked into the kitchen and wrecked a trayful of dishes. Hundreds of diners passed through the place every week. Surely they wouldn't remember one fat-head?

I had an early night and a dreamless sleep.

CHAPTER SIX

Disaster almost struck within five minutes of arriving at Le Trouquet d'Or. François had greeted me and we had talked for a few minutes. I suggested that in order to get to know the staff, each of them should take me around his own area and François had agreed. The first person I was introduced to was Henri Leclerc, the maître d'.

The moustachioed face examined me as we shook hands and I could see recognition dawning quickly. I told François I would talk to him later and he nodded and went back to his office.

"I am sorry, M'sieu, I did not know the other evening that you were helping us investigate these strange happenings," Henri said apologetically. "Naturally, with these things going on . . ."

"I understand," I said generously. "You were right to be suspicious."

"Your head," said Henri, "it is all right I hope?"

"Perfectly," I assured him. I gave him a suitably conspiratorial nod. "And we will say no more of this matter, eh?"

"Certainly."

"Not to anyone," I pressed.

"Of course."

That was one obstacle out of the way.

Henri lead me along a wood-panelled corridor with old menus framed on the walls. "This is Mr Leopold's office. He is general manager. He is not in yet." He lead me a little further along. "This is an office used by our accountant. He comes in only occasionally. Anyone else uses it in the meantime. Come, we will go to the kitchens."

Shiny metal gleamed everywhere. Oven fronts, pots, pans, blades shone brightly and glass and ceramic jars, bottles and containers sparkled under the bright kitchen lights.

"Our head chef, Mr Klingermann, will be here at any moment," said Henri.

Even if he wasn't here to crack the whip, his staff was already hard at work. Two apprentice chefs were sorting vegetables for salad and another came through carrying a tray of meats. A kitchen helper was chopping pears and dropping them into a bowl of red wine. The air was still pristine with no aromas yet apparent. In a few hours, it would be heavy with luscious smells of sauces and spices, pungent with the flavours of condiments and seasonings.

We walked on through the dining and banquet rooms. They were silent and empty, awaiting their turn to be brought to glittering life. I looked around. There was not much to see but I wanted to get the feel of the place. A door slammed and Henri went to look. "Ah, here is Mr Klingermann. Come and I will introduce you."

Klaus Klingermann was a big man with a bald head that looked polished and a jovial expression. He was Swiss, he told me proudly.

"I've heard your name, of course," I told him. "Switzerland is fortunate to have two such fine chefs."

He beamed. To be put alongside the legendary Fredy Girardet was the finest compliment I could pay him.

"You are going to help us find out the meaning behind these terrible things that are happening here?" Klaus' large face was almost pleading. "I love this restaurant. Who can be doing these things to us?"

I assured him I intended to find out. "Can you tell me anything about these events?" I asked. "Were you involved in any of them?"

"François has told you about them . . .? yes, the mice I can tell you about." His jovial expression was gone. He looked almost ready to cry. "We found them in one of the cupboards in the kitchen . . . come, I will show you." He did so, pulling open a door. "They were in here. But, I can tell you — someone put them in here. We have a clean kitchen here, a spotless kitchen. It is absolutely impossible to have mice."

"Klaus," I said, "we both know that cockroaches and houseflies have been found in the kitchens of London hotels and restaurants. I appreciate the fact that you are proud of your

kitchens but I have to be critical. How can you be really sure
—" He stopped me with an upraised hand and looked around.
"Tommy, over here a minute."

A youth of about eighteen with a thin Cockney face put
down his knife and walked across. "Tommy is responsible for
the cleaning and storage of these cupboards. Tommy, you
remember the mouse incident? Tell this gentleman about it."

Tommy scratched his ear, mildly embarrassed by the attention.

"I cleaned out them cupboards just the day before the
inspector was due," he said in a strong East End accent.

"How often do you do that?" I asked.

"Once a month. I 'appened to do it that day because we was
changing things around — the way they was stored, I mean.
So before puttin' all the new stuff in, I cleaned the cupboard
out, cleaned it real good, I did."

"And you saw no signs of any mice? Not even any
droppings?"

His young face creased in a grin. "Mister, I know signs of
mice when I see 'em. Lived in Barking, I did when I was a
youngster."

"West Ham supporter?" I hazarded.

He glowed. "Right! 'ow about last Saturday, eh? Four-
one!" He caught Klaus Klingermann's eye then with cheerful
Cockney cheek said, "The boss is an Arsenal supporter . . .
yeh, well, I can tell you there was no signs of mice in that
cupboard. None whatsoever."

He sounded sincere but I had to push it a little further.

"Couldn't they have come through from another cupboard?
A hole in the wall?"

Klaus cut in at once. "After the mice were discovered, I had
that cupboard examined very carefully. It is not possible, no.
Thank you, Tommy," he said to the boy who went back to his
counter. Klaus turned to me. "There is only one way mice
could have been in that cupboard. Someone put them there."

It was understandable that any chef, and particularly one of
Klingermann's reputation, would want to distance himself
from such a suggestion. On the other hand, there were the
other incidents. Accusations against other restaurants had not
put them out of business although one hotel's kitchens had

been shut down for a while. Nevertheless, it was the general feeling in the trade that a one hundred per cent spotless kitchen was impossible.

One other point bothered me. "It's my understanding that inspectors don't announce visits in advance," I said. "I can see that if someone wanted to show Le Trouquet d'Or in a bad light, they might plant mice when they knew an inspector was due. But how could they know?"

"It is usual for inspectors to turn up unannounced," agreed Klaus. "The inspector for our area does not advise us when he is coming but he is a man of rigid schedule." He smiled, back to his happy beam. "We mark him on our calendar and we know to within two or three days. One of the tricks, you might say."

"So only a person familiar with the restaurant and its operation could have known of the visit?"

Klaus rubbed his chin thoughtfully. "I hadn't thought of it that way but yes I suppose so."

"Do you think a competitor is behind all this?"

Klaus looked alarmed. "A competitor?"

"Yes. You are in a very competitive business."

"But we are not gladiators in an arena!" Klaus was shocked. "We do not fight each other. Chefs, owners, proprietors — we are like a brotherly community, we help each other —"

"You have an enemy," I said sternly, "who hates you. He isn't acting in a brotherly manner."

Klaus shook his head sadly. "I wish I could say you are wrong but —" he sighed. "Alas not, you may be right."

I decided to press home the advantage. "Can you suggest any competitors who might be this ruthless?"

"No." Klaus was firm. "No, I cannot."

"Isn't there anyone — anyone at all — with a grudge against François?"

"I am sure not," he said emphatically.

"Isn't it true that he and Raymond have bitter feelings towards each other?"

"Raymond? Raymond Lefebvre?" Klaus looked alarmed at the idea. "They were friends once," he admitted slowly. "I believe they worked together as young men. They had an argument —"

"About what?"

Klaus grinned. "A woman, I suppose — I mean, I have always assumed that. What else is important enough at that age to break up a friendship?"

I could think of other things but obviously Klaus had been brought up in a Gallic atmosphere of cooking despite his German-Swiss name and saw life through Latin eyes.

"Could that break-up have been so acrimonious that Raymond might want to ruin François?"

Klaus looked horrified. "After so many years?"

I could understand his scepticism, I felt the same way. But was that all? Had there been just an argument? What could it have been about?

"Perhaps there's more to it than just an argument over a woman."

"What could there be?"

"I don't know," I admitted. "You can't suggest anything?"

"I work for François," Klaus said proudly. "I am his head chef. You would expect me to be loyal — and I am. But I tell you I know nothing more. François never refers to Raymond, never."

"Raymond is his closest competitor, isn't he?"

"One of three or four close competitors, I would say."

"Does François ever refer to the others?"

"Well, of course . . ." His voice trailed away.

"But never Raymond?"

"Well, no."

Miss Marple would probably have been able to make all kinds of deductions from that but I couldn't discern much that I didn't already know.

More staff had now come into the kitchen. One came up to Klaus and held out a dish. "Try this galantine," he invited. Klaus tasted, savouring it. "Stuffing for a piece of sirloin," he told me in an aside and tasted it again.

"Needs more salt," he ordered. "M'm and maybe some fresh truffle peelings — but certainly more salt."

"What's a Swiss chef doing in England?" I asked. "Wouldn't you rather be in France?"

"Not today. Ah, back in the thirties, yes. I would have given a lot to have been in Paris then. It was the time and place when food was most appreciated — paradise for a chef." He laughed. "Why am I here, you ask? I am old-fashioned. I like the way people take their time here. It is essential for food — whether cooking it or eating it. I spent a year at 'The Fenestre' in New York City." He shivered. "Twenty-four clerks just to take reservations! Can you imagine! Purgatory — maybe worse. François rescued me and brought me here."

"No wonder you're loyal," I told him.

A tray of pastry went by on its way to an oven. Klaus stopped the man carrying it, scrutinised the load then nodded approval.

"Thanks, Klaus. I'll let you go back to work."

"You wish to return to François' office?"

"I'd like to talk to Mr Leopold. Think he's in yet?"

"Possibly. He comes in about this time."

He led me to Leopold's office, knocked and went in. Leopold was there, behind a tidy desk with neat stacks of folders, papers and bills. Klaus introduced me and left.

Larry Leopold was one of the most dynamic individuals I had met in a long time. Lithe and wiry, he moved with a quick nervous energy like an electrified marionette. In his early forties, he had an angular face with short reddish-brown hair and darting eyes. His outstanding feature was a well-trimmed reddish-brown Van Dyke beard which jutted out from his chin in a way which gave him a distinctly piratical look.

He paced up and down as he talked, despite having seated me. Bookshelves stuffed with files and folders covered one wall and on another were diplomas, certificates and framed photographs. It was a working office and had an energetic, efficient air that matched its occupant.

"Any progress in finding out what's going on around here?" he asked in a staccato voice that delivered words in machine-gun like bursts. "No, of course not. Haven't had time yet, have you? François told me he was hiring you." He viewed me critically. I wondered if I passed the inspection. "Damn funny business. Any ideas?"

"Not so far," I said. "I need more information. What can you tell me?"

He was still pacing. I wished he would sit.

"Klaus told you what he knows, did he?"

"He told me about the mice."

He paused for a moment, eyed me then went on pacing.

"Ah, yes, the mice. Good man, Klaus. Fine chef. We're lucky to have him."

"He seems quite certain that the mice were put there — and if so, it must have been by a person who knew that the food inspector was coming that day."

"And you're thinking that's what he would say —"

"Am I?" I asked.

Larry Leopold rubbed the sharp point of his beard against the back of his hand reflectively. "No chef would accept that he runs a dirty kitchen, would he?"

"You think Klaus does?"

"Of course not." His voice was sharp.

"What about the other incidents?"

"I can tell you about the missing VAT files. That's in my area."

"Missing? Files do get mislaid."

"These were missing. One day they were here, the next they couldn't be found."

"They never turned up?"

"No."

"What happened then?"

"There was a hell of an argument with the VAT people naturally. We estimated the VAT payments as best we could but they weren't happy about it. They've been breathing down our necks ever since."

"François mentioned foodstuffs, supplies, going astray. What can you tell me about those?"

His pacing increased in tempo. He was a very nervous individual. "The worst incident was the last one. We were doing a big banquet for one of the Scotch whisky groups. They had asked for lamb chops — we'd had a big write-up in the *Evening Standard* a few weeks earlier. Perhaps you saw it?"

I said I thought I had but I didn't remember.

"The write-up was so good that the whisky people wanted the same meal. We had to order the chops specially. They didn't arrive."

"Did you find out what had happened to them?" I asked.

"The supplier insisted he had sent them to us. We said they

hadn't arrived. We had to give the whisky people a different meal. They were furious, I can tell you."

"You both looked into it further, I suppose?"

"Sure," said Leopold. "All we could find out was that the driver of the delivery van had been told by someone here that the order had been cancelled. We never found out who."

"You said that was the last incident. There were others?"

"Yes, earlier. Of course, we thought it was human error then. The kind of mistakes that can happen anywhere."

"For instance . . .?"

He was still pacing. He rubbed his chin again.

"We use a special honey for one of our dishes —"

Now, I was rubbing my chin. It was to cover a slight smile I had not been able to suppress. I knew which dish used that kind of honey and I knew how it was used. I concentrated on Leopold. "— It comes from abroad by air. One complete shipment arrived with every jar broken."

"Accident?"

Leopold stopped in mid-stride. "Never happened before." He resumed his patrol. "Another time, we had ordered a shipment of oysters. We received mussels."

"Readily replaceable, surely?"

"Certainly not," Leopold said irritably. "Ours are on special order from Turenne. We can't just substitute them with a boxful from the local fishmonger!"

It would make anyone irritable, I thought. In fact, there seemed to be a pattern all through this — all these items were not readily replaceable. Whoever was behind this knew a lot about the restaurant.

"Can you give me the dates of all these?"

"Of course." I nodded wisely. I had no idea what I'd do with this data but it sounded competent to ask for it.

"Here's my phone number," I told him, handing him a card. He had to stop moving long enough to take it. "My answering service can get in touch with me twenty-four hours a day —" I must tell Mrs Shearer about that. She'd be astonished and want more money.

He didn't look impressed but I was. Just like a Continental Op.

"If there are any more incidents — call me at once," I

admonished him. He nodded and we shook hands and I left.
With all those papers on his desk, he'd have to sit down now.

François was on the phone. I waited till he was finished.

"I'd like to pop in from time to time," I told him. "No
schedule, just at random."

"Of course." He rummaged in his desk drawer and pulled
out a key. "This is to the back door." I hadn't meant out of
hours but I took it anyway.

"Did you get what you need from Klaus and Larry?"

"Very interesting," I said sagely.

He fixed me with his piercing look again. "I'm very
worried about this situation, very worried," he said. "I hope
you're going to get to the bottom of it."

"I will," I said confidently. François looked less confident
but he nodded, "Good."

I was about to take my leave when he said:

"One other thing —"

"Yes?"

"There is a banquet on Friday night for the Circle of
Careme. We are hosting it here. You'd better be on hand."

I could hardly believe my luck. "Of course."

"Call me the day before and I'll give you whatever details
you need."

When I left Le Trouquet d'Or and stepped out into a
blustery wet wind, I was in a euphoric daze. I had just
completed my first day as a real private eye . . . it hadn't gone
too badly and I thought I had asked most of the right
questions. Had I made any progress? I'd have to think about
that.

Then a real bonus! The Circle of Careme! And I was going
to be there.

CHAPTER SEVEN

The Circle of Careme.

The banquet room at Le Trouquet d'Or glittered under countless butter-gold candles. There was already a steady hum of conversation, growing louder as more and more members arrived. There was the occasional clink of a glass or a plate as the waiters put the finishing touches to the huge circular table. Seating was both inside and out, with gaps for access to the inner sections.

The Circle of Careme.

The most prestigious, the most celebrated of all gourmet organisations in the country. I felt quite privileged to be there, even under these circumstances. It would also be intriguing to learn something of the Circle for it was an enigma.

It had no known president, no identifiable secretary and no registered address. At various times, its periodic banquets would get a mention in the press, mainly because of the luminaries who attended. Guests were often invited it seemed but the membership was as nebulous as the panel of officers. One read that so-and-so or what's-his-name had been present but it was impossible to establish who were members and who were guests.

The Circle did not make obvious efforts to remain secret but it certainly maintained a cloak of anonymity that would have made Howard Hughes envious. It never sought publicity and probably exercised influence to avoid more than a minimum amount.

The purposes of the Circle were apparently two in number — the enjoyment of the very best of superb food and an opportunity to meet and talk with friends, colleagues, peers, rivals and competitors.

That was all I knew about the Circle and it was perhaps more than most. So now I was listening and watching with all the enthusiasm of a child paying his first visit to the circus.

François had phoned me the day before as promised and we had discussed how to handle this surveillance. I suggested going as a waiter but François thought it would provoke too many questions. Due to the clandestine nature of the group, he considered it better that anyone who wanted to do any wondering about my presence could speculate on whether I was a guest or a new member. Several others present would be the subject of speculation, he said, so one more wasn't reason to raise any eyebrows. I didn't know what strings François had pulled to get me invited and I didn't ask.

I began identifying those present. I saw Ellsburg Warrington first of all. He was the easiest to see, towering above everyone else. Very tall and very old, grey in hair and face, he was still active as the founder and owner of Warrington's Markets. "Cheaper than Tesco, better stocked than Sainsbury's and higher quality than Marks and Spencer" was their slogan and it annoyed many — those three especially.

Near him was his son, Tarquin, thin-faced, thin-lipped, the creator of the slogan and known to be influencing his father into more abrasive techniques of advertising and selling. He was deep in conversation with Johnny Chang, urbane and smiling as usual. I had done a job for Chang not too long ago, locating a European source of lotus leaves, the indispensable wrapping of the famous "Beggars' Chicken" dish which was one of the outstanding offerings at Chang's restaurant.

The conversation was thickening. I moved a few steps, partly to hear better and partly to look less statuesque and noticeable. Glasses were clinking and I was wondering if an aperitif in my hand would make me look more like I belonged.

"Well, don't tell me the Circle has admitted you! If I'd known about it, I would have blackballed you without any hesitation!"

Maggie McNulty was not what you could call a sophisticated dresser. Her clothes always looked as if they had been thrown on to her with a pitchfork and no matter what she wore, she looked as if she had just come in from riding a horse. Not unattractive in a jolly hockey-sticks outdoor way, she could be a stunner if she dresed better, learned something about make-up and lost a stone and a half. As long as she belonged to such conclaves as the Circle of Careme though, there wasn't much likelihood of the latter.

"Hello, Maggie. I didn't realise that this was the sort of organisation that would admit people like you or I'd have stayed home and curled up with a good cook book."

She smiled, showing excellent teeth, one of her best features.

"The Circle needs us entrepreneurs and marketeers — we're a much needed balance against all these writers and talkers."

I knew what she meant. From a background of magazine publishing (which was where I had first met her) and a dead husband's legacy, she had founded a company making and selling quick-frozen foods. The big step had found the market sceptical but she had gained a surprisingly strong foothold and her company was reputed to be growing rapidly.

Maggie swirled her glass. "Not drinking? You don't have to pay for them here, you know."

"Just on my way to get one," I assured her, thankful that she was not going to press for a reason for my presence.

She nodded and I moved away. Talking earnestly with two men was Per Larsson, a stocky Swede. I would have guessed he would be there even if I had not seen the attendance list from François. The high priest of food, the guru of cooking and travel, he was universally known for his *Larsson's Guide to Hotels and Restaurants*, the bible of many eaters and travellers.

I was not a bit surprised to see Benjamin Breakspear and would have heard his resounding voice and recognised him immediately although I had never seen him in person before. He was known to millions of film and TV viewers as King George the fifth, Nero, one of James Bond's adversaries and Hermann Goering among other memorable roles.

The bulbous eyes, the stylised gestures, the hammy mannerisms and the plummy enunciation were no longer in such demand due to his advancing years. He had kept his place in the public eye by becoming a regular on TV quiz and game shows. He wrote books, mainly autobiographical, which some critics insisted should appear under a fiction label.

"— just got back from America" he was saying to a small

group. "I was in this restaurant in South Carolina and the waitress asked me, 'How many hush puppies would y'all like, honey?'"

"'One for each foot — if I wanted any at all,'" I told her but of course, she did not understand my impeccable English and returned with a huge bowl containing dozens of the things."

"And what are they?" asked an obliging bystander.

"Balls of corn bread, deep-fried a golden brown. They got their name supposedly from a hunter who didn't give his dogs any of his bounty. They howled and whined so much that he fried bits of corn mush and fed them, saying 'Hush puppies'."

"You were lecturing over there, Benjamin?" asked Goodwin Harper. Rotund and red-faced, he ran what many believed to be the most English of English restaurants and the home of traditional roast beef.

"Yes." The famous smile beamed and the whole face lit up. "Larger than life over there, dear boy, larger than life. I was invited to what they call a Happy Hour. Would you credit it? A happy hour and it lasted from six till nine p.m.!"

"Pick up any good recipes?"

Benjamin shuddered.

"Wouldn't want most of them."

"Can we quote you on that?" asked someone mischievously.

"Good gracious, no. I'm going back again in August. No, if you want to quote me, say how enormously impressed I was with the enormously wide variety of food there. Maine — with its rocky sea coasts, Illinois with its magnificent steaks, Wisconsin with some of the —"

I moved on. Another group was arguing over diets. Dr Hay's 1929 book *Health via Food* was being compared with Dr Frank's more recent *Beverly Hills Diet*. "They're the same," a voice I didn't know was saying. "Both advocate the same thing — don't eat starch in the same meal as meat or fruit. And it's nonsense. Both books are based on the theory that the digestion of starch needs alkaline conditions. That's false, completely false."

The speaker made the mistake of pausing for breath and a little man with wire spectacles promptly said, "What I always say is — eat anything you like and let the food argue it out in your stomach." There were laughs while the original speaker tried to get back to his point.

I was still tempted to head for one of the bars but I recalled that cops always declined the offer of a drink under such circumstances. "Not while I'm on duty, ma'am" they always said. But surely that was official police? It was probably in their handbook. Private eyes were different. Few of them were abstainers. Quite the reverse — most of them were out-and-out boozers. But then wasn't it their drinking that often got them into trouble? A couple too many and they found themselves in a rat-infested cellar about to be flooded unless half a ton of dynamite exploded first.

I compromised and got some grapefruit juice in a whisky glass. The room was full now. The doors had been closed so I presumed everyone had arrived. The bartenders were coping manfully and the conversation level was making it necessary for voices to be raised. Benjamin Breakspear was having no problem though. He was some distance away but I was still receiving him loud and clear.

I passed François. He gave me a look and I gave him a nod. I assumed his look to be asking "Is everything all right?" and I hoped that he was interpreting my nod as saying "Yes".

Mad Mike Spitalny was holding forth to another group and I edged near enough to hear. His restaurant, The Bohemian Girl was one of the showplaces of the London eating scene. Mike, like Benjamin, was louder than most but that was to be expected. He had a reputation for volatility of character and was said to insult diners who didn't heap enough praise on his food. I had always doubted that he did any such thing but he was a good enough showman to have created the myth.

"Wars are not fought in vain," Mike was saying. "In India, Britain learned the secrets of curry and tandoori. France lost Indo-China but gained 3,000 Chinese restaurants — then they lost Algeria but gained couscous."

Next to him was another restaurateur with whom I had no acquaintance but recognised readily. Ted Martin, distinguished, relaxed, was general manager of Middleton's and he said:

"I hear Luis wants to join the Circle."

"Don't admit him," said Mike Spitalny promptly. "The

Spanish have never produced a dish worthy of note."

Nelda Darvey, also in the group, I knew well. Food columnist for the *London Gazette*, she was as outspoken as Mike. "Gazpacho soup," she said and I knew she was being controversial and not stating an opinion.

"Gazpacho soup!" said Mike scornfully. 'It's cold soup. How can it be soup if it's cold? You eat it and are left with the feeling that if you had come earlier, you could have had it while it was still hot."

A latecomer was being admitted. Over the heads, I could see Roger St Leger, a familiar face. He was a former television cook who had had a tremendous following with his amusing and informative programme. His pleasing personality and casual breezy style had been in welcome contrast to some of the more stern-faced and serious media cooks who behaved as if they were in a cathedral rather than a kitchen.

His television series had ended and he had been unable to get another. Even the satellite networks, usually avid to snap up the cast-offs, had not made any offers. His many fans looked forward to his return but right now he seemed to be "between engagements".

He was fair-haired, with a pleasantly masculine face and a square jaw. He was tall and well-built and carried himself easily. His expression, friendly and relaxed when he was on the box, was now tense and almost grim.

He seemed to be pushing his way through to the bar — but no, he was grasping the arm of yet another individual I recognised. This time however, it was a face I had seen only on television.

Ivor Jenkinson had made himself famous with his pro-gramme "IJ". These were his own initials but he had originally called himself "The Investigative Journalist" and his show was now so well-known that "IJ" identified both it and him to millions.

He was good at his job, supremely good. His speciality was exposing skullduggery wherever and however it occurred. He had a nose like a bloodhound, the tenacity of a bulldog and the instincts of a ferret. He had caused a sensation in the business world with his exposé of inside trading and countless Stock Exchange heads had rolled as a result. IJ became a household word with his next programme which revealed dirty work in the insurance world. He was soon firmly established as a British Ralph Nader and it was said that captains of industry and trade tycoons held their breath until his next target was revealed.

Lean and very intense, a pale face and a narrow nose, thin hair swept straight back, he never smiled. His grim visage must be terrifying if you knew or suspected that you were on his list. But what was he doing here? I didn't know anything about him beyond his television persona but he didn't seem like a gourmet.

I watched as Roger St Leger took an envelope from his pocket and handed it to IJ. He opened it and studied its contents. He nodded with satisfaction and the look that passed across his face was probably as close to a smile as he ever achieved. He said a few words to St Leger who answered briefly and walked away. IJ put the envelope into his pocket and gave it a reassuring pat. What was all that about? I wondered. They seemed an unlikely pair but they did have the common background of television. Well, that was what I was here for — to observe. What else was happening?

Deep in serious debate was a trio of personalities. Bill Keating, lanky, loose-limbed and owner of a chain of wine and spirit outlets, Ray Burnaby of Burnaby Wine Imports, older, pot-bellied but still personally active, and Sally Aldridge.

Sally was known — no, she was notorious — for her outrageous best-seller *Any Gourmet Meal in 30 Minutes*. If she was a member of the Circle, she must have been admitted before her book exploded on the food scene. Her name also appeared frequently in the magazines where she delighted in offering startlingly controversial viewpoints on any subject connected with cooking or restaurants.

Sally was petite with masses of dark hair which cascaded around a deceptively elfin face. The slightly gap-toothed smile and the determined pug nose made up an attractive package.

She was asking, "Why do people drink the wines they drink?"

"They read about them in wine magazines if they want expert opinions,' said Ray Burnaby.

"Expert?" challenged Sally.

"Yes. Impartial reviews by authoritative wine writers."

"But wine magazines get 95 per cent of their revenue from advertising so how can it be impartial?"

Bill Keating joined in. "Wine writers don't do it for the money. They do it because they love wine. They love drinking it primarily but secondarily, they love writing about drinking it.'

Sally was warming up now. She could be a tigress when she got into a discussion like this. "There are two kinds of wine writer. There are wine specialists who write about wine. They know about wine but can't write. Then there are the writers who like wine. They may be able to write but they are ignorant when it comes to wine. Give them both the same bottle to taste and they'll give you two completely different opinions."

"Wine's not a science — it's an art." Ray Burnaby was digging in his heels. "Why shouldn't two experts have different opinions?"

"What does the reader about wine really want?" Bill Keating asked. "To learn something helpful about wines so he knows which ones to choose? Or does he want to read an interesting article?"

"The wine business is all hype and advertising," Sally said. "It's easy to pull the wool over the eyes of the average wine drinker — that's obvious from the successful campaigns that have persuaded people to drink rubbish like Beaujolais Nouveau, Côtes du Rhone Primeur, Blush wines and those dreadful coolers."

"There's some truth in that," admitted Bill Keating. "Drinkers — beer as well as wine — are no longer guided by their own taste but by media promotion. They drink what they are told to drink. Image is more important than enjoyment."

"Nonsense," said Ray stoutly. "Wine is a production-oriented commodity not a market-oriented one. Taste and quality are two of its inherent characteristics and always will be."

"You published an in-house wine magazine, Ray," Bill reminded him. "You should know."

"He doesn't know at all," scoffed Sally. "His writers push

whichever vintages Ray wants to get rid of."

"That's not true," Ray puffed. "Only sincere and well-informed people write for me."

I could see Sally's eyes glinting. "Can your wine-tasters really tell — when they taste a wine today — what it's going to taste like in ten years' time?"

"Its potential? Of course they can. That's their job."

Sally had her mouth open to say something vulgar as I moved on. I strolled through more groups of gourmets, gourmands and guests, not always knowing which were which. Repeating a ploy that already proved effective, I walked into the kitchen while trying to cultivate a look suggesting I was seeking a toilet.

CHAPTER EIGHT

O
n this occasion, I was not apprehensive about the staff — as I had been before. I wanted only to pass muster among the guests and avoid any queries about my presence. I didn't really need to worry, the kitchen staff were all so busy they didn't notice me.

The place was a turmoil of steaming pans, vats of aromatic juices, rich aromas, all elbowing bustle and impatient voices. It was pandemonium to a layman's eye but I had spent sufficient years cooking to be sure that it would all come together in the right way at the right time. Klaus Klingermann was directing operations like Captain Bligh on the foredeck of the *Bounty*. I knew that François had been in the kitchens until minutes before the banquet, preparing and organising. The strategic planning done, all was now in the hands of the tactician, Klaus.

I walked down the corridor and peeked out into the alley. It was grey and grim and looked like rain. Normal weather. I looked up and down the alley. It was normal too.

Back in the banquet room, there was light, gaiety, the throb of anticipation and the pulsing beat of conversation.

Benjamin Breakspear was still going strong. His face was growing redder and his voice was louder. I had to listen.

"— hog jowls, turnip greens and black-eyed peas. They're staple food in the South — no wonder they lost the Civil War! Eat them? Certainly not! Oh yes, I tasted them — just so I would be able to tell you how awful they are. Do they have any good food in the South? Their breads and their desserts are excellent — can't fault them at all."

"What about the steaks, Benjamin?" someone asked. "Are American steaks still the best?"

"I have to admit it, yes. Steaks are very good there. They don't always treat them properly though. For instance, they have 'Turf and Surf'." He shuddered and his whole substantial body quivered. "It's steak and lobster! Together! Can you imagine? Criminal waste of both in my opinion. I told the proprietor so in one establishment but he just laughed and said that Americans like catchy titles. "More than food?" I asked him and he laughed again.

A dazzling red-head walked by but joined a group before I could move to intercept. She must have been well-known for everyone greeted her warmly.

Circulating further, I caught the tail-end of another discussion. I would like to have heard the beginning but all I got was "– but that's because in France, cooking has grown out of the marrow of the nation, just like music in Germany, sport in Australia and art in Italy."

I picked up a little more of the next one. "When a top French chef lowers his standards then the decline of French cooking is obvious."

"In what way is he doing that?" asked an elderly lady with a heavily made-up face. I told her in detail.

"And what about the cat food manufacturers who invited French restaurateurs to advertise their produce on television?" asked another.

"Oh no!" was the horrified chorus.

"Well, they have refused but who knows what will happen if the offer is raised?"

There were shrugs, mutters, dark looks and dire forebodings from the group. It was getting grim. I moved on. I could see Raymond some distance away, looking as angry as ever. A lady with blue-rinsed hair was telling him a story with hand accompaniments.

Nearer at hand, Larry Leopold was speaking, his pointed beard wagging.

"Of course you should drink a different wine with every meal. After all, wasn't it our spiritual founder, Antonin Careme, who said 'Economy is the only enemy of the gourmet'?"

"But doesn't drinking so many different wines give you a headache the next day?" asked a timid soul who was surely not a member.

"No," replied Leopold promptly. "It's only drinking indifferent wines that does that."

The laughter that greeted this comment was interrupted by a muted gong. The guests began moving slowly towards the tables, seeking their name cards.

François passed me. We exchanged another look and another nod. The movement was general now and many were sitting. The Circle was a well-trained organisation — or else they were anxious for François' cooking.

François had done his work well, he must have friends in high places in the Circle for I was surrounded by people I didn't know. More to the point, none of them knew me. He had shown me the guest list and I had ticked off the names I recognised but even so he had been very efficient.

My table companions included a jolly man who said he owned several pastry shops, a visiting lady journalist from Australia, the proprietor of a restaurant in Paris and the general manager of a travel agency which specialised in gatronomic tours. The opportunity for any probing questions as to who I was and why I was there was fortunately cut short by the arrival of dishes of Tartelettes à la Dijonnaise. These were tiny tarts of tomato, cheese and onion with garlic and herbs. They had been heated precisely long enough to bake the pastry and heat the tomatoes while melting the cheese to form a crispy golden crust. The man with the pastry shops heaped praise on the timing.

The wine waiters were pouring the first wine. It was a Deidesheimer Kieselberg Kabinett, apple-fresh, marginally low on acid but lively and piquant. Champagne would have been an unimaginative alternative.

Next came a tiny portion of Brouillade d'Oeufs Mystère. This was a real touch by a master chef — taking so much effort for what amounted to only a few spoonfuls — but what spoonfuls! François had poured Mornay sauce and melted Parmesan cheese in baking dishes, layered them with thin-sliced mushrooms previously sautéed in cream and minced shallots then poured in scrambled eggs and covered with more sauce and cheese. The trick with the scrambled eggs was to add raw egg at the end of the cooking in order to give it a really smooth consistency and François had done it to perfection.

The wine glasses had been removed and another wine was being poured. It was a Château Lafite and its glorious colour was full of promise. My table companion with the travel agency said he had organised several trips to the Bordeaux region and quoted Professor Roger, the eminent authority on the wines of that district — "The man who has never tasted a great bottle of Lafite cannot know the perfection of which claret is capable."

The Frenchman with the restaurant in Paris said, "Mr Malcolm Forbes agreed with that — he had his son buy a bottle at an auction for $165,000." We all looked at the approaching bottles with renewed respect.

The satisfied nods which went around the table upon tasting it suggested that the Lafite's taste met this reputation. It was perfectly proportioned, mature and full of charm. A claret might have seemed an odd choice for this early in the meal but the next course was arriving. Sasarties are a South African dish despite their Malay name and consist of paper-thin slices of beef, marinated for forty-eight hours then quickly grilled over a very hot fire and served with a slice of pumpkin.

It was the next course which brought the wine into prominence though and a very unusual selection this was but this seemed to be the hall-mark of the Circle of Careme. The dish was Lamproise Bordelaise.

The Australian journalist lady was an Anglophile who reminded us of the story of King Henry I, said to have died of a surfeit of lampreys. It used to be called the dish of kings, she said but after one of them died of it, the dish's popularity declined and it has been virtually unknown since World War I.

François had marinated the lampreys and then cooked them in fish stock, bay leaf and port wine. Now they were being served with a rich, dark Bordelaise sauce over them. Cut and served in such a manner as to remove all its natural resemblance to the eel, lamprey had a taste midway between sweetbreads and turtle meat.

The pastry man was effusive in his praise. "The wine was chosen to accompany the sauce not the fish," he pointed out. "Very wise." The excellence of the food muted the conversation then as the last morsels were disappearing from plates, the benevolent influence of the Château Lafite renewed discussions.

I could see Sally Aldridge, heated and vociferous again.

Near enough to hear was Vito Volcanini, rated by many as Britain's leading Italian restaurateur and owner of the hugely successful Trevi.

"The food of Parma and Bologna may serve the stomach," Vito was saying, "but it is the food of Apulia that touches the heart. There, it is a part of life and of living. Sitting down to a meal is a joyous occasion, a ceremony — no, that is wrong, that suggests something pompous, something scheduled — and Apulian food is never that."

"It is Arab-influenced though, isn't it?" asked Ellsburg Warrington.

"Arab — yes and Greek, Turkish, Norman, Spanish . . ."

"Seafood mainly though," insisted Warrington.

Vito put down his fork and kissed his fingers.

"Zuppa di pesce — there is no other like it. It is magnifico. Every local fish will be in it — bream, langoustine, mussels, clams, lobster, octopus, squid, sea urchins — and any other fish that swims into the net."

"So it varies from one day to the next," needled Warrington. "How can you keep customers that way?"

"Of course it varies!" Vito's response was explosive. "What do you want? A soup controlled by a computer?"

Frankie Orlando sat within range. His Medici Palace was also a very popular Italian restaurant and it was inevitable that Frankie should disagree. His background put him in a different camp to Vito when it came to cooking.

"Apulian food is okay," said Frankie, condescendingly. "Fourth, maybe fifth in Italy. As everybody knows, Tuscan food is the best. Roast pig stuffed with garlic, rosemary, fennel and sage — now there is a dish for royalty. But you don't have to be royalty to enjoy it. It is sold from vans in the streets, delicious slices of tender pork with some well-salted crackling and wrapped in a piece of paper — just like your fish and chips used to be."

"Peasant cooking," sneered Vito. "In Tuscany, the grill and the spit do all the work and the wood smoke does all the flavouring. What need is there of cooks in Tuscany?"

Frankie Orlando had his mouth open for a spirited reply

when Maggie McNulty said silkily, "Personally, I prefer Venetian cooking."

There was quiet for a few seconds. Vito and Frankie regarded her with astonishment. How dare any non-Italian enter the arena — and a woman at that!

"Fegato Veneziana — made from calves' liver naturally. Now there is a dish," Maggie went on smoothly. "Have either of you ever had it at Dino Boscarati's in Mestre? Superb! Or how about duck with apple and chestnuts — a perfect example of using local ingredients. Accompanied by a bottle of St Magdalener, it's a —"

Maggie had over-reached. They leaped on her.

"Santa Maddalena!" snorted Vito. "With duck?"

"Impossible!" cried Frankie. "It needs a Teroldego or an Amarone."

"They're red," objected Vito. "Don't you know anything about wine in Tuscany? You need a white wine to allow the full flavour of the duck to come through. A Gambellara or a Friuli would be the —"

The Italians had the ball back and were bound together in an alliance that might last several minutes. The main course was being served now though and attention was re-directed.

"Roast Pork Perigourdine" it said on the menu card. Meltingly tender symmetrical discs of roast pork with a centre piece of truffle and an undertaste of garlic with the jellified gravy from the joint, they were accompanied by Pommes Parisiennes.

I knew that François had spent most of the morning supervising the preparation of this masterpiece of seeming simplicity. The wine was a Château Ausone, a veteran vintage, master of the table and a benevolent dictator of the meal. Rich and full yet smooth and rounded, it had an elegant nose and a lasting but restrained finish.

What was that? Someone not waiting to enjoy this marvellous dish? Tarquin Warrington had risen to his feet and was heading for the door. It was not one of the doors leading to the facilities — it looked as if he were leaving. He was passing my seat and I put out a restraining arm.

"Leaving so soon?" I asked him.

"Yes," he said curtly and shook off my arm.

He was never particularly polite but I had a job to do even if he didn't know it. "Why are you leaving before the meal is over?" I asked.

"None of your business," he snapped and was gone.

That was strange. What would Lord Peter Wimsey have done? He would probably have been enjoying the meal as much as I was and would have shrugged it off as a problem to be solved later. I didn't know what else to do — I could hardly stop him leaving — so I emulated Lord Peter.

"That lamprey was really delicious," said the Australian lady. "Better even than carp."

"Never eaten carp," confessed the pastry man. 'I kept goldfish as a boy. They're related, I understand, so you can see why I'd never think of eating carp."

The Frenchman shook his head. "The English have always been sentimental about food."

The travel agency man said, "Nightingales' tongues used to be very popular in Ancient Greece. I had them at a banquet once."

The pastry man shuddered. "I could never eat anything that sings."

"Don't see why not," said the Australian lady cheerfully. "You eat things that moo, don't you?"

The Château Ausone flowed substantially and soon there was not an uncleaned plate in sight. Comments were being exchanged and François would be glowing with pleasure if he could hear them. It had been truly a memorable meal.

There was a puzzled murmur which seemed to roll through the many conversations. Heads turned. It looked as if there was going to be a speech. IJ had risen to his feet and stood surveying the room. Voices quieted. Most faces were surprised. No one was expecting this and François had not said anything to me about a speech.

Silence fell. Every guest was watching IJ, waiting for him.

He stood, surveying the Circle.

"The two of them are in it together," he said in a loud, clear voice. There was a soft buzz of mystified muttering. No one knew what to make of this. IJ looked from side to side, taking in the entire banquet room. He seemed to be looking at everyone yet somehow focusing elsewhere.

"I have the proof," he said confidently. His hand patted his side. It appeared to be a gesture of confidence but I realised that he was patting the pocket where he had put the envelope handed to him by Roger St Leger.

"I can prove . . ." his voice, strong before was faltering now. He made an effort to get out the words. "I can prove that they are —"

He didn't finish the sentence. He collapsed across the table with a crash of glasses and crockery. An overturned bottle spread its dark-red stain across the white table-cloth. A woman squealed and there were gasps of horror.

Next to IJ, Goodwin Harper on one side and Raymond on the other side pulled him up and eased him back into his chair. Goodwin Harper had his hands on IJ's wrist, feeling for a pulse.

There was not a sound in the room. Goodwin Harper felt IJ's neck then he straightened slowly, a look of bewilderment on his face.

"He's dead," said Goodwin Harper.

CHAPTER NINE

The scene in the banquet room was vastly different from that of half an hour earlier. Then it had been glowing with camaraderie and basking in good humour. Now, fear and uncertainty hovered in the air like great vampires.

The guests stood clustered in small uneasy groups, discussing IJ's death in low voices. Suspicion and doubt were in every face. Hercule Poirot would have said that the smell of death was in the air but to be honest, the odours of good food still lingered.

The calls for an ambulance and the police had brought forth a constable from his beat, hastily summoned by his walkie-talkie and he was in the restaurant within two or three minutes — even before the initial furore had subsided. The doors had promptly been closed and within a further few minutes, a sergeant and a horde of constables had descended upon Le Trouquet d'Or.

Against a wall, the body of IJ lay on a table, the subject of many a nervous glance. The occasional guest wandered over, unbelieving but irresistibly drawn then turned away.

Near me, Benjamin Breakspear was regaling his neighbours with a reminiscence brought on by someone thoughtlessly asking him the kind of question he doted on.

"Oh yes, I was in a James Bond film once," he boomed. "I was killed off in the first five minutes but I . . ." Something on the faces of his listeners must have given him a hint. He was ordinarily as impervious as a buffalo but on this occasion, he went on quickly — "Just a film, of course. Not at all like real life . . .'

Maggie McNulty approached me. "God, I need a drink! Don't you have any influence around here? These young men in uniform are very sweet but they haven't been trained in the social amenities."

"You'll have to forgive them, Maggie. I don't think we can expect them to be serving any liquor just yet. After all, the body isn't even cold."

Maggie shivered. "Did you have to say that?" She walked away in search of better co-operation.

Vito Volcanini was waving his arms and rolling his eyes. I supposed he was saying something dramatic and Latin. Johnny Chang was listening, imperturbable by contrast to Vito's volatility. The police sergeant weaved his way through the knots of people, his eyes on me.

"Can I have a word, sir?" he asked politely.

"Certainly." We distanced ourselves from the others. I noticed that constables had been stationed by all the doors, not blatantly, in fact quite discreetly though it was evident that no one could get in or out unless they allowed it. Two or three of the constables had disappeared, presumably gone to the kitchens to establish similar control.

"Sergeant Nevins, sir," he introduced himself. He was a little over thirty, red-faced and beefy. He looked like a tough man to face in a rugger scrum. "I believe you're responsible for security in this establishment."

"Not exactly, sergeant —" I began.

"Mr Duquesne says he hired you to keep an eye on things here."

"Well, yes, that's true but —"

"In the Force, we would consider that as responsible for security, sir."

"It may look that way to you, sergeant, but in fact I have only just been hired."

"Hired to be responsible for security, sir?"

"There's more to it than that!" I was getting rattled. Did what I had been hired to do include security? Perhaps so but I had not anticipated anything like this. What niggled at me too was the feeling that whatever I had been hired to do, I hadn't done it very well. Still, no one could blame me for not preventing IJ's death but Sergeant Nevins' questions were getting under my skin.

"You had any inkling of what might happen here, sir?"

"Of course not, none at all."

"You weren't told to watch out for food poisoning or such?"

"Certainly not."

"Perhaps you can tell me why you were hired, sir?"

I'm not sure what I would have told him. It would have been blistering, that's for sure. But it was at that moment that a door opened and a constable entered, ushering in a man in plain clothes.

This was the man who was to be in charge of the investigation. It was obvious from his manner and his bearing. He looked competent and efficient. If there was a crime to be solved, here was the man to solve it.

He was close to six feet, slim and spare and carried himself with military erectness. He was about fifty, had a small neat moustache and a keen, alert face. Any casting office would have signed him to play the commandant of the Foreign Legion garrison. His light grey suit was Gieves and Hawkes and his tie was Pierre Cardin. He was clearly used to authority — that was clear from the way his gaze swept around the room. Even as it alighted on Sergeant Nevins, that policeman was already hurrying across, his interrogation of me forgotten.

They talked in low tones for a few minutes. The newcomer went over to the side of the room where the body of IJ lay. He examined the corpse without disturbing it then spoke to the sergeant who looked round the room. He walked towards François, brought him back. They talked briefly. François nodded and left. The sergeant spoke to a nearby guest who pointed out Ted Wells, presumably as the nearest thing to a responsible official as the Circle of Careme possessed. The sergeant brought him and there was a longer conversation. The newcomer raised his voice and addressed the room. Everyone else fell silent.

"I'm Inspector Hemingway from Scotland Yard." His voice was strong and firm. He didn't have to speak loudly to be heard. "I must ask your co-operation so that we can get to the bottom of this tragic incident as quickly as possible. The constables will be taking their places at tables where you will give them your name, address, phone number and affiliation. If you have any information which you think might be helpful, give them that too."

Ellsburg Warrington stepped forward, bristling with indignation. "This is preposterous! We are all well-known people — you cannot treat us like this!"

Hemingway regarded him calmly. "I know who you are, Mr Warrington and I recognise several of your fellow guests but a death has occurred and it is my responsibility to establish how and why. The quicker we conduct these formalities, the sooner you can go."

"We may leave then?" asked Mike Spitalny.

The inspector nodded. "Yes, you may."

"Can we stay if we wish?" called out Nelda Darvey. Good old Nelda, always the news-hound. It would be a great coup for her column.

"No, Miss Darvey," answered Hemingway smoothly.

I was astonished. What kind of a detective was this who recognised Ellsburg Warrington and Nelda Darvey?

The constables were getting set up already and guests were jostling for position. Inspector Hemingway and Sergeant Nevins were coming towards me. I had no intention of letting the initiative get back into the hands of the sergeant. I promptly introduced myself to the inspector. The piercing grey eyes assessed me swiftly.

"Ah, yes, you're the fellow who helped Winston's Restaurant in Holland Park to locate a European source of mahi-mahi."

"I'm amazed," I stammered. "How on earth did you come to know that? Not that it was a confidential assignment — but surely Scotland Yard has more important things to do than keep track of fish shipments!"

"I'm in charge of the Food Squad," said Hemingway.

I goggled. "The Food Squad?"

"Yes. The Yard has a Fraud Squad, an Art Squad, a Computer Squad and we even have some chaps who specialise in matters pertaining to religion. They call them the God Squad."

"Good Heavens!"

"Quite so. Why then, shouldn't we have a Food Squad? We may be behind the others in total crime turn-over but we're catching up."

I was flabbergasted. "As it happens, I spent nine years in homicide," Hemingway was continuing, "so I assigned myself to this case when I was told an unexplained death had occurred — especially as it involves a famous name."

His tone took on just a fraction more ice and I knew he was going by what he had been told by the red-faced sergeant. "Now, perhaps you'll tell me exactly what you're doing here tonight? I believe you're here in a security role."

The private eye of fiction is always ready for this question. "I can't tell you that," he always says. "My client's identity is confidential and I can tell you nothing about my assignment without his permission." He would light a cigarette and puff smoke arrogantly at the inspector.

The merest of fleeting thoughts sped through my brain — I would say something like that and Hemingway would bluster and threaten then finally back down, muttering threats about having my licence taken away.

The thought was gone as fast as a turkey leg at a Salvation Army Christmas dinner. Hemingway said, almost conversationally — "I urge your complete frankness. A man has died here tonight. Because of his role in the media, a lot of questions are going to be asked about how it could happen. I intend to get all the answers I need and I'm starting with you. Now, what are you doing here?"

His tone might have been conversational but his eyes were glacial. It took only milli-seconds for me to decide to abandon private eye convention for the moment and tell all I knew.

He listened attentively. When I had told him everything, it didn't sound like much, even to me.

"So you had no reason to anticipate that anything more sinister might happen than these incidents you mention?"

"Absolutely no reason." I put all my conviction into it.

"Did you know Jenkinson?"

"I recognised him from seeing him on TV but I've never met him."

"Did you meet him tonight?"

"No."

"Do you have any idea what he was doing here? I wouldn't have expected him to be a member of the Circle."

"No, I don't know why he was here. And no, I wouldn't either."

Hemingway nodded. "I'll check on that. Anything else?"

"Tarquin Warrington was here. He is surely a member. He left though — just as the main course was being served. I asked him why but he simply told me it was none of my business."

"Very well. I'll look into that too. Any opinions on the cause of death? You saw him die."

"Poison, I suppose . . . I mean, what else could it be?"

"The police surgeon will be here any minute — then we may know a little more." He looked into my face. "How do you feel?"

"Feel? Terrible," I assured him. "I'm hired to —"

Hemingway cut me off with an impatient gesture. "That's not what I mean. The sergeant is instructing the constables to ask each person the same question. Doesn't it strike you as unlikely that only one person is poisoned? Everyone ate the same food."

"I see what you mean."

"I didn't announce it. A person's imagination can become active. If anyone admits to a constable that they don't feel well, they will be taken immediately to St Cyril's Hospital."

Inspector Hemingway knew his job. I was glad he didn't look upon me as an interfering private eye. I was on shaky ground already.

"My assistant, Sergeant Fletcher is in the kitchens, taking samples of all the foods eaten tonight —"

"And the wines and coffee," I added, trying to sound efficient.

"Of course. I'm going to have the sergeant liaise with you afterwards."

I groaned inwardly. Surely not another Sergeant Nevins! My career as a private eye looked like being a short one.

"Don't leave until the last guest has left," ordered Hemingway. "Then check with me before you go."

I nodded agreement. "Very well." He was gone. I saw him talking to Goodwin Harper. It was only then that I remembered the envelope that I had seen Roger St Leger hand to IJ before the dinner had been served. Should I go and tell the inspector? He was deep in earnest conversation and Per Larsson had joined them now. They didn't look as if they would relish being disturbed. In any case, what could I tell them? My only suspicion was based on the looks on their faces. How could I convey those?

I was supposed to be a detective. Right, I'd detect. If there was nothing of significance in IJ's pocket, I didn't need to say a word to the inspector. I made my way casually across the room.

None of the doors had been opened yet and no one had left. A few guests had gone into the lines but many still stood in groups, discussing in low voices. I edged my way through.

As I approached the body, I saw Roger St Leger standing a few paces away. He was looking at IJ with a strange expression on his face. Was it sadness, compassion, sympathy? Maybe none of those. Satisfaction? Surely not and yet . . . he turned and saw me. He gave a start and walked quickly away.

I looked around surreptitiously. All clear. I moved close to the body. I could see the corpse-white face and the bloodless lips. I took another step —

"Looks quite peaceful, doesn't he?" said a voice and I almost jumped out of my skin. It was Charlie Flowers, formerly of Wheelers who now had his own small chain. I nodded. To my relief, Charlie's attention was on IJ and not focused on my guilty start.

My hands had flown up with the shock. I was able to conceal my reaction by raising them in a gesture of pious supplication. For good measure, I rolled my eyes up at the chandeliers.

"In the midst of life . . ." I murmured in tones of incantation that many an archbishop would have envied. Charlie nodded and moved on. This time, when I glanced around, I made certain that no one was near and, as far as I could tell, watching.

Keeping my gaze fixed on IJ's face, I stole a hand to his suit-coat pocket. I twitched it open and slid my fingers inside. I could feel nothing . . . I reached further . . .

My attention was still on his face when an ice-cold hand clamped on my wrist. The breath froze in my throat but there was worse to come. The eyelids flickered open and Ivor Jenkinson slowly rose to a sitting position. The head turned, jerkily and his accusing glare burned into me.

CHAPTER TEN

IJ sat in the centre of the room in a large armchair that one of the staff had brought in.

He still looked like a corpse. His face was deathly-white and devoid of any texture suggesting life. His eyes were dull yet staring — a chilling combination. He had mumbled only a few words and none of them had made sense. Baffled murmurs could still be heard for the spectacle of a dead man coming back to life had overwhelmed the gathering. Those who had been standing in line to give their particulars to the constables so they could leave had now come rushing back.

Goodwin Harper came up to Hemingway.

"He was dead," Goodwin Harper was saying in bewilderment. "I swear he was dead. I'm no doctor but I was a medical orderly in the war and I've had first-aid training since. I know how to find life symptoms and there were none. None!" His voice rose. "He was dead, I'd swear it!"

The inspector laid a steadying hand on his arm. "The police surgeon will be here any minute. We'll hear what he has to say."

While they were talking, another discussion had broken out.

"Brandy," said Frankie Orlando, looking solicitously at IJ's inanimate features. "Get him some brandy."

"Should be Armagnac," suggested an unidentified voice.

"Nonsense," scoffed Benjamin Breakspear, the authority on everything. "Cognac, preferably the VSPO."

"Courvoisier," corrected Bill Keating who had the dealership.

"Stravecchio," Vito Volcanini said. "Horses have won the Palio on Stravecchio."

"As a restorative, Calvados is the best drink," contributed another.

"Here," said a voice just as Hemingway broke off his discussion with Goodwin Harper and saw what was happening.

"No — don't give him anything!" he cried but it was too late. IJ had obediently accepted the brandy glass that was put into his hand and drained it, oblivious to its origin or year.

In a few lightning steps, Hemingway was at his side but was only in time to catch the glass that fell from IJ's seemingly nerveless fingers. All eyes were on IJ. For several heartbeats, the scene was motionless. Then IJ said in a surprisingly clear voice:

"It will be my best programme. It will prove the guilt and . . ."

His voice trailed away. His stare seemed to be focused but on some distant object. He was still chalky-white and his posture was stiff and unnatural. He sat like a robot. The assembly was silent and when IJ spoke again, all crowded to listen.

"Now they can get the money, it will be the biggest . . ."

His voice faded again. We were momentarily distracted by the opening of the door and a conversation with one of the constables which didn't carry.

A man bustled in. He was round and tubby and his short legs moved in quick jerky steps. He wore an old black suit with a waistcoat that barely buttoned. The black bag he carried meant he must be the police surgeon.

Hemingway saw and hurried to greet him.

"Dr Pepperdine, glad you're here. This way please."

The little man hurried over, looking curiously at the room and its occupants. He appeared irritated at having to be here.

"All right," he snapped. "Where's the body?"

There was a pause. "I am," said IJ. His voice was firm but he did not seem to see the doctor.

"Don't be absurd," barked Dr Pepperdine. He glared at the inspector. "What's all this tomfoolery, Hemingway? Why are you wasting my time? You said there was a dead man!"

The inspector had probably never been at a loss for words in his life but he came very close to it now.

"Mr Jenkinson was pronounced dead," he said finally, choosing his words with care.

Dr Pepperdine peered at the figure in the armchair.

"Jenkinson? Aren't you that TV chappie?"

The question was lost on IJ whose gaze wandered as if he were trying to locate the source of the voice.

"Yes, he is," supplied Hemingway.

"You say he was pronounced dead? Pronounced by whom, may I ask?"

Goodwin Harper took a hesitant step forward.

"I thought he was dead —"

"Thought!" snorted the bristly little doctor. "You thought he was dead? Ha!" The last exclamation came out like a gunshot and IJ's attention finally turned in the doctor's direction. He studied him as if finding him curious.

"I examined him too," Hemingway said. "Cursorily but I did check his pulse, wrist and throat, his eyes and his respiration. Can't blame Mr Harper — I agreed with him. Mr Jenkinson did seem to be dead."

Dr Pepperdine was opening his black bag and taking out his stethoscope. He unravelled the cord and clamped the plugs in his ears. "This chap *thought* he was dead — you say he *seemed* to be dead," he barked at Hemingway. "Doesn't look dead to me."

He pulled open IJ's shirt and was about to place the probe on his chest. That close, he looked into IJ's pallid features. A tiny portion of the doctor's bluster ebbed away. "On the other hand . . ." he muttered. He listened for a moment. IJ was impassive again as if he were unaware of the presence of the doctor or his stethoscope.

"Irregular heart beat," the doctor said in a low tone. He took a small torch from his bag and looked into IJ's pupils. The eyes still stared, unaffected by the beam.

The doctor tossed his instruments into the bag and zipped it. "Get him to a hospital as quickly as possible," he ordered. He wasn't quite as testy now.

"The ambulance should be here any minute," said Hemingway even as a constable came hurrying over. "Ambulance outside, sir."

"Something I don't like here," Pepperdine said to the inspector. "Have the ambulance bring him to St Cyril's Hospital in Marylebone. They have some special equipment there I'll need. I'll be there by the time the ambulance arrives. Tell them to make it fast."

He picked up his bag and was out of the room with his short jerky steps before Hemingway could reply.

Attention returned to IJ. He looked very slightly more normal. His flaccid skin had taken on a tinge of translucency and there was a hint of expression in the eyes that had been absent before.

I was delighted — for my sake as much as his. My first assignment as a private eye — it would have been unthinkable to have a corpse on my hands.

Inspector Hemingway evidently noticed the improvement too.

"Feeling better, Mr Jenkinson?" he asked. I felt he could be excused the cliché question after the ordeal he had been through.

"It's the Courvoisier," explained Bill Keating. "It's a wonderful remedy."

"I thought he got Cognac," said Benjamin Breakspear.

It was hard to tell if IJ heard the inspector's question. He seemed to be trying to speak but then gave up.

The drama was over. Feet were shuffling. It was an anti-climax and the guests wanted to go home.

Then IJ's head turned and he tried to look over his shoulder. Was he trying to see someone? Slowly, he stood up and it was like watching Frankenstein's monster rise from the grave. I expected him to creak.

He took a hesitant step and one hand raised as he tried to point. His mouth opened but nothing came out. His knees sagged and he crumpled and fell forward on his face.

The unfortunate Goodwin Harper was nearby and he was first at IJ's side. He examined the prone man then shook his head and looked up at us in bewilderment.

"He's dead," Goodwin Harper said. "He's dead again!"

CHAPTER ELEVEN

Scotland Yard was very disappointing. All right, perhaps I didn't really expect squad-rooms, drunks, huge pistols and badges with haunted-looking detectives wolfing down massive sandwiches and swilling hot coffee by the bucketful while others lounged by the water-cooler, arguing over 401s, 622s, citizen's rights and the Miranda-Escobedo law.

Even so, we are all brainwashed to some degree by this American television view of crime-fighting. It nags persistently at the memory despite being surrounded by the calm and orderly lobby of Scotland Yard as I was now. I looked it over casually, not wanting it to be too obvious that I had never been here before. It was much like another lobby I had been in recently only that had belonged to a cereal manufacturer.

A very polite young lady took my name and asked me to be seated. I barely had time to glance at the headlines of the *Daily Telegraph* when she called my name.

"Sergeant Fletcher will be with you in a moment, sir."

Oh dear! I hoped he wasn't going to be another Sergeant Nevins — a beer-drinking, rugby-playing bully with no imagination and a dislike of security men.

I returned to the *Telegraph*. At least Hemingway seemed like a reasonable fellow, aside from his icy efficiency. I went over in my mind the latter part of the previous evening. When Dr Pepperdine had returned to Le Trouquet d'Or, he had been madder than a wet hen. "What's the matter with you, Hemingway?" he bellowed. "How many more times are you going to get me back here to look at the same corpse?"

The inspector displayed admirable self-control. "You'd better examine him very carefully, Doctor —"

"Examine him carefully! Of course I will! D'ye think I didn't before?"

"This time," said Hemingway, remaining remarkably

unruffled "I am sure you'll agree that Mr Jenkinson is indeed dead."

The scrappy little doctor went to work, using several instruments I didn't recognise. Despite his testy words, his examination lasted considerably longer than before. Finally, he sighed. "Poor chap's dead and no mistake."

The doctor had IJ's body loaded into the ambulance then he climbed in himself. "Not taking any chances," he growled. The inspector spent a little time speeding up Sergeant Nevins and the constables in their task of recording the particulars of all the guests. He came over to me. "No need for you to wait any longer. Come and see me at the Yard tomorrow morning at ten." So here I was.

The story hadn't made this edition of the *Telegraph*. I wondered if Nelda Darvey had been able to hold the presses or whatever it was they did and get the story on the streets in her paper. Before I could scan the other journals on the table, my name was called.

I turned to see as toothsome a little blonde as I had ever set eyes on. Slightly under medium height, hair trimmed short and curling slightly, her bright blue eyes sparkled and her full lips parted in a smile as if she was glad to see me.

"I'm Sergeant Fletcher," she introduced herself in a warm, friendly voice.

"I'm very glad to meet you," I said and I really meant it. Her uniform fitted her trim figure beautifully. Was it half a size too small though? Or did Scotland Yard have better tailors than I would have expected? Further speculation was cut short as Sergeant Fletcher asked solicitously, "No trouble parking, I hope?"

"No," I assured her, still astounded at the improvement over Sergeant Nevins. "I came by tube."

"Good." She smiled as if genuinely relieved by this news. "We have a large group of police officers from Korea visiting today, studying our methods and they all came by limousine. The parking area is chaos."

"I'm sure that you can teach them a lot."

"This way." She led me out through a door that clicked open and then shut on seemingly invisible commands. We went along a corridor and I followed with pleasure, admiring the sway of her shapely rear in the tight black skirt and the twinkling black-clad ankles. We entered a lift, went up two floors and at a glass-panelled door, the comely sergeant knocked and led me in.

Inspector Hemingway's office was sparse and very functional. There were no files — they must be central. Against one wall was a glass-fronted cabinet full of bottles and jars. The inspector sat behind a tidy desk and behind him was a photograph of him with Edwina Currie in front of the House of Commons. There were two chairs for visitors. Sergeant Fletcher sat on the left and I faced the inspector.

The sergeant crossed her knees demurely and smiled gentle encouragement. I enjoyed the smile and the knees but hoped that it didn't mean I needed to be bolstered up for an ordeal. It started mildly enough.

The inspector greeted me briefly and opened a file in front of him. He studied it for a few seconds and said:

"Your father died when you were fourteen. You left school and went to work at Smithfield Market."

I stared at him astonished.

"That's my file you have there?"

He nodded. I looked at the sergeant. She smiled again. I hoped I was still correct in reading encouragement into it.

"After a year in the market, you got a job as an apprentice chef at Kettner's. You worked and learned and were soon promoted."

"Inspector, I can't believe this. You actually have my life story in that file?"

Hemingway leaned back in his chair. "You became the youngest sous-chef at Kettner's then you joined the White Funnel Line — on cruise ships." He looked slightly quizzical. Perhaps every detail wasn't in my file after all.

"I wanted to see something of the world outside London," I explained, "and I wanted the opportunity to create some original dishes and get experience of foreign food. Kettner's was one of the top restaurants in London but the scope was limited."

Hemingway glanced over at the sergeant. She wasn't smiling at the moment, she was serious and official. She said:

"There are gaps between the cruises — between the dates. What were you doing then?"

"I took chef jobs at some of the places on the White Funnel routes — San Francisco, Santiago, Miami, Sydney, Lisbon. I wanted to practise my preparation of foreign foods." I looked from her to the inspector. "Why? I'm not being interviewed for the Secret Service, am I?"

The sergeant's smile returned. "Just filling in the record."

Hemingway took up my life story. He glanced only occasionally at my file. He must be familiar with it. Why was I that important? I wondered uneasily.

"You then went to work for Collis and Wood — in procurement, I believe?"

"Yes. I went on assignments, locating unusual products for their buyers to follow up on, tracking down new sources of exotic foods."

"Then came World Wide Foods."

I nodded. "It was a mistake. I couldn't know they were shaky financially. It seemed a similar type of activity to F and M but with more responsibility and opportunity for initiative. But when they folded, it opened my eyes to even better possibilities. I took a chance and started my own agency."

"You became The Gourmet Detective."

"Right. Oh, I'm not really a detective, you understand —" I added that quickly before either of them could get any wrong ideas. "I detect only in the sense of finding rare foods and recipes, giving advice on marketing and so on."

Hemingway closed my file. I had been trying to see what else might be in there.

"I talked to Mr Dusquesne. He said he hired you after some peculiar happenings at his restaurant. I would say that makes you sound more like a private detective than a food detective."

His tone had gone accusatory and his expression, which seldom changed much, was now bleaker than before. I didn't like the sound of this.

"I had no idea there'd be any violence," I protested. 'François asked me instead of a real private eye because he felt that a knowledge of food was more important."

Hemingway drummed his fingers on my file. It was as if he

were drumming on my head, I could feel the reverberations.

"He told me that too. What did he mean by it? What is he afraid of?"

"I don't know," I confessed. "It's all happened too fast for me. All I know is that he told me someone was trying to put him out of business. He described some strange things that have been happening in his restaurant. I talked to some of his staff and it does sound as if he has reason to think that."

"And your presence at the Circle of Careme banquet was part of that assignment."

"Yes. Naturally he was concerned that nothing should happen on such a prestigious occasion."

"But it did." Hemingway had that bleak look again.

"Nobody regrets it more than I do. I feel guilty about letting it happen — and yet I don't know what I could have done to prevent it."

"I asked you last night if you had any ideas that might throw any light on this case. It was immediately after it had occurred so perhaps you were still stunned." He gave me that penetrating look again. "Anything further you can think of?"

"I mentioned Tarquin Warrington leaving early . . ."

The blue-eyed sergeant answered that. "I'm seeing him later this morning. He didn't go home last night."

"The other thing . . ." I was a little hesitant on this one and hoped it didn't show.

"Yes?" prompted the inspector.

"Just before the guests sat down at the table, Roger St Leger handed an envelope to IJ. He looked at it, seemed pleased by whatever was in it and put it in his pocket."

Hemingway looked disappointed. "And what do you gather from that."

"Well, the envelope wasn't in his pocket afterwards."

I knew I had fluffed it as soon as it was out of my mouth. Hemingway put his arms on the desk and drummed on my file. The sergeant uncrossed her legs and leaned forward.

"Afterwards?" snapped Hemingway.

"You would have found it if there was an envelope in his pocket, wouldn't you?" I babbled.

Hemingway was speculative. "Yes, you were the one who let out that yell when IJ recovered, weren't you?"

"You were the closest to him?" asked the sergeant and I chose to answer her first.

"I suppose I was." I would probably have implicated myself further only the sergeant said: "There was nothing like that in his pockets."

I avoided Hemingway's eye. He drummed a few more seconds. I stole a glance at the sergeant. She still looked good enough to be the dessert at a royal banquet but she was looking at Hemingway and not at me.

"How many of the people there did you know?" the inspector asked and I was off the hook for the time being.

"I know Nelda Darvey, Sally Aldridge and Maggie McNulty." At least that worked and the sergeant turned her gaze back to me. "I had carried out an assignment for Johnny Chang, I know Ted Wells — oh and Ellsburg Warrington and I have been on a few panels together. I have talked to Ray Burnaby on occasion at various wine tastings."

"M'm." The inspector's comment was as non-committal as a glass of tap water. "You're not too helpful, are you?" he asked abruptly.

It was rhetorical but I felt that some further emphasis might be in order. "Only because I can't tell you anything — the reason for that being I don't know anything. The first thing I'm going to do," I added, "is to tell François that our deal is off. I mean, I didn't bargain for this."

The merest glance was exchanged between the two of them but before I could attempt to analyse its meaning, Hemingway went on in a tone that was, for him, almost chatty.

"You were surprised that Scotland Yard has a Food Squad. Surely as The Gourmet Detective, you should have known that?"

"I only know food. I don't know anything about crime or Scotland Yard. Like I keep saying, I'm not a real detective."

"The Food Squad gets calls for assistance from most of the squads at the Yard," said Hemingway. "Fraud, Business, International, Banking — all of them interface with us from time to time."

"That's interesting," I said. I didn't know why he wanted to tell me all this.

"We supplied much of the evidence for a major legal battle,

we contributed to the Stratford inquiry and we have investigated several of the brewery takeovers."

I nodded at the photograph on the wall. "You were in on that too."

"Yes. This Circle of Careme case though is a different matter entirely. Violence is rare in our field — almost unknown."

"A violent death," said the sergeant.

"The death of a prominent man."

"In front of a large number of people," completed the sergeant.

They made a good double act, I had to admit. Why, I wondered, was I the audience?

"So it's not just different, it's extraordinary — and at this stage, baffling," Hemingway stated. "Which is why we need all the help we can get."

I looked suspiciously from one to the other. "I don't know why you're telling me all this," I said. "But I should have known you didn't invite me here for a cup of coffee."

"You wouldn't like our coffee here at the Yard," said Sergeant Fletcher sweetly. "It's a cheap Brazilian brand."

"Well, if you're not offering coffee, I'll go —" I rose to my feet.

Hemingway didn't move a muscle. He just said quietly, "Sit down," and I sat.

"But you accept that I know nothing that would help you." I didn't have much protest left but I would use what I had. "And I told you I can't make any more suggestions. So why don't you let me get out of here and you can both go back to work solving the mystery."

The sergeant's blue eyes had cooled. Hemingway's expression hadn't changed much but then it hadn't ever.

"I was puzzled by the initials P.I.E. in your file," the inspector commented.

Another change of direction. I was getting bewildered.

"So I asked the sergeant and she explained." I waited. "So you're a private eye fan?"

"Yes, I am," I said.

"Yet you insist that you're not trying to act as one."

He was back on that tack again. "I do insist," I said stoutly.

"I don't have a licence or anything. I just accepted this job and I wish I hadn't. I'm a food detective — not a private detective. Fictional private eyes are just a hobby."

"Scotland Yard has the final decision when it comes to licensing private detectives," Hemingway informed me. "We don't like them involved in our investigations — once a case is in our hands, we want them out of it." He stared at me. "Do you understand?"

"Absolutely," I said quickly. "No need to worry about me. I'll be glad to get out of this thing and stay out."

"I'm glad to hear that," the inspector said. The pert sergeant ventured the tiniest of smiles. I began to breathe easily again.

Hemingway picked up my folder. Good, I thought, he's going to file it and forget me. Instead, he slapped it down on his desk so hard it sounded like a gunshot and I leaped half out of my seat.

"Except I don't want you out. I want you in."

CHAPTER TWELVE

I goggled.

"Unfortunately, you're in a unique position," Hemingway said. Was there just a hint of regret in his voice? "You were there at the time of death, you know many of the people present, you are at home in the environment — and perhaps most important of all, you were already involved in an assignment which may be connected."

The sergeant's red-lipped smile was back. The inspector regarded me rather as a snake regards a rabbit.

"It's not really a unique position I'm in," I stammered. "It's unfortunate — not just for me, well, me too but I don't see how —"

"You are going to help us," Hemingway purred. "You are going to continue your assignment and you are going to tell us all you learn which may be connected with IJ's death. Anything, everything, however minute or seemingly irrelevant."

"I don't think I want to —"

"I'm not asking what you want." This inspector could be terrifying.

"It's best you co-operate," said the sergeant gently. "The inspector is not a man to cross."

What could I say? Not very much but I had to salvage an ounce of pride.

"If I'm to pass along all I learn and if we're co-operating then it means you'll tell me what you learn."

"That's not the inspector's proposal." Sugar wouldn't have melted in the delightful sergeant's mouth but whose side was she on anyway? Don't answer that, I told myself.

"But that's not fair!" I objected.

"I didn't say a word about being fair," said Hemingway. He was rapidly becoming one of my least favourite people.

"We don't expect you to work in the dark," he went on.

"We'll see you get any information that seems relevant. If we hold any items back, it will be because you have no need to know."

"I'll think it over, of course . . ." I said generously.

"You don't have to do that," retorted Hemingway. "This isn't a take it or leave it proposition."

"It's more of a like it or not proposition," the sergeant explained. She wasn't making any points with me either. She was trying to make up for it though — she gave me her full red lipped smile. "You're in, Mr Gourmet Detective!"

I felt like a very small fly in a very strong web. More struggling would not get me out, it might enmesh me more tightly. Besides, the inspector was speaking again.

"In mystery fiction, the private eye and the official detective are always at loggerheads. The private eye goes merrily on his way, breaking the law, bending the rules, intimidating witnesses, motivated only by sex and money and solving the crime only by luck and blundering." He paused then asked quizzically, "Am I right?"

"One hundred per cent," I agreed. "The official detective, on the other hand, is pompous, pedantic, stifled by red tape and a lack of imagination. Oh —" I added, "— and solving the crime only by luck and blundering." I waited a second. "Am I right?"

To his credit, Hemingway nodded amiably. "Sounds as though the criminal is unfortunate to be caught in either event, doesn't it?" He wagged a finger at me. "The point is — it's not going to be that way with us. You are going to help us and you are going to co-operate. Don't step on our toes — just continue your investigation as if IJ's death hadn't happened."

"But —" added the sergeant briskly, "don't lose sight of the fact that it did."

"How exactly are you treating this investigation?" I wanted to know.

"It's simply an investigation at this point. When we get the forensic results later, we may know more where we're going. Until we have evidence to the contrary however, we are going to handle it as we would a murder investigation."

I had wanted to be out, no question about it. Now that I was in though, I couldn't help feeling a glow of excitement.

Me — investigating a murder! Just like Philo Vance . . . well, maybe more like Archie Goodwin — but I was investigating. I sublimated my glee, may as well keep up a reluctant front.

The inspector was saying, "— And so in order to maintain close communications, I am going to assign Sergeant Fletcher to be your contact. Keep in close touch with her and keep her informed of your whereabouts at all times."

Maybe today was my lucky day after all. Being a private eye — I mean a real one, might have been a hidden fantasy but now it had come true. Keeping in touch — he had said close touch — with the sergeant could be another fantasy. I hadn't really wanted to be trapped in this business but we all have to make sacrifices.

"Yes, Inspector," I said meekly, trying to sound reluctant.

He nodded again. He was more human now that he had established his position of control. "One more thing . . ."

"Yes, Inspector?" I invited.

He pushed something across the desk. It was the menu for the banquet at the Circle of Careme. "Lamprey and pork?"

"And then a man dies," commented the sergeant.

"Is it a menu you'd recommend?" asked Hemingway.

"Possibly not," I said. "But a chef of the stature of François has to strive constantly for originality."

"You wouldn't say there's an element of hazard in serving lamprey and pork?"

"It can't have any significance," I said. "How could it?"

"I'm always suspicious of coincidence," Hemingway said.

"What about the other guests? Any of them report any symptoms?"

"Five," said the sergeant. "They've all been checked at St Cyril's."

"They're still in hospital?"

"No, they've all been released."

"What was wrong with them?"

"We'll have that report too, along with the other on IJ and all the foodstuffs and drink in the banquet room and the kitchen."

The inspector pulled back the menu. It seemed the interview — or the recruitment — was over. His purposeful face, the small clipped moustache and the determined expression in those piercing eyes made him seem all the more like the stern commandant of the Foreign Legion fort . . . only now he took on a resemblance to the same commandant who is sending an unwilling "volunteer" on a suicidal mission across the empty desert — well, empty except for thousands of bloodthirsty Arabs. It was a false analogy, I told myself . . .

"It's interesting that you're such a fan of PIs," he went on and his tone was a little lighter. "I enjoy reading novels about the official detectives."

He was getting more and more human all the time. Of course, he could afford to now.

"Perhaps it's because the official detective usually gets a raw deal in fiction. Too often, as you said, he is portrayed in an unfavourable manner. Where the private eye is intuitive, the official detective is incompetent — where the one can take short cuts, the other has to abide by bureaucratic procedures.

"But fiction seldom gives credit to the official detective — not even those who operate without tripping over private eyes."

"Novels which contain both detectives have necessarily to show the official as a bungler," I agreed. "So that the PI can look good by comparison."

"Exactly."

"So it's reasonable that when the official detective is on his own as the crime-solver, he needs to be more competent, more efficient, more —"

"More realistic," Hemingway supplied.

"Touché," I admitted. "You're right though. Who are your favourites?"

"Morse and Wexford among the current crop."

"Cuff?"

"I have the greatest respect for him but perhaps more for Steve Carella. The 87th Precinct is a hot-bed of crime."

"That brings in the other dimension — the surroundings of a family life," I said. "An image which suits the official detective but is all wrong for the private eye."

"That's why I like Carella," said the inspector. "He's more real and that deaf and dumb wife is different enough to be memorable."

He stood up.

"The sergeant will escort you out. It's been nice to have this chat with you."

"The last part especially," I said. "The earlier part — well I'll do the best I can."

"We value your co-operation," were the inspector's final words although he seemed to me to re-constitute his Legion commandant image and really mean:

"We hope your desperate mission will be successful. Then you can return."

CHAPTER THIRTEEN

W e had started the downward journey in the lift.

"So, Sergeant Fletcher," I said, "you will be able to tell me later today what the forensic report says."

"Yes. Do you want to give me your phone number? We can arrange to meet and I can tell you about it."

"Surely, Sergeant Fletcher, with that voluminous file which tells you which dentist I visited at the age of ten — you don't have to ask for my phone number?"

There was a merry twinkle in her eye. "Oh, perhaps it's in there somewhere . . . and I take your point. If we're going to be working together, the 'Sergeant Fletcher' might be cumbersome. My first name's Winifred, most call me Winnie."

"I'll call you Winnie too. Anything to simplify a working relationship," I said and mentally dubbed her "Winsome Winnie".

The lift stopped. She walked across the lobby with me. It was almost full. I would have loved to know which were criminals and which were informers and what the others were but I had the mantle of a private eye on my shoulders now.

"I'll call you later this afternoon," said Winnie.

"Fine," I said. "We can meet this evening if you don't mind overtime."

She pulled a wry face. "No such thing as regular hours when a case like this is in progress. It becomes a twenty-four hour a day proposition."

"I'll await your call."

"Good-bye for now." She held out a hand. "I'm glad you're with us on this."

"So am I — I think."

She smiled and walked out of the lobby.

So I was on the case. There were two people I had to tell

about it. I walked past the Guildhall and took a taxi to Bookery Cooks in Streatham.

Bookery Cooks is a unique establishment. Run by Michael and Molly Markham, two of my best friends, it is the Mecca for lovers of books about food and cooking. Entering, it looks like any bookshop at first — but then the delicious aromas of exotic dishes come wafting through the air. By the time the visitor has recovered from the unlikelihood of Indian cookbooks smelling of curry or Italian cookbooks of basil and garlic, the kitchen on the first floor of the store has become evident. The two attractive girls cooking and serving equally attractive food have also become apparent.

Today, it was Indonesian food, judging by the peanut odours of Satay and the pungent tickle of ginger. Dorothy, a tiny girl with freckles and a pony tail and a real knack with spices, waved a hand while tasting a sauce. Marita, a raven-haired beauty with an enticing smile but also a boy-friend who was a chef and six feet two, was herself a star performer particularly with Asian foods and marinades. She came over, waving something from the spit for me to taste.

I took the skewer and nibbled. I made horrible faces for Marita's benefit and she scowled ferociously and raised another skewer in a threatening gesture. I held up a placating hand and we went into our accustomed ritual.

"Lancashire pork —" I guessed.

"That's easy," she said. "And —"

"Marinated at least forty-eight hours —"

"That's easy too. And —"

"Marinated in soya sauce, garlic, er — chillies —"

"And laos powder . . ."

"Oh, of course — and then, let me taste again . . . The sauce . . ."

I tried another taste. "Roasted and crushed peanuts —"

"How do you know I didn't use peanut butter?" Marita demanded.

"Because you never take short-cuts —"

Her face crinkled in a happy smile.

"Go on. The sauce —?"

"Onions, garlic, more chillies, lemon grass, shrimp paste, lemon juice, sugar and — naturally — coconut milk."

Marita clapped her hands prettily. "Bravo!"

"Do I get another skewer?"

Marita pretended to consider. "I don't know — Well, maybe just one."

"Don't give him any more, Marita," called Dorothy. "It's almost lunch-time — he's free-loading."

"Stop teasing the staff," said a voice from behind me. "Good help is hard to find."

"It is when they cook like these two," I agreed, turning.

Michael Markham is small and compact. He moves with much purpose and determination, never wasting a movement. He had worked for a large international engineering concern and finally left to run his own factory. Food and its enjoyment was his ruling passion and as a sideline he had built up an archive on food and cooking that had no equal in the English-speaking world. He plucked information from obscure places, found recipes that were thought to be lost and was in continual demand to supply food facts to writers reviewers and compilers. He tired of the world of manufacturing, sold out and created Bookery Cooks in Streatham. At last the archive had a permanent home. The shop was a condensed, more easily manageable and greatly reduced version of the mini-empire he had run before. We teamed up and I put out my board as The Gourmet Detective with half of the financing coming from Michael and Molly and the agreement that he would furnish the food facts that I needed as well as pass along inquiries that needed follow-up, leads and commissions.

The truth was that Michael could have been a better gourmet detective than I would ever be. But he was happier now in a more modest, behind-the-scenes role, doing indirectly what he might have been doing directly. This more leisurely life with an absence of stress made both Michael and Molly happier.

"Ever think of opening a restaurant?" I asked him.

"What? You must be mad!" he grinned. "When Dorothy and Marita have this kind of talent! Why should I waste them in a restaurant?"

"That Satay Sauce is delicious. What do I look for on the label at Safeway?"

When Michael grins, he looks like Ronnie Corbett and his

large glasses seem to cover even more of his face. The grin faded now as he asked: "What about this terrible business at Le Trouquet d'Or and Ivor Jenkinson?"

"I was there," I told him.

His mouth opened and his eyes widened until his glasses slid down his nose. He pushed them back with one finger. "You! You were there at the Circle of Careme! How did you manage that?"

"I was lucky enough to get an invitation," I said, "although in the light of what happened, maybe I was unlucky."

"Come on in the office and tell me about it — I can't believe this! You were there! Molly!" he yelled and she appeared from the storage room. Molly is small like Michael and with a round, pleasant always smiling face. She gave me a hug.

"What's all the shouting?" she wanted to know.

"He was there! At the Circle of Careme!" Michael was almost dancing with excitement. "I can't wait to hear about it."

I told them everything, from beginning to end. Michael's glasses kept slipping down his nose as his eyebrows got higher and higher.

"A bit awkward for you," was Molly's sympathetic comment.

"I'm helping Scotland Yard with their inquiries."

"You mean you're under suspicion?" grinned Michael.

"Certainly not. I mean I'm really helping them. They think my assignment for François is somehow connected with IJ's death."

"So now you're a real private eye," said Michael admiringly.

"Just like Hercule Poirot," added Molly.

"Only he investigated murders," amended Michael.

It was Molly's eyebrows that went up now. "IJ was murdered?"

"Scotland Yard are handling it as a murder investigation until they know more."

"I haven't read the papers yet," Michael said. "I saw it on the television news this morning. They didn't say what he died of."

"They don't know yet."

"Sounded like poison. A weird one though. I mean, seeming to die then coming back to life." Michael shivered.

"Must have been scary." Molly looked apprehensive too.

"It was," I admitted. I hadn't gone into the details of IJ's icy hand seizing me in that terrifying grip. It had been a lot more scary than either Michael or Molly knew.

"Anything I can do to help?" Michael asked.

"Yes. See what you can dig out on Legionnaires' Disease, the Salmonella scare, the Mad Cow affair, the Currie and eggs business and anything else that seems relevant to you."

"Right." This was what Michael loved. Molly would be on her own in the book store for a while until Michael had ransacked every bit of information at his disposal.

"Oh, and see what you can find about lamprey, too, would you?"

"Lamprey?"

"It was on the menu."

"Was it indeed!" Michael pushed his glasses back up again.

"I know — the Yard are sceptical about it too. It doesn't have to be suspicious though. It is edible."

Michael nodded. "These master chefs go to great lengths to be different, don't they? One serves curry sauce on salmon and another served Cow's Udders once. I'll get on it right away. Anything else?"

I was about to say no when I had another thought.

"Maybe this is nothing but —"

"All the great detectives say that — then it turns out to be a vital clue. What is it?"

"See what the financial situation is at Le Trouquet d'Or and at Raymond's."

Michael was clearly surprised but didn't voice it. "That's it?"

"Not quite. How about one more skewer? I'm on my way over to Le Trouquet d'Or now and after last night, they may not want to invite me to lunch."

Michael grinned. "I think that can be arranged. You'd better try these meat balls too. Molly, is there any more of that South Tasmanian Burgundy left or has it gone off completely?"

Molly scowled at him. "We can do better than that.

Michael's got the continent right and that's about all," she confided to me. "We have this case of Australian Shiraz from Cathcart Ridge — it's a really super wine. Hang on, I'll bring some up."

The meat balls that Michael had referred to were, he told me, really called Rempah and are a sort of Indonesian hamburger. Coriander, cloves, cumin and ginger are the principal spices and of course, they contain shredded coconut like so many dishes from those islands. They are as easy to make as their Western equivalent and are ideal as a snack, an hors d'oeuvre or a main course. A plateful of those, two more skewers of Marita's pork and a couple of glasses of the excellent Shiraz staved off the possibility of starvation.

I headed for Le Trouquet d'Or feeling fortified. I was likely to need it too. François was not going to be in a very friendly mood. He had hired me to make sure nothing further happened to his restaurant — and what had occurred? A violent death, no less. Splashed all over the newspapers and television and likely to be a *cause célèbre* as long as it sold papers and programmes. What had it done to François' business? I didn't like to think. I didn't relish going there either but I had to — like it or not.

At the tube station, I called Mrs Shearer. Now that she was my twenty-four hour a day answering service, she acted like she was my assistant. I expected her to ask me about the case and so to head her off, I said:

"I'm expecting a call from Scotland Yard. Has it come in yet?"

She was suitably impressed. "No, they 'aven't called," she told me in a hushed voice.

"They will. I'll call you every couple of hours. It's very important."

"Don't you worry," she said earnestly. "We'll look arfter you."

It was the busy lunch period on the Underground by the time I caught a train. I had to stand all the way but I didn't feel I could conscientiously charge a cab to François' bill.

The restaurant was quiet. I went through to the kitchens and even there, it was muted and there was an uneasy stillness that hung in the air like a pall. One reason was immediately apparent — a plain-clothes detective was there taking samples, putting them in jars and labelling them. Klaus Klingermann gave me a grudging nod of acknowledgement. His face was grim and set. He didn't look as if he wanted to talk.

Larry Leopold was in his office. This time he was sitting. He looked terrible, haggard and tired as if he had been up all night. Perhaps he had.

"I don't think there's much you can do," he said. He didn't sound friendly.

"I had to come," I told him. "I suppose this is the kind of thing that François hired me to prevent."

"It's disastrous. Coming on top of everything else — well, I just don't know how we can survive."

"I hope it's not that bad," I said. He shrugged, his grey face thin and old.

"Better go talk to François." He nodded, not caring much what I did.

The panelled walls of François' office made it seem much gloomier than before but that was probably due to the countenance of its occupant. He looked like a man whose world has come to an end.

He glanced up as I came in, anger, sorrow then pure melancholy chasing each other across his face. He gave me a nod even more cursory than the one I had from Klaus. I felt like commiserating with him then decided on a more forceful approach. I knew it would help me, I hoped it would help him too.

"Did you have any suspicion that this might happen?"

He hadn't expected that. "No." He answered involuntarily then found more words. "No, I didn't. I was worried over the incidents that we have told you about but I couldn't have guessed that we'd have something terrible like this."

"I took this job because it was intriguing and because — well, because I hated the idea of a great restaurant being persecuted this way." His glum expression didn't change. "But I didn't bargain for anything like violent death — maybe murder."

That got a reaction. His eyes widened but he didn't say a word.

"And you know nothing that would suggest it might have been murder?"

He shook his head firmly. "No."

"Do you think IJ's death is connected in any way with the other incidents?"

"I can't imagine any connection."

He was a tough character. His jaw set in a stubborn pose. I could see I wasn't going to get any more out of him. Did he know any more? I wondered. Was there something he wasn't telling me? Or was he truly perplexed concerning all these bizarre events?

He sighed. "I'm sorry about this," he said and before I could ask what he meant, he slid a piece of paper across to me. It was a cheque. "That will cover expenses and half of the fee we agreed. I think you'll agree that's fair."

I stared at the cheque. "I don't understand —"

"The other incidents were bad enough. Bookings had begun to drop off —"

"But who knew —?"

He cut me off. "In this business, word gets around — fast. The death of IJ is the end. It will finish me. I shall have to close up. Our contract is terminated. It's not your fault but you can see I will have no further need for your services."

He stood up and held out his hand.

CHAPTER FOURTEEN

W hich was worse — being fired from my first job as a real private eye — or the knowledge that I had been a miserable failure — or the fact that I was off the case as far as François was concerned which meant that Scotland Yard had no more need of me?

Following swiftly after the latter was the awareness that I would no longer be working with Winsome Winnie, a prospect I had looked forward to eagerly. What did he mean "no longer"! I hadn't even started yet — and already I was finished.

I was stunned by François' action. On reflection, I could hardly blame him but still it was a shock I hadn't expected. I looked at the cheque and then at his hand.

"Now just a minute. I thought you used to be a fighter . . ." I paused but not long enough to give him a chance to say anything. I wanted to get my lick in fast. "Surely you're not going to throw in the towel while you're still on your feet?"

He leaned forward, resignation written all over his face.

"I can't keep a restaurant open without customers. We've been accustomed to being booked a month ahead — now we're not going to get enough people to cover expenses."

I struggled for the right words. "Remember what you said to me? Your work as a chef? Your restaurant? Nobody can take them away from me, you said. We can't see a place like mine forced out of business, you said."

He shook his head. "It's different now. A man is dead. Le Trouquet d'Or is going to be associated with his death in the minds of the public."

" 'Who knows which restaurant might be next?' Remember asking me that? So you're going to lose Le Trouquet d'Or . . . you were very concerned about other restaurants then. Now you're thinking only of yourself!"

There was just the slightest hesitation in his manner and I

hoped I was reading it right. I leaped in.

I picked up the cheque and tore it in half.

"Give me two weeks."

"No, I —"

"I'll continue on the case. If I don't find out who's responsible for the incidents in your place in two weeks, I'll return your money and you don't owe me a penny."

He was reeling on the ropes. In his weakened condition, he could only last a few seconds. No, I was wrong — he came back with another swing.

"And the death of IJ?"

I was about to say "I'll throw that in as a bonus" but it sounded too flip and anyway, I didn't want to sound over-confident. There wasn't long to think about it or he would slip away. I had faith in Hemingway's ability to solve the mystery of IJ's death and if he could do it at all, I felt it would be within two weeks so I was safe there. If he were right about a connection between the death and the incidents at Le Trouquet d'Or then solving the major crime would produce a solution to the minor ones.

"I'm working closely with Scotland Yard,' I told him. "You can verify that with Inspector Hemingway if you wish. Their orthodox approach with all their facilities and my — well, my approach . . . Together we'll crack this case, I guarantee it."

My impersonation of Dick Tracy worked. François thought for a moment then said, "All right. Two weeks."

It would have been nice if his gloomy expression had lifted with my brave words but you can't have everything. I shook his hand and hurried out before he could change his mind or think of other difficulties.

I walked back to Covent Garden where I found a phone and called Mrs Shearer. Yes, there had been a call. Mrs Shearer sounded disappointed that the young lady hadn't confided in her but she had left a number. I thanked Mrs Shearer and hung up quickly.

When a voice answered "New Scotland Yard", I was really excited. I gave the extension number and Winnie answered promptly. "I have the autopsy report and some other stuff I can tell you about," she said.

"What time can you get away?"

"About seven. I'd better meet you right from here —"

I thought quickly. "Look, there's a new restaurant just opened up in Pimlico. That's not far from the Yard. I promised a friend I'd check it out and give him an opinion — he's got money in it."

"Sounds good. I only had time for a carrot salad and a cup of coffee for lunch. I'm starving."

"It's an Italian place," I said. "I know a lot of people think that Italian restaurants are just places where New York gangsters go to get shot but I have respect for George — especially his financial sense — and he wouldn't put money into an operation unless it was good."

"I like it already."

I gave her the address and agreed to see her there at seven thirty. When I hung up, I breathed a big sigh of relief. So far, so good. I had avoided being fired and maintained my slender but vital relationship with the police. Now all I had to do was make sure that the big-mouthed promises I had made came true.

I turned away from the telephone kiosk and walked into Covent Garden, lamenting as I always did when I came here, the good old days when it was a smelly, untidy, sprawling amalgam of fruit and flower stalls where you expected to run across Eliza Doolittle or some Dickens character any minute. Now it was a neat, orderly array of shops and boutiques selling geegaws to tourists.

Tony Livesey's health-food shop was busy as usual but Tony found me a corner table where I could enjoy a cup of yerba maté and think. He had trouble believing that I didn't want any food.

"We've got Homity Pies today," he tried to persuade me.

"No, thanks, Tony."

"We've a Creamy Leek Croustade that is really delicious."

"No, really, I —"

"The Mushroom and Cashew Nut Paté then — that's very light."

"Just the maté at the moment, Tony," I told him.

"Been stuffing yourself with all those unhealthy starches and carbohydrates, have you?" he said sadly. "Eating flesh, gorging yourself on corpses —"

Fortunately, I knew he was kidding. Tony is a vegetarian himself and loves concocting new and tempting dishes for his restaurant but he is not a bigot.

"Half an ox and a brace of grouse for lunch," I said. "How can you call that gorging?"

He grinned and brought me another cup of maté, an excellent stimulant for the brain. It wasn't working too well for me today though and I strolled down Long Acre and took a taxi to Billingsgate which, like Covent Garden, isn't what it used to be. Many of the fish wholesalers have moved away but some remain and I found a couple where I knew people who had been in the trade all their lives.

We chatted about fish, cleaning and preparing them, shipping them. We talked about instances of people eating fish and suffering ill-effects although this wasn't a popular topic with the people I was talking to. When I mentioned lamprey, ears pricked up for everybody in London must know about the unfortunate IJ by now. But none of them asked why I wanted to know. They told me all they could but it didn't add up to a lot.

A visit to Billingsgate is not the ideal prelude to a dinner with an attractive blonde so I took the tube back to Hammersmith and sought refuge in a hot bath-tub with plenty of fragrant bubbles. I put Handel's Water Music on the CD while I dressed — it's wonderful mind-clearing music, not too ebullient yet not soporific.

I arrived about fifteen minutes early at La Bordighera so as to have the opportunity to talk to Luigi, the man George had put in charge of the place. George insisted that I was responsible for the idea and had been pressing me to eat there for some time. I had known George when he was head chef with one of the hotel chains and I was asked to seek out some herbs he was having trouble locating. We became friends and in the course of a meal George commented that too many restaurants teetered uncertainly between French cooking and Italian cooking. I agreed and suggested that there was room for a place which accepted this and combined the best of both cuisines. La Bordighera was the result.

Luigi had spent some years in Nice, that Italianised capital of the Riviera and so knew French and Italian cooking intimately and he assured me of his desire to wed the two in accordance with George's plan. Luigi was a lively, voluble man with all the charm and sparkle of a true Neapolitan.

Being Italian, he listened with the greatest interest when I told him that this was to be the first meal I had enjoyed with my lady guest, arriving shortly. It would be the delight of his heart, he said, to see that we had a meal that would gladden the lady's senses, satisfy her stomach and make certain that the rest of the evening would be as successful. I forebore to tell him that she was a detective, not wanting to dampen his professionalism.

He had some extra flowers put on the table which was in a secluded corner as I had asked. Luigi naturally drew his own conclusions from this and equally naturally, I did not tell him that I was making the request because I didn't want waiters or other diners to hear us discussing a death in a restaurant.

A smiling waiter brought me a tall glass of Prosecco, the sparkly Italian dry wine to which a few drops of peach juice had been added. It was a good sign that La Bordighera was genuinely trying for the cross-culture effect as this drink was a compromise between a Kir Royale, as loved by the French and a Bellini, as served at Harry's Bar in Venice.

Winnie walked in at 7.35 and I gave her full marks for promptness. I also gave her full marks for appearance and more than one male head turned as the beaming Luigi conducted her between the tables. She looked crisply attractive in a navy-blue suit, cut slightly severely but softened by a warm red blouse. I wondered what would have happened to Luigi's beam if she had entered in uniform.

The waiter appeared with her aperitif at once and after I had welcomed her, I told her about George and the conversation that had launched La Bordighera.

"It was a good idea," she agreed. "I think the reason that restaurants have that problem is that they're trying to accommodate English tastes. French cooking tends to be traditional and Italian cooking rather more casual. Combining all those three ambitions isn't easy."

"Very true."

"I like the name too," Winnie said. "Calling the place after a town almost on the border between the two countries reminds all concerned of their objectives."

She looked serenely radiant and I told her so though I toned it down to "very nice".

"I keep a couple of changes at the office. They come in handy when we're on a case like this."

"I like the idea of Scotland Yard being called 'the office', " I told her.

"I got myself into the habit of calling it that whenever I can. It startles some people when they hear 'the Yard'."

"I can understand it. How's the drink?"

"Delicious." She smiled that friendly smile and I remembered my first order of priority with difficulty.

"I asked that we don't get a second aperitif or even the menu until I ask for them."

"Sounds like blackmail," Winnie said sweetly.

"An ugly word, blackmail — or so they always said in B movies. Maybe it's whitemail in this context but I really am bursting to know what the autopsy showed."

"Understandable curiosity." She opened the leather tote bag which she had kept on her lap till now. She took out a plastic folder and set the bag on the floor. "I'll give you the headlines first so you won't starve me. Then we can go into more detail later. Okay?"

"I hang on your every word."

"IJ died from poisoning — by Tintilinum botulinum . . ." she began.

"Go on," I urged. "Enlighten me."

"You've heard of one of its cousins — Clostridium botulinum. It's the bacterium that causes the fatal food poisoning known as botulism."

"I thought that was found only in cured meats that have been kept too long," I said.

Winnie shook her head. "It is known for that — but it also occurs in fish and in vegetables. At room temperature, the spores germinate into the active bacteria and produce a nerve toxin which usually causes death."

"And this Tintilinum —?"

"Occurs principally in fish which has been kept too long before cooking."

"Ah," I said and Winnie nodded.

"Exactly. Cooking temperatures don't destroy it — even

boiling water doesn't affect it. In those respects as well as others, it's similar to botulism. The main difference is that Tintilinum is much faster and much more powerful. It can kill in an hour — or less."

"And where did it come from? You already said it occurs mainly in fish so I presume —"

"Right. The autopsy indicates that it was in the lamprey."

"Oh dear."

"Just a minute — there's more."

I was startled. "More? How can there be more?"

Winnie consulted one of the sheets of paper from her plastic folder.

"You know that many shellfish and some other fish have a poisonous vein running down their back. It's removed when preparing the fish for cooking."

"Yes."

"That poison was found in IJ's stomach too. It's the type that's found in eels."

"And lamprey is an eel."

"Correct."

She set the papers down on the table. I sat back and looked at her. Just for the moment, her blue eyes, red lips, blonde hair and neatly chiselled features didn't register. I was thinking only of the inevitable conclusion from what she was telling me. I hoped I was wrong.

"What does the Yard deduce from this?" I asked.

"The facts suggest sloppy preparation of food —"

"Not removing the poison veins thoroughly."

"Yes — and bad housekeeping in having the lamprey around too long at room temperature before cooking."

"In other words, the worst possible deductions as far as Le Trouquet d'Or is concerned."

Winnie sighed. "I'm afraid so."

"You have more to tell me —" I started to say and then waited until she said, "Yes, I —" then I held up a hand.

"I promised progress food-wise after the initial bad news."

Winnie smiled enticingly. It was probably hunger pangs. I waved at the waiter and he arrived quickly with a tray. From it, he placed on the table two more of the house cocktails. "Compliments of Signor Luigi," he said. He put down a tray of tiny bouchées, crisp-looking circles of pastry — "Gratinéed Shrimp," he explained. From under the tray, he whipped two menus and placed them in our hands and laid a wine list on the table.

"Good service so far," Winnie said. "Your friend George is determined to earn your approval and he's impressed it on the staff."

"I hope he's impressed on them the need to give all their customers this kind of service," I told her.

I was desperately anxious to hear what else Winnie had to say but I forced myself to study the menu. George was living up to his intention of blending Italian and French cuisine and the choice wasn't easy.

"How does it look?" I asked Winnie.

"I could ask for almost anything on here," she murmured, still reading but after a couple more minutes she said, "I think I've decided."

The waiter was hovering nearby and came over as soon as I looked up. Winnie ordered the Soufflé Stuffed with Crab followed by the Veal Sweetbreads. I ordered the Terrine of Salmon and Rascasse and the Leg of Lamb Provençale.

"I'll order the wine then you can tell me what's in the rest of that folder," I said. "Do you have any preference?"

It has been my experience that women ask for white wine more often than red but Winnie surprised me.

"On this occasion, a full-bodied red," she decided and I ordered a Gattinara. It is not perhaps quite as deep and strong as a Barolo but usually more subtle.

When the waiter had gone, I gave her my full attention which was not at all difficult.

"The other five people who complained of not feeling well at the dinner. What did you learn from them?"

"The Poison Unit at St Cyril's Hospital found small amounts of one or the other of the two bacteria in them."

"Small amounts, you say?"

"0.1 to 0.25 International Units. The level of fatality is over 1.2."

"And IJ had how much in him?"

"Over 3.5."

We tasted the bouchées. I didn't remind Winnie that they

were shrimp and she didn't comment. They were hot and very tasty — the shrimp in a mixture as near as I could tell of onions, curry, Tabasco and cream.

"I talked to Tarquin Warrington too."

"Ah, yes. I wanted to ask you about him."

"He said he didn't feel well after eating the lamprey. He left and went straight to his own doctor. Said he didn't want to make any fuss at the Circle."

"Very laudable — if true."

"Well, it was true as far as going to his doctor was concerned. The doctor verified it. The symptoms that Warrington described were consistent with Tintilinum botulinum."

"Did the doctor diagnose it as that?"

"No. But then he wouldn't be able to without tests. He wanted Warrington to go to a hospital but he said he'd see if he felt better in the morning."

"And he did?"

"Yes."

"Is that probable?"

"Yes. He could have got a very minor dose."

"Convenient," I suggested.

Winnie stopped, a bouchée poised to enter her opened mouth.

"You suspect him of not telling the truth?"

"Not really. I suppose I'm prejudiced because he's so curt and rude."

Winnie completed the eating of the bouchée and I enjoyed watching her enjoy it. The waiter arrived with the first course. Winnie said the soufflé was outstanding and my terrine was light, fresh and tangy.

The main course was just as good and the Gattinara was rich and powerful. I let Winnie reach the last of her sweetbreads before I asked the question:

"What are your next moves?"

She finished chewing, wiped her mouth daintily and asked:

"My next moves?"

"In the investigation."

"Oh." She cleaned her plate carefully. I like to see a girl enjoy her food. "We're checking now on IJ's relatives and friends. He doesn't seem to have anyone really close. We're talking to his co-workers but he didn't confide much there either. He wasn't popular though — and we're following up on that. We've talked to most of the guests at the Circle of Careme. Only two or three of those exchanged any conversation with him and they don't have anything useful to offer."

"What about his neighbours at the table?" I asked.

"Nothing there either."

"Did he eat the same as the other guests?"

"Oh yes. Just the same."

"So it's odd how he ingested much more toxin?"

"It is."

"No sign of any poison in any of the food other than the lamprey?"

"None at all."

"The brandy . . . you've heard what happened when IJ recovered after being apparently dead? Someone handed him a glass of brandy and he drank it before the inspector could stop him."

"Yes." Winnie nodded, her expression wry. "Bizarre. We've heard several versions but they all amount to the same story."

I leaned forward, interested in this point as I had been so close to it.

"The brandy glass . . . It dropped from IJ's fingers after he had emptied it. Then he died only minutes later. What happened to the glass?"

Winnie smiled. "The inspector slipped it into his pocket."

I laughed. "The sly old dog!"

"He can be — he can be. No trace of any toxin on it though."

"H'm," was the best comment I could make.

The waiter poured the rest of the Gattinara. "Dessert?" I suggested.

"No, thanks. I yield once in a while but just coffee will be fine right now." She flashed that wonderful smile again. "It was a superb meal."

"I'll let you congratulate Luigi yourself. He'll appreciate that."

"Before I do," Winnie said, "I must ask you — what are your next moves?"

"Well, I thought we might —"

"In the investigation."

"Ah — well, I've been thinking — and the more I do, the more I want to talk to Raymond."

Her eyebrows raised. "Raymond?" she asked surprised.

"You've heard the stories of the feud between him and François?"

"Yes but what reason do you have for supposing that it goes any further than professional rivalry?"

"I don't have anything. Just a feeling — and I want to explore it."

She considered for a second. "I don't see why not. It's certainly more relative to your investigation than ours. Let me know what you learn."

We had coffee, authentic black Italian coffee from a machine which could be heard faintly as it gurgled and spluttered in the kitchen. Luigi came over to make sure that we had enjoyed the meal. We complimented him and I paid the bill. Winnie protested that we should go Dutch. I insisted on paying it and Winnie shrugged.

"All right but the next one's on me."

"Does the Yard pick it up?"

She nodded. "Inspector Hemingway is very liberal regarding entertainment expenses."

"He should be. After all, you are the Food Squad. Okay, I accept your offer. When and where?"

She pouted. "We'll be in touch."

We walked outside. "Where do you live, Winnie?"

"Not far. Just over the Albert Bridge, opposite Battersea Park."

"We'll take a cab —" and even as I said it, one came cruising past.

In the taxi, I said, "I've been so engrossed in all these details, I haven't even had the chance to ask you about yourself."

"There'll be plenty of time."

The cab lurched around Dolphin Square and on to Grosvenor Road where the lights of the Thames bridges glistened wetly in the evening mist. The turn threw her against me. She seemed to reach for the strap but must have missed it.

"Here we are," she said what seemed like only seconds later.

We got out and Winnie held out a firm hand.

"We'll do it again soon." Then she was gone.

CHAPTER FIFTEEN

The first thing I did in the office next morning was to call Ben Beaumont, the president of the P.I.E.

"Remember the girl who gave us that talk on Quincy — how the medical examiner in real life compares with the one on TV?"

"Carol Dodson?"

"That's her. Do you have her phone number?"

"Not your type, old chap. Now I'd recommend —"

"Ben, they're all my type — but that's another problem. What I'm calling for is to ask if you have Carol's number."

"Oh well," he grumbled, "if you've made up your mind . . . just a minute." He quickly produced two numbers and I thanked him and called the office number for Carol.

"Could you get me some non-confidential information?" I asked. "It's probably readily available in your lab files." I knew that the forensic laboratory she worked in did jobs for official bodies and so should be well-equipped with data.

She agreed at once and I told her that I was looking for all she could tell me about Tintilinum botulinum. It would be no problem, she assured me and would call back in a couple of hours. "Oh, do you have a fax?" she asked. "In case there's quite a lot of it." Helpful girl and I told her so.

"The IJ Case" as I found myself calling it might be occupying most of my thoughts but while I was in the office, I decided to catch up on some other business.

I skimmed through the fax's from Michael. He had sent statistics on snails to help me make up my mind what I wanted to do with that particular query. There were figures on world-wide production and consumption plus figures for France and elsewhere — the UK still had a long way to go in both.

On the subject of cobalt, not a lot was known. It is one of

the active minerals in the body and is part of Vitamin B-12. It is essential for red blood cells like iron and is not a normal food supplement. It occurs naturally in meat, kidney, liver, shellfish and milk. Vegetarians are most likely to suffer from a deficiency. Too much of it might enlarge the thyroid gland.

I could hardly charge for that scanty information so I made a note to send it to the enquirer with compliments. The data Michael had provided on aluminium was, however, a different matter. Numerous powerful bodies and a few multi-national corporations were locked in the struggle here and major issues were involved. I don't mind the occasional participation in a good cause but it sounded as if I might emerge a loser in this one no matter what I decided. I drafted an answer declining.

Opening the post brought a few laughs. The first came from a letter which read:

"Could you please recommend a non-alcoholic wine for the wedding at St Richard-in-the-Marshes Church of our son, So-and-So and Miss Penelope Something. Both are ardent teetotallers."

I drafted a reply for Mrs Shearer to send:

"I regret that I cannot recommend a non-alcoholic wine for consumption at a wedding."

The next letter was interesting. I read:

"We are having a barbeque for two hundred people in the grounds of Graceworthy Manor. This will be a gala affair and all the guests are in or associated with the travel industry.

"We wish to serve wine and we are in a dilemma as to what this should be. If you will make suitable recommendations and if these meet with the majority approval of our guests, we will send you a case of one of those wines as token of our appreciation."

A cheeky one — but I liked it!

The lazy drift of smoke, the sizzle of meat over hot coals and the satisfying sense of eating in the great outdoors . . . what a thrill!

Well, maybe to some people but not to me. My ancient tribal memories of eating around a blazing fire were apparently buried too deeply to be revived by the smell of charred pork, burned sausages or singed eyebrows.

Still, it was my opinion that was being sought not my

participation. What could I tell them? It was a tricky question and depended on whether they intended grilling — which is fast or barbecuing — which is slow as well as the degree of smokiness to be induced by wood chips or water or fennel.

I would have to ask them about these points because they would affect the selection of the wines but in my mind, I was already turning over various possibilities. The frank taste of a Zinfandel would be good with beef, if it were to be grilled. A Brunello di Montalcino — an Italian wine becoming increasingly more popular — would be even better. A Gigondas or a Côtes du Rhone Villages or a Moulin à Vent would all go well with grilled meat.

If they were planning chicken then I would suggest a Chardonnay, a Pinot Gris or a Vernaccia, preferably one from San Gimignano. With lamb, red Bordeaux or a Cabernet Sauvignon whereas with pork . . . but I was getting carried away. And with a feast I wouldn't even be enjoying. All for a case of wine! Ah, well, it was fun and I made notes to ask several questions.

The rest were routine and not nearly as interesting. I took the notes to drop off with Mrs Shearer on the way out and ran into her outside the door.

"Off detecting again?" she asked with a conspiratorial wink. Since I had put her on twenty-four hour call, she had acted like . . . no, I couldn't call to mind a parallel. Hardly Dr Watson, certainly not Harriet Vane . . . Tuppence to my Tommy . . . or maybe Nipper or number one son from Honolulu? I gave up, handed her the notes.

"Not a word to anyone about this strange business, Mrs Shearer," I said in a low voice and exited before she could reply.

I took the tube to Tottenham Court Road Station, walked down Charing Cross Road then turned before reaching Cambridge Circus. Even as in Dr Johnson's day, all human life was there. I managed to ignore some of it and went along Pagnell Street where the atmosphere improved as I came nearer to Raymond's Restaurant.

My arrival time was 11.15. I had planned that so it would be before opening time and I would have the opportunity to talk to him before the restaurant went to full action stations. I rattled the front door. A waiter just inside was moving chairs. He put one down long enough to wave negatively at me. I rattled again. He came to the door and through the glass made mouthing signs. I shook my head, pointed to myself then pointed inside.

The waiter made waving-off gestures with both hands as if he were on the deck of a carrier and I was an approaching aircraft coming in too low. I shook my head again and made meaningless motions but they held his attention. Finally, he unlocked the door and opened it almost two inches.

"We don't open until —"

"I know. I don't want to eat."

That statement really grabbed his attention. He stared at me as if I had said I had just arrived from another planet.

"You don't want to eat at Raymond's?"

"No. I just want to talk to him."

"Oh." He pulled open the door and I went in.

"His office is at the end of the corridor, top of the stairs."

Raymond's Restaurant was a sort of Paris idyll without making any overstatement that might contradict its location in London. It was decorated in the shades of turquoise always linked with Paris and consisted of a set of rooms, interconnected at irregular angles, their dimensions made uncertain due to the subtle use of trees and plants and carefully placed mirrors.

It was grand but not opulent, luxurious but not ostentatious and everything in it was a tempting invitation to dine at what was clearly an exceptional restaurant. Top class was obvious from the glint of silver to the sparkle of crystal glass.

Raymond's office was impressive too in its way. An old desk, carved from dark wood stood in one corner. A brass lamp cast a pool of orange light on to the tooled leather desk top. Raymond's large, face looked out at me through the cone of light. The expression changed on recognition but he rose, greeted me and led me across the room to a long low mahogany table with some carved ivory figures on it. Three large leather couches were spaced around it and Raymond motioned me to sit.

"I saw you at the Circle of Careme dinner on that terrible night," he said.

"Yes," I agreed. "It was a terrible night."

He waited for me to tell him what I was doing there but I didn't oblige. I wasn't even sure why I was suspicious of him — or what I suspected him of doing. Perhaps it was just a private eye's hunch — or perhaps it was because my introduction to this entire affair had been through him, if indeed his commission had been part of it.

"Is there something you wanted to talk to me about?"

"I'm making some inquiries," I told him.

"Inquiring into what?" he asked politely. "The death of Ivor Jenkinson?"

I'd better tread carefully here, I thought. Don't want this reaching the ubiquitous ear of Inspector Hemingway.

"There may be some related matters," I said. He didn't ask what that meant fortunately. "How can I help?" he asked.

"You didn't talk to François Duquesne at the Circle of Careme dinner, did you?" That broke the ice as effectively as dropping a steamroller into it. His eyebrows shot up.

"Talk to him! I haven't talked to him since — don't you know we —" he spluttered to a stop then went on more calmly.

"No," he said. "I didn't talk to him."

"I've heard about the feud between you and François. I suppose everybody has. What exactly caused it?"

His eyebrows went up again at my audacity. "What does this have to do with —"

"I don't know yet," I said, watching him carefully. The private eyes in fiction always seemed able to pick up all kinds of clues from people's faces but I had never really believed it was that easy. None the less, a flicker passed across Raymond's features. I was still trying to analyse it when he went on:

"It was a long time ago. Yet it wasn't so long that either of us has forgotten it. It was a bad business — very bad — unpardonable." He sighed. "The details don't matter now."

"They might matter," I pressed.

"No," he said decisively. "They don't."

"And if they do, you're not going to tell me."

"They don't concern you — or anyone."

"A man has died," I reminded him.

"There is no connection."

One more try at this subject, I thought. "You're both very bitter about it still, aren't you?" I asked.

"Bitter?" He gave a short barking laugh though there wasn't any mirth in it.

"Had you met IJ previously?"

"No."

"Did you talk to him that night?"

"No."

The best private eyes knew when to keep silent. They often did it after the person being interrogated had been unforthcoming. The idea was that the guilty wanted to explain how they weren't guilty and the innocent had nothing to hide. To my surprise, it worked perfectly.

"We've had other media persons at the restaurant but never Jenkinson."

Something in his tone prompted me to ask, "Have any of them come for other reasons than to enjoy the food?"

"Yes, sometimes." He seemed more willing to talk now. Was it relief that we had got away from the one subject he wanted to avoid?

"Who else has been here?"

"Sally Aldridge, Roger St Leger . . ."

"You don't mean together?" I was half joking but he answered seriously enough.

"No, no," he said, "separately."

"These visits were recent?"

"Sally Aldridge . . . about three weeks ago. St Leger — a week, no, ten days ago."

"Why did they come to your restaurant if not to eat?"

"I knew St Leger. He had me cook a meal on his programme — oh, last year some time. You know, explaining each step, that sort of thing. Perhaps you saw it?" he suggested.

"I think I did." A little prevarication might help. "What did he want to talk to you about?"

"He wants to get back on television. He's trying to get a new series. He had a few ideas and wanted me to comment."

"And did you?"

"Yes but he was vague. None of his ideas had been thought through very far. He struck me as being desperate to get back on television but not having a clear plan of how he wanted to do it."

"What about Sally?" I asked.

"She said she was planning a new book. She wanted to know if I would contribute some recipes."

"Are visits like these unusual at all?"

"Oh, no. Within limits, we like to get all the publicity we can. It's good for business to keep our name in front of people. Nelda Darvey was here too. She's writing a series of articles on London restaurants. She's always given us a good press."

I wasn't much further along in my thinking. Raymond didn't seem to be hiding anything — so why was I still suspicious of him? Was this a man who would stoop to foul means of putting a hated rival out of business? He didn't look like he was but then Charles Crippen had looked like a respected doctor, Billy the Kid was angel-faced and Dion O'Bannion had been a choir-boy before he had gathered together a gang to battle Al Capone and kill dozens of Chicago citizens.

The visits of St Leger and Sally Aldridge to Raymond's — both within the last three weeks — were another big question mark. The reasons sounded innocent enough but neither seemed to have achieved much. Was one of them a cover to mask some other purpose?

"You did an excellent job for me on — on that matter recently," Raymond said.

I inclined my head to acknowledge his words.

"I have been trying to decide whether I should come to you again."

I waited for him to continue. He was looking for the right way to express it. He did so, slowly.

"I suspect that someone is trying to put me out of business."

CHAPTER SIXTEEN

It was becoming as prevalent as the common cold. How many other London restaurants were catching the same virus? I eyed Raymond cautiously. Or was it a tit-for-tat conflict with Raymond hitting back? Had the famous feud now grown to a bitter battle?

The cause of that feud seemed to be lurking behind these questions and looming in importance. If I could find out what had caused it, I might be a lot closer to several answers. For the moment though, I needed to know what Raymond's statement meant.

"Simple things," he said in reply to my query. "Simple to do but with severe effects on the operation of the restaurant. Labels on spice jars switched, for instance. Cinnamon with ginger, basil with tarragon."

"Similar in appearance so the changes wouldn't be noticed. Devastating in result though — especially if a dish reached the table —"

"One did. It could have been much worse but the chefs were very careful about aromas during cooking after that."

"What else?"

"Cancellation by phone of an order of beef tenderloin. It was for dinner for a large and influential group of a dozen people. By the time we found out about it, there was no time to go elsewhere. We had to substitute. The group said they wouldn't come back. Then our reservations book disappeared. That caused confusion and we inadvertently double-booked some tables. The reservations book reappeared."

"Carelessness? Accidents? Human errors?"

Raymond shook his head vehemently. "My staff are too efficient, no — I don't believe it."

That led me into my big question though I wasn't too hopeful for its success in bringing any revelations.

"Is there anyone you suspect?"

"No. I can't imagine who would do this."

"Would François?"

He didn't reply right away. He sighed.

"We're back to that, are we?"

"Of course we are," I said flatly. "Any list of suspects would have François' name at the top, wouldn't it?"

He didn't answer. I was getting a little peeved.

"If I'm suspicious of him, you have to be more so. Unless there is someone else . . ."

"I told you — I can't imagine anyone else doing this."

I changed tactics. "Are you so concerned about these events in your restaurant?"

His eyes widened. "Of course I am. Shouldn't I be concerned?"

"Have you told the police?"

"No."

"And you didn't approach me. I came here to talk to you."

"I had thought of it — but I was still trying to find other explanations. It's so preposterous, not only who would do these things but why."

It wasn't as preposterous as he thought. It was already happening in a similar manner to his hated rival but I couldn't tell him that.

"The death of Ivor Jenkinson has changed a lot of things for me," I told him. "I just couldn't take on an assignment for you at the present time."

He nodded unhappily. "I understand but —" he gave me a pleading look "— will you do this for me? Will you keep in mind what I have told you? Maybe you will run across a clue, a hint — you might hear something —"

Well, I had said — or at least hinted — that I was involved in the investigation of IJ's death. Did he have some reason to believe that there might be some connection with his problem? I asked him.

He shrugged. "I don't know. But you will do as I ask?"

I agreed, trying to think what else I ought to ask him. Philip Marlowe would have had dozens more questions but I didn't. I was already rising to leave when there was a knock at the door. It opened and in came a really stunning-looking woman. She was in her early to mid-thirties and had lustrous coppery hair and large oval-shaped brown eyes. A dark-green wool knit dress fitted her lovely figure perfectly — tight enough to be sexy but not so tight as to be tarty.

Raymond introduced me then said: "This is my niece and general manager, Paula Jardine."

Her eyes appraised me coolly as we shook hands.

"I'm making some inquiries," I told her, "which may be connected with that terrible business at the Circle of Careme dinner —" I broke off as I remembered, "I saw you there — wondered who you were."

"I've been a member for some years." Her voice was low and musical. I could have listened to it for hours but Raymond was suggesting, "Perhaps you could escort the gentleman out, my dear? I have to go to the kitchen —"

As we went out, she asked: "Do you know our restaurant?"

"By reputation," I said.

We reached the door and she turned to me. She was breathtakingly beautiful close up and her complexion was flawless.

"You must come and eat here. We live up to our reputation, I can assure you."

"I'd like that," I said and meant it. "I'll see if I —"

"As our guest, of course."

"That's very nice of you."

She smiled delightfully. "My guest, that is."

"That's even better —"

"How about tomorrow?"

"Tomorrow?"

"No, I'm sorry — I have to host those Canadians tomorrow. The next day?"

"That would be fine," I said promptly. I couldn't think of anything I'd rather do and I might even get a few view-points of Raymond from a different angle.

She was dazzling as she opened the door. "See you at 12.30. You'll have a wonderful meal and we'll have a cosy chat."

Being a private eye wasn't such a bad life after all, I reflected as the tube train bucketed and jolted out of the station. The food was good and the girls were gorgeous and there seemed to be a good supply of both.

After leaving Raymond's, I had found a phone booth and asked information for Roger St Leger's number.

"I'm sorry, there is no number listed for that party," said the girl sweetly.

"Does that mean it's an unlisted number?"

"I'm sorry but I'm not permitted to give you that information."

"How do I go about getting an unlisted number?" I asked.

"You would have to call the party concerned and ask them to give it to you."

"But if you won't give me the number, how can I — thanks anyway."

He could live out of London but having had a regular television programme, it seemed more likely that he was in the Greater London area. I did what I often do in such circumstances — I called Michael.

"I'll call you back," he said after I had told him what I wanted.

"I'm in a phone box. I'll call you."

"Give me five minutes."

I gave him six. He picked up the phone promptly and gave me St Leger's number. "His address — if you want it — is 103 Melbourne Place, Fulham Wharf."

"You're a marvel, Michael," I told him. "How did you do it?"

"I called his publisher."

"He's a writer too?"

"Wrote a book based on his last TV programme. I know the publisher — promised him I'd move two hundred copies of a new cook-book just coming out."

"I'll buy one of them," I offered, "providing it's less than a fiver."

"Good-bye," Michael said and hung up.

Fulham Wharf was one of those new Thames-side developments, all concrete and glass and trees in barrels. The river looked dark and greasy and a chilly breeze swirled through the barren streets which were liberally scattered with black-and-white humps to break the heads of fast drivers. A barrier kept out unwanted visitors but it looked as if all visitors here came in cars for there was no one to stop me walking in.

I had decided to just go rather than phone. He couldn't say "no" as easily this way. I found Melbourne Place from the large map displayed inside the entrance. It was grim and impersonal like the rest of the buildings in here but the inhabitants no doubt preferred the facilities, the location and the trendy to the picturesque.

Number 103 was on the ground floor and the expansive window must have had a fine view of the dirty water. I paused outside and gathered my thoughts as to why I was here.

Raymond had said that St Leger had visited his restaurant, saying that he hoped to get a new TV programme. Well, maybe . . . but wasn't that putting the dessert before the entrée? There was no question though that most of my suspicion of St Leger stemmed from his behaviour at the Circle of Careme dinner. But why? What had he really done? I'd seen him hand an envelope to Ivor Jenkinson and had seen the look on IJ's face when he had opened it and seen the contents. And I had seen the look on St Leger's face when he had stood looking down on the dead body of IJ — well, we had all thought it was dead.

Not much to go on, I admitted. If I had read of these items in a report, they would have meant little or nothing. It was only because I had witnessed them myself that they seemed to have some significance — and because IJ had died.

Was I kidding myself? I wondered. Or was my lack of experience showing? Father Brown's understanding of human nature or Sam Spade's intuition would have been useful right now.

The heavy curtains were drawn inside the windows of number 103 even though it was still daytime. One of them was crinkled, leaving a sliver of space at one end through which I could peek if I pressed against the glass. The lights were on and I could see part of a large white couch with pastel pillows piled on it. In front of it was a glass topped coffee table with chrome trim and angled chrome legs. A lush pale blue carpet covered the floor but I registered these details almost automatically.

It was because my mind was refusing to accept what else I saw — a body half under the table, sprawled in an impossible position and with one leg twisted at a grotesque angle.

CHAPTER SEVENTEEN

I recoiled in horror. I looked again — the body was there, no doubt about it. "St Leger!" my mind screamed. "He's been murdered because of what he knows!"

The large window appeared to be double-glazed and made of very thick glass. Not much chance of breaking it in without a sledge-hammer. I would have to go for help. As I passed the door, I took a look at it. It looked solid and probably had half a dozen locks and bolts. I turned the brass handle — and to my astonishment, the door opened.

It was St Leger sprawled there. I pulled him out from his position half under the coffee table and dragged him on to the couch. It was only then that I remembered the cardinal rule about never touching the body. Oh well, no private eye is perfect. I was looking round for a phone when a groan made me jump almost out of my skin.

St Leger groaned again and I pulled him up straighter. He was still alive! I started to loosen his tie but it was already loose. Memories of IJ being dead and coming back to life began to flood back but I was close to St Leger now and I suspected that the circumstances were different. The blast of alcohol fumes that he breathed at me almost knocked me back. He wasn't dead but he was certainly dead drunk.

I found the kitchen, a couple of dozen electronic gadgets surrounding a stainless steel island and put half a jar of coffee into what was surely an automatic coffee maker. The refrigerator had a continuous ice-maker and I soaked a dish towel in water and filled it with ice cubes. I made a cup of coffee strong enough to sober W.C. Fields and took it and the ice cubes back into the living room. It was then that I noticed two glasses on the table. One had lipstick.

Some minutes later, the bleary eyes greeted me with a

singular lack of cordiality. After they had focused, St Leger croaked:

"What the devil do you want?"

He looked awful. I forced more black coffee into him and re-arranged the ice pack. He almost gagged at the coffee and tried to push the ice-pack away.

"What is that?" he spluttered.

"Just coffee. Have some more — it's good for you."

He didn't agree, I could tell. Especially he didn't like the way I made it. He expressed his opinion of me and the coffee in language that NTV would never have allowed on the box. Then the coffee started to come up and I moved out of range.

"What are you trying to do — choke me?" he gurgled.

"What are *you* trying to do? Kill yourself with booze?"

He glared furiously at me but his breath was coming back.

"I knew a fellow once," I said conversationally, "spent forty-eight hours in intensive care with an intravenous drip in his arm after over-indulgence in the grain."

The glare was still there but his breathing was nearly normal. His colour was coming back too but I didn't want to be too soft.

"Didn't help though. He died anyway."

There was silence for a while, not of the kind called companionable. Finally he said, "If you'll put some more coffee on and make it properly this time, I'll drink it."

I did and poured one for myself though I didn't drink it.

"What are you doing here?" he asked me, a little more civilly but not exactly warm.

"I came to talk to you."

"What about?"

Now was the time — or was it too late? Should I have pressed him unmercifully while he was still weak and unable to resist?

"About the death of IJ."

He closed his eyes and then opened them as if they were small slabs of marble.

"Why would I know anything about it?"

"You were there."

"So were you."

I *had* left it too late. He was getting sassy already. I moved the coffee out of his reach.

"What was in the envelope you handed to IJ at the Circle of Careme dinner?" I asked abruptly.

"What envelope?"

"Don't play games!" I snapped.

He squinted at me out of puffy eyes.

"How did you get in here?"

"Jimmy Valentine — Master Cracksman."

"That's breaking and entering!" he said indignantly.

"I didn't break a thing. Now tell me — what was in the envelope?"

He groaned and tried to move the leg that had looked as if it had been bent through three angles.

"I don't know."

"Of course you know."

He was still wincing with pain. Maybe it was distracting him from my questions or I could hope that it made him more vulnerable.

"I collected it from one of IJ's informants," he said, rubbing his knee. "I came in a little late — went straight over to IJ and handed it to him."

"What was in it?"

"I told you I don't know."

"Who was the informant?"

"I'd never seen him before."

"But you know some of IJ's informants."

"I've seen one or two. Never saw this one before. IJ wasn't free with introductions."

One thing I was beginning to realise was that deciding when people were telling me the truth and when they were lying was very difficult. The private eye of fiction can spot the flicker of an eyelid or the quiver of a lip and interpret it unerringly. His instinct was more efficient than a polygraph and a prevarication didn't stand a chance. I didn't find it that easy. If there had been a meaningful flicker or quiver — then I'd missed it.

St Leger sounded as if he were telling the truth but he probably wasn't. Raymond had sounded as if he were telling the truth too and so had François. Most likely, there were lots of lies in there — but where?

"How did you get along with IJ?" I asked him.

His face contorted as stomach pains twisted his insides. He fought to keep them under control. "I didn't like him much," he said at length.

"Hard to get along with, I've heard."

"He used me as if I were an errand boy."

"You were helping him with his programmes?"

"He had me doing a few things for him, yes."

"Because of your background regarding food?"

"Yes."

"If he was killed, who do you think killed him?"

The puffy eyes opened as much as swollen flesh permitted. "Who said he was killed?"

"Nobody. I said 'If he was'."

"There wasn't anybody who liked him. He was an unpleasant bastard."

"So everybody disliked him?"

St Leger didn't answer that speculation, just shook his head.

"So everybody had a reason to kill him?"

His glare came back. "Don't be absurd! You don't kill people just because you don't like them."

"Out of all the people who didn't like him — maybe there was one who disliked him enough — enough to kill him," I suggested.

He shook his head wearily. His eyelids were drooping. The reaction was setting in and he was going to fall asleep on me any minute now.

"You must have had quite a party," I commented.

He nodded and yawned.

"All of you," I said pointedly. He saw me looking at the two glasses and tried to do the same but he didn't focus well.

"M'm . . ." he murmured.

"Your ex-wife?" I hazarded.

He shook his head then moaned with the pain.

"Girl friend?" I persisted. "Au pair? Neighbour? Cleaning lady? Income tax inspector?"

None of them registered although he heard them. His head was drooping. The interrogation was over.

I went into the bathroom and opened all the cabinets. No sign of any female occupancy. I thought of what he had told me, little as it was. Once again, I had heard how disliked IJ was. I wondered if all IJ's colleagues at the studio felt the same way, what they might know and what they could guess.

There was only one way to find out. Oh, I remembered Inspector Hemingway's warning but if Nero Wolfe had listened to Inspector Cramer, he would never have solved a crime.

The phone was another electronic marvel. Pushing the right buttons, St Leger could probably talk to the astronauts and ask them what flavour mush they were sucking through their straws today. After I figured out how to place a local call without getting the Kremlin, I got the National Television Studios.

"This is Roger St Leger," I said in what I hoped was near enough to his voice. "I have a friend who has kindly agreed to come to the studio tomorrow to pick up some files for me. Make arrangements to let him in, would you?"

There were clicks and I had to repeat my request. A voice said: "I'll call you back at your private number to confirm." They did so and I hung up, pleased that that had gone so well.

I put St Leger's feet up on the couch, brought a duvet from the bedroom and tossed it over him. I didn't tuck him in but I did make sure the door locked as I went out.

Back at the office, I read the fax from Carol. There was a fair amount of technical stuff that wasn't very enlightening but the gist of it was that Tintilinum botulinum was a very nasty customer indeed to have on your plate.

It is similar to the botulinus bacillus but much less common. The toxin is found in fish which has been kept too long before cooking. The onset of symptoms occurs much more quickly than in botulism.

First, there is an inability to focus the eyes. The stomach may or not feel queasy. The voice remains normal but the brain rapidly becomes unable to concentrate and can operate properly only for short spans. There is difficulty in connecting thoughts.

The pulse slows and may become so weak that it is undetectable. Breathing is very shallow and the victim may appear to be dead. Both pulse and breathing may return to normal for brief periods but death will follow.

It all fitted IJ's symptoms and explained his mysterious return from the dead. I turned to the contents of a fat envelope from Michael Markham.

He had been as thorough as ever. There were a lot of newspaper cuttings on Legionnaires' Disease and the Mad Cow Affair which seemed now to be irrelevant. However, I learned that the bacteria known as listeria which is found in some pre-cooked, chilled foods especially soft cheeses kills over two hundred people a year. Reading about the Salmonella in Eggs scare made it seem more political than medical. One alarming figure though came from the Ministry of Health quoted by the *Sunday Times* as saying that totally two million people a year in Britain experience food poisoning, ranging from one day attacks to death.

On the subject of lamprey, Michael had dug deep into historical files. Just before World War I, thousands of lamprey had been washed up at Hammersmith Pier, all dead from poisoning. Forensic investigation at that time was not well advanced but the conclusion was that they had died from their own poison — and that was presumably Tintilinum Botulinum, the poison that had killed Ivor Jenkinson.

Michael had included comments on King Henry I's death and it seemed that modern opinion was that he had died — not from a surfeit of lampreys as popular legend had it — but from the poison in the fish. Michael reminded me that several kings had died from eating certain foods, the most interesting of which were King Matthias of Hungary — killed by eating figs and King George I of England — died after eating watermelons.

There were financial reports on both Raymond's Restaurant and Le Trouquet d'Or. Both were in excellent shape and both had shown record profits in the last reported year. Stock was not available to the public.

The day's post contained nothing of value and I left the office at six-thirty, stopping to make a few purchases. Fish, cheese and eggs didn't sound too appetising in view of my recent reading and I decided against figs and melons too. Tomorrow, the information input on them would have receded to a lower memory level and they would sound as tasty as ever.

I browsed through the CD files, searching for the right — or a try at the right — combinations. I passed over Corelli's Concertos — at the moment, they seemed like music to drink Diet Coke by. Eventually, I put on Dvořák's Slavonic Dances. They are a reliable raiser of spirits despite the criticism of both Brahms and Liszt that they confused Hungarian music with gypsy music. To accompany the fiery rhythms and tuneful melodies, I poured some Jack Daniels and added lots of ice. The music and the liquor were worth repeating so I repeated them.

When I went to work in the kitchen, it was to prepare some Madeira Sauce. I made a brown roux, then added beef consommé, boiled it and added chopped tomatoes, onions and carrots, thyme, bay leaf, parsley, salt and pepper. I let it simmer while I thawed some soup I had made and frozen for the day when I would want soup but not want to make it. This was a purée of asparagus with tarragon.

Previous attempts at musical accompaniment for the soup had been unsuccessful. This time I tried Debussy's String Quartet, written during the period when Debussy was a close friend of the Impressionist painters and was trying to do for music what they were doing for painting. I was probably over-extending myself — I was not always able to match music and food — now I was blending music, food and painting!

I pulled the cork from a bottle of Dão. Most of Portugal's finest reds come from this region and when they are good, they are superb. It can be a gamble whether you get one of these or one of the others. Labels may mislead and some older vintages can be musty-tasting due to the addition of oak essence, a ploy to replace the natural flavour imparted by ageing in oak barrels. This one was excellent and I let it sit for a few minutes while I put another of my purchases on to sauté. These were two small tournedos — surely the best named beef. "Turn your back" is the one thing you cannot do as they cook so fast. Tournedos are the tenderest beef but not the tastiest so a sauce is recommended — only Rossini knew why he considered a truffle topping with a little foie gras to be enough.

The sauce I was using required the addition of Madeira before serving and the result was very satisfying. The next CD came on even as the sauce thickened and the tournedos were ready. It was a personal favourite — Beethoven's Second Symphony. It is the work which gave him the most trouble to write and he had to write it three times before he was satisfied. He was aware at the time that he was going deaf, making its gay, poetic charm all the more remarkable.

I debated the subject of dessert — doctors and dieticians have instilled a guilt feeling throughout the entire Western world on the questions revolving around it. After deciding "yes" rather than "no", the next decision was "which?"

A sabayon seemed like the best idea, self-justified as I had had no potatoes, rice or pasta with the dinner. It is a dessert suited to such an occasion as it can only be prepared at the last moment and served immediately. I followed the classic recipe, using dark Barbados rum.

With coffee, I had a rare indulgence. I watched television. The film was an old one about a woman who suspected her husband of poisoning her. As George Sanders was playing the husband, I wouldn't have been a bit surprised if her suspicions had proved correct. I was relieved that it wasn't fish poison but the number of red herrings in the plot made up for that.

He hadn't been responsible on this occasion and I went to bed even as the final clinch dissolved into credits.

CHAPTER EIGHTEEN

The National Television studios in Acton Park were only a short walk from the tube station. The massive letters "NTV" hung above the gateway entrance to the parking area. They obviously expected all their visitors to arrive by car and when I walked across the street and presented myself at the glassed-in guard office which controlled the double-barred barrier, I received a questioning look from the commissionaire.

My name received no immediate recognition but I suppose they get lots of people there, many more famous than me. Eventually he found my name on his list though the way he said "Ah — by Mr St Leger" suggested that I wasn't among the day's celebrities and neither was Mr St Leger.

"Did you park your car across the road, sir?" he asked. "You can bring it in and —"

"I didn't come by car." I could see that I'd slipped a few more notches down the scale. "There a bad traffic situation on the A40," I explained. "Or so they said on the radio."

"Radio!" His lip curled in derision. "Radio! What do they know about traffic?"

"Oh, they're often wrong, I know but —"

"Often? Not often right if you ask me — still who did you say you wanted to see, sir?"

"Miss Watkins."

"Ah, not easy. She's a hard one to find, she is . . ." he paused with his hand on the phone then through the window, he spotted someone and rapped hard on the glass.

A little elfin-like lady in a grey dress, black shoes and a red and white bandana holding her greying hair appeared and cocked her head on one side.

"Oh, Millie, take this gentleman up to the third floor west, would you? See if you can find Miss Watkins."

She looked scornful. "Like looking for a blinkin' will-o'-

the-wisp, that is." She studied me for a moment. "Well, orl right, let's see what we can do."

Crossing the yard, she cocked an eye upwards. "Looks like rain," she commented cheerfully.

"Surely not," I said. "That fellow after your news programme last night said it was going to be fine all day."

" 'im!" she said contemptuously. "Since when did 'e ever know anythink about weather?"

"Well, he sounds as if he does."

"Reads it!" She cackled, holding up a hand to slow an approaching limousine so that we could cross unhindered. "Reads it, that's all 'e does."

"He seems to be accurate enough —"

"Then why did 'e come in this morning carrying 'is umbrella?" she demanded triumphantly. "Knows nothink about weather, he does. Proper shower if you arsk me!" She cackled at this then led the way into a large brick building. She tittered once or twice at her own witticism and I smiled encouragingly. We went along a lengthy corridor then up in a lift that hiccuped threateningly but finally deposited us on the third floor.

A long narrow passage seemed to stretch into infinity. Off it were dozens of doors each with a minuscule name on a card in a holder. Presumably this made frequent changes simpler.

Millie knocked at one door, poked her head in, called out a question then banged the door shut. " 'aven't seen 'er," she reported. "Come on, let's try down 'ere."

A few doors further along, she tried again, still without luck. The next time, she came out grinning with satisfaction. "She's in Layout. Near the end."

We went down the seemingly endless passageway. Young men and women, mostly with sheafs of paper or folders or computer print-outs went by in both directions. The building was evidently all administrative. The studios must be in another building. At last we stopped. Millie went in without knocking. It seemed to be one large room achieved by knocking down walls and combining several smaller ones. Large tables like drafting tables filled the room, most of them occupied by people engaged in sketching or drawing.

"That's 'er," said Millie. She pointed and left abruptly,

leaving me standing there. No one took any notice of me so I walked over to the woman indicated.

She was small and wiry, with a tight pinched face and hard challenging eyes. She wore old slacks and a brown sweater that had seen better days. A crumpled cigarette dangled from her mouth and she didn't bother to remove it while she was talking.

She held up a large board and stared at it in disdain.

"What the bloody hell is this?"

A young girl was holding a stack of similar boards and had presumably just given her this one.

"The Enchanted Forest," the young girl said placidly.

"The trailer park in Southall looks more like an enchanted forest than this does. Take it back to him and tell him to do it again. Put a bit of enchantment into it this time."

"He's done it twice already. You said the last one looked like Butlin's after a tornado." The girl, despite her youth, was not cowed. Evidently, she had been through this before.

"Then tell him to do it three bloody times. And he'd better get it right this time or he'll be down at the Job Centre begging for work designing Christmas cards."

The young girl took it back and handed her another.

"Looks like Wormwood Scrubs on a bad day."

"It's the Duke's Castle."

There was an indignant snort then she became aware of me.

"Who the hell are you?"

I told her my name.

She shook her head impatiently. "I don't want to know your name. Means nothing to me. What do you want?"

I decided quickly that St Leger's name probably wouldn't cut much more ice than mine. I needed a tougher approach. Philip Marlowe wouldn't have tolerated this dame for five seconds.

"You Deedee Watkins?"

"Yes but what —"

"I want to ask you some questions."

"What the hell do you mean —"

"About the death of Ivor Jenkinson."

She took the cigarette from her mouth at that. It smelled like a year-old Gauloise — or worse.

"How would I know about that? I wasn't there," she said defiantly.

"I know. But I was."

"Then ask the bloody police — not me."

"I don't need to. I'm the one asking the questions. I'm asking you because you worked with him."

She drew the wrong conclusion from my words — as I wanted her to do.

"Nobody worked with him. He was an independent bastard. The only thing he'd have shared with anybody would have been a communicable disease."

"Not popular, you'd say?"

"IJ had one highly developed instinct — for being completely obnoxious."

"Would you say he had any enemies?"

She tried to laugh but it made her cough, a rasping smoker's cough. When she recovered, she took another drag at the cigarette which still smouldered rebelliously.

"Enemies? No, not IJ — he didn't have an enemy in the world." She chuckled at my evident surprise. "He didn't need any enemies — all his friends hated him."

I seemed to have broken through the veneer of resistance in Deedee Watkins though I wondered if St Leger had deliberately given me her name knowing the reception she would afford me. If so, well, two could play at that game.

"Was Roger St Leger one of his friends?"

"St Leger! The poor man's Fanny Craddock? No, they weren't friends. IJ was just making use of him." She suddenly noticed that the young girl was still standing, the layout boards in her hand and drinking in every word of this fascinating cross-examination. Probably a Bergerac fan. "Go on, Jean. Bugger off back to that refugee from the *Tatler* and tell him to get his arse in gear. I want new designs by tomorrow."

The girl left, clearly reluctant to miss a merciless cross-examination by a tough investigator. I went on swiftly, keeping the pressure on Deedee now that I had her talking.

"What kind of use?"

Deedee pulled deeply on the cigarette again. It kicked off a few sparks and she brushed them off her sweater carelessly.

"IJ was a user of people. He put his programmes together alone — never told anybody anything. But you can't work completely alone in this racket so he had to use people. But that's what he did — used them to get what he wanted."

"What did he want?"

"Information, knowledge, tips, scandal, scuttlebutt, dirt — whatever would be helpful in putting one of his programmes to bed."

"Was he good at it?"

"Good? Oh, he was good all right. The best."

"And what was he working on when he died?"

"Christ! You're not listening to me, are you! I'm telling you he told nobody what he was working on. People brought him bits, dribs and drabs, fragments — and he put them all together. He'd send people out on assignments and out of all they brought back, only IJ would know what was relevant and what wasn't."

"But those people would know at least the general target," I insisted. "Insurance, the Stock Exchange, airlines . . ."

"Oh, sure," Deedee said. "Just like we told your people who were here yesterday." A hint of suspicion had crept into her voice.

"Our F-12 group," I said promptly.

"I don't know what —"

"I'm F-14." My tone emphasised that there was all the difference in the world. "We communicate of course but our methods of approach vary. Vital in a case like this."

It seemed to satisfy her, at least she didn't ask for credentials. Before she could think about that, I asked:

"What did IJ do with all the information he gathered for a programme? Do you have data banks where —"

She chuckled, sounding like the Wicked Witch of the North. She tapped her forehead. "Kept it all in there till he was ready."

"Who else worked with him —" I intercepted her look. "In any way — I mean, somebody had to schedule —"

"You might talk to Mike Quinn. He had some contact with IJ."

"And where can I find him?"

"Left out of the door, five doors along. Name's outside."

I thanked her for her help and exited quickly. At the door marked "M.J. Quinn", I knocked and went in without waiting for an answer.

A man in his late twenties sat in front of a TV screen, idly watching. He was tall and strongly built and had a healthy complexion and a lot of unruly red hair. The TV screen was only occupying a small percentage of his concentration. Most of this was focused on a bizarre ceremony that he was conducting and I stared in fascination.

A newspaper was spread out on the desk and there were several slices of soft white bread that had dents where he had touched it. A slab of what might be luncheon meat sat there — it was probably 100 per cent protein which was 90 per cent fat which was 85 per cent saturated. A block of pale yellow cheese lay alongside the meat. The cheese looked like it might have been a fair substitute for axle-grease on a donkey cart.

The three components were being assembled in layers and a quarter of a pint of thick red liquid was being squeezed out of a large tube. The liquid looked as plastic as the tube. I wondered what he was going to do with this grotesque structure when it was finalised. He applied the last rites and sat back and contemplated his masterpiece. Something on the screen temporarily distracted him and it was when he looked back at his desk-top creation that he saw me.

He smiled, a happy farm-boy sort of welcoming smile.

"Hello. Looking for me?"

"Mike Quinn?"

"That's right." He didn't seem curious about me or what I was doing there. I decided to keep it that way. I pulled a battered wicker chair next to the desk.

"I'm investigating Ivor Jenkinson's death."

"Oh." He thought for a moment. "You fellows were here —"

"Yesterday. Yes, I know. That was our F-12 group." It had worked once, might as well keep telling the same story. "I'm F-14. Just want to ask you a few questions. You did the scheduling for IJ, didn't you?"

"As much as anybody could."

"Hard to work with, I believe."

Apparently I rated higher in entertainment value than the

TV set on his desk. He reached out and switched it off. He grinned. "Just timing a show before we send it out for re-runs. Yes, IJ was a shit to work with. Never told you anything. Rude bugger too. Expected the earth but never said thank you."

"What was he working on when he died?"

"He was a close-mouthed sod — never told a soul what he was up to."

"In view of the nature of his exposés, that's to be expected, isn't it?"

He eyed the white, light-brown and yellow edifice on his desk but not with any noticeable longing or intent. "Others work differently," he said. "Some take their staff into their confidence. They think they get better results when they know what they're doing."

"But not IJ?"

"Not him. The CIA isn't run as tight as his programme."

"But there must have been some clues —"

"He had three investigations going as near as I know. Might have had more, sometimes he did. They were low-cost housing in the North-East, the food industry and some scandal about a coal mine in Nottinghamshire where a shaft had collapsed, two men were injured and IJ thought it had been hushed up."

I didn't need long to zero in on the one that had a connection with his abrupt and violent death. "The programme on the food industry . . . what did that entail?"

Mike Quinn shook his red head vigorously. "No idea but he was enthusiastic about it. Seemed to believe it was going to be one of his best shows."

I recalled with a chill the words that had been among IJ's last — "It will be my best programme."

"So nobody worked closely enough with him to know any details of his investigations?"

"No."

"Who did he use as sources, as helpers?"

Mike Quinn grinned again. "Whoever he could. He had a few regulars, crummy lot, most of them. One or two were stringers for the newspapers, one or two gossip page photographers, in fact, any freelance who wanted to earn a few quid and didn't mind how they did it."

"You mean some of them weren't above irregular methods?"

"Come on, you don't expect me to admit that to a copper!"

I adopted my sternest expression. "You'd better, my lad."

He didn't look in the least intimidated. Nevertheless, he answered. "Irregular, unethical, illegal even — I don't doubt."

"Ever meet any of them?"

"Saw some of them now and then, didn't actually meet any. IJ didn't share his sources."

"Do you know who any of them were?"

"You mean names?"

"Yes."

He rubbed his chin in thought. "There was an Italian chap, a photographer, always needed a shave, long hair. Worked for that magazine — what's it called . . . *Scandalous.*" He grinned. "It's well named, ever see it?"

"Yes. It's the one which specialises in pictures of famous people in places and positions they'd rather not be seen in."

"That's the one — and with people they'd prefer not to be seen with."

"What his name, this photographer?"

Quinn shook his head. "Don't remember."

"Try." He tried. His brow crinkled and he screwed up his face with the effort. Finally, he gave up.

"Can't think of it. I'll call you at Scotland Yard if I do."

Before I could comment on that, he was asking inevitably,

"What's your name again?"

"Don't worry," I told him. "I'll be in touch. Back to IJ — he didn't have a secretary?"

"No. Used the secretarial pool. That way, no one got to know anything."

"Office?"

"He had a sort of an office . . ."

"Sort of —?"

"Well . . . want to see it?"

Of course I did and he led the way down the corridor, turning through a door into what seemed like a small, untidy conference room. It was little more than that with a large table, lots of chairs and a huge blackboard covering one wall.

"This is his office?" I asked in astonishment.

"You'll have gathered that IJ didn't go in for show," Mike Quinn said. "He didn't spend that much time in the building. He was always out so he didn't need much here. He used this room to talk to people."

"A weird operator."

"He was that sure enough."

My gaze strayed across the big blackboard and my interest quickened when Quinn said casually, "Some of that's his."

He meant all the squiggles, notes, scrawls and undecipherable jumbles that covered the board in half a dozen colours. I was about to ask a question when the door opened and a young man of about Quinn's age came in.

He was lean with dark hair and a light olive complexion. He walked with a slight limp and Quinn greeted him jovially.

"Hello, Joel! Have a good holiday?"

"Yeh, it was good."

"What d'you do? Twist an ankle coming down the slopes?"

"Not likely! wouldn't catch me out there in all that white mush. No, I fell over a stool in the lodge. It was the last night fortunately."

"Mix the punch pretty strong there, do they?"

"Something like that." He was looking at me with frank curiosity and Mike Quinn waved a hand of introduction.

"Joel Freedman — this is, er . . ."

"I'm investigating the death of Ivor Jenkinson," I said quickly. "Did you just get back from holiday?"

"Last night. My flat-mate told me about it. Otherwise, I wouldn't have known. I didn't follow any news in Austria."

"You knew IJ, did you?"

Freedman shrugged. "A little, yes. Nobody really knew him."

"We were just looking at the board here when you came in," said Quinn. "You're one of the few who knows his writing. How much of this is his?"

I moved towards the board, curbing my eagerness. Here was a real chance to learn something — something that Scotland Yard didn't know as they had been here yesterday and Joel Freedman had only returned last night.

Freedman looked over the board languidly.

"They took photos of it yesterday," commented Mike Quinn and I felt like telling him to shut up.

"Any additional information," I said, "is always welcome."

Freedman pointed to a line of red writing. I took out my diary to write in and found a pen. I wrote down the line.

"Dr F — B4 CC." What did that mean? Freedman was already pointing to some yellow chalk inscriptions. "That's his too."

"VDZH St Armand — 12, 9.30." I wrote that down too.

Freedman was scanning the board. "I've been gone ten days," he said. "All this is new since I left." He waved an arm at the board. "IJ always scribbled his notes — such as he had — on this side of the board. The rest seems to be from a presentation somebody else gave on marketing old programmes."

I was about to put my diary away when Freedman said, "Oh here's another one." He smiled. "Looks like a pay-off to one of his informants."

"£150 AS." I added that to the others. It might take an expert code-breaker to figure those out.

"Any more?" I asked.

"Seems to be all."

"Anyway, you've got the photographs," said Mike Quinn. "Your people will be able to match up his handwriting and know which is IJ's."

Smart alec — probably watched all the Maigret re-runs.

"Well, thanks," I said. It was time to get out while my cover was still intact.

"Did an escort bring you in?" Joel Freedman didn't sound suspicious but I wasn't taking any chances.

"Millie brought me."

"Oh, then I'll take you down to —"

"That's all right," I told him. "Millie's taking me out too."

I shook hands briskly with both of them and left. The corridor was busy with people hurrying or sauntering on various errands and I walked quickly, merging with them. I had had a sudden idea and I was going to strike while the mental iron was still hot.

At the end of the corridor was a small alcove with a coffee machine. Two girls were sipping coffee and discussing Tom

Cruise's latest film. I took a plastic cup to make me look casual but after a peek at the grey fluid in their cups, I decided against actually drinking any.

"Is the medical department on this floor?" I asked them.

"Medical department? Oh, you mean the clinic? It's the next floor up, first door."

I thanked them and went up the stairs.

The clinic was so white, it was dazzling. White-tiled floor, white walls, white ceiling and brilliant white neon strip lighting. A wheeled trolley was covered with a clean white sheet and two chairs with white nylon seats were placed by a desk with a white top and a sheet of glass over it.

"Anyone here?" I received no answer and was about to call again when a door opened. I hadn't noticed it — it fitted the white decor so closely.

A head of pure white hair appeared followed by a tall elderly woman in a spotless white smock.

"Sit down," she ordered and came up to me. She gave me a gentle push in the chest to help me sit.

"I'm not here for —" I began.

She was already peering into my eyes. "Open wide," she instructed and when I did so, she snapped, "Your mouth — your mouth."

"Look, I'm not a patient —"

"I'm not a patient person either," she said. "But don't worry. No one can help being ill." She already had two fingers pulling down my lower lip. She almost recoiled. "Blue!" she said in amazement. "Your mouth is blue!"

She wrote rapidly on a pad on the desk. "Very unusual. Have you spent time in the tropics?"

I took advantage of her writing to pull myself away.

"I'm not a patient. I don't work here. I'm investigating the death of Ivor Jenkinson. Did you ever treat him?"

"You'd better sit down," she said calmly. "Now, what can I do for you? From the police, are you?"

"IJ. Did he ever consult you — about anything?"

"Yes but never anything serious." She eyed me solicitously. "Your mouth is blue though . . ."

"I had blueberry muffins for breakfast."

"M'm," she said complacently. "That would explain it."

I took out my diary and made a pretence of making a note. "Your name is —?"

"Dr Margaret Evans." So much for hot ideas. She wasn't the Dr F on the blackboard. "Did Ivor Jenkinson have a doctor of his own?"

"I suppose he must have had. Probably didn't consult him much though. He was a very healthy individual."

"Can you tell me his name?"

She rose and went to a cabinet. After a moment, she came back with a card in her hand. "Dr William Stanley, Weymouth Street."

Another blank. "How detailed is that file on IJ?" I asked. "For instance, did he have any allergies?"

She examined the card. "None shown here."

"Food allergies?"

"Nothing here." She put the card down. "Terrible business," she said. I nodded. "Never speak ill of the dead, of course — but he wasn't a man who was liked. What have you found out? What was the cause of death?"

"That is confidential at the moment," I said pompously.

"Professional interest, that's all," she assured me.

I thanked her and exited. I made my way out into the yard and across the parking area. At the guard gate, a window opened.

I turned and waved past a couple of cars. "Thanks, Millie."

"Oh, saw you back here, did she?" the commissionaire asked, trying in vain to spot the invisible Millie. "We have strict rules about people being escorted at all times."

"You're very efficient about it too," I told him.

I hastened off to study the immortal notes of IJ, hoping they would give me some clue about something. At the moment they were as incomprehensible as a menu at a Korean restaurant.

I phoned Winnie from the office. Perhaps I was feeling slightly guilty about having gone sleuthing at St Leger's apartment and at the NTV studios. Inspector Hemingway had been firm — well, more than firm really — in his insistence that I must not get involved in the investigation into the death of IJ. But hadn't he said himself that he believed it was mixed up with my assignment for Le Trouquet d'Or? How could I know which investigation was which unless I investigated?

That sounded convincing to me anyway. So I needn't feel guilty and besides I wanted to know what was new with the Food Squad — and well, yes, I did want to talk to Winnie.

She answered promptly.

"Any progress?" she asked.

"A few things," I said vaguely. "I'm not sure what they add up to — perhaps you can help me figure them out."

"What are they?" She was brisk and businesslike today.

"I don't think we can discuss them properly over the phone," I said. "Is there anything at your end?"

"We've pretty well exhausted the list of relatives. None of them are close and none have had any contact which indicates any animosity. As for his friends — well, there's not much there either except that he really didn't have any."

"That's what I've heard," I agreed.

"As for his colleagues at NTV — well, you know the situation there as well as I do."

Her tone was light but I didn't have a response ready.

"Impersonating a police officer is an offence punishable under Code 2244 —" she was continuing. She didn't sound too harsh and I took a chance and threw myself on the mercy of the Law. She hadn't mentioned St Leger. Did she know about my visit there too? Probably not but I'd better not push my luck too far.

"I haven't actually impersonated a —"

"I know. You allowed them to jump to wrong conclusions." She even chuckled slightly. "Don't worry — I haven't told the inspector." What a wonderful girl! "Did you learn anything?"

"Nobody liked IJ," I said quickly, thankful for the diversion. "That doesn't seem to be news though. But I can't believe that anyone there had any reason to kill him. If indeed, he was killed . . ." I left the sentence dangling, hoping Winnie would take it up. She did.

"It looks that way. Forensic agrees that the heavy dose of bacillus that killed him is out of proportion to the minor doses that the others received. They're also saying that such a dosage seems excessive — even for the most virulent lamprey."

I took a deep breath. "Then it's murder?"

She didn't answer right away. Then she said:

"I'm not going to mention to the inspector that your detecting might have strayed into our investigation — and in return, I want you to keep what I'm going to tell you in the strictest confidence."

"All right!" I assured her at once. Not even Sexton Blake or Lord Peter Wimsey were taken into the confidence of the Yard!

"The inspector doesn't want to issue a definite statement that it was murder because then we — as the Food Squad — would have to turn the investigation over to Homicide."

"How long can you hold out?"

"A few days only. The inspector is determined to solve it in that time."

"Do you think he can?" I asked.

"When the inspector determines to do something, he usually does it."

"But at the moment, you don't really have a suspect?"

"No," said Winnie. "Do you?"

"I think I'm getting close."

"Oh?" She sounded surprised.

"Give me a day or two. I should have something for you by then."

She wanted to ask more but she said, "Very well. Keep in touch — oh, and be careful."

She hung up before I could ask her what she meant by that.

CHAPTER NINETEEN

For breakfast, I made some muesli. I always make my own — it's not that much more difficult than opening a packet.

Muesli started out as a mixture of oats, milk, apple and nuts. It was an instant hit because of its natural freshness and its high nutritional value. Health food stores make it easy to obtain all the ingredients and I like to be able to ring the changes and use whatever happens to be in the kitchen.

This morning, I had some rolled oats, some wheat flakes, rye flakes, some plain yoghurt, a little honey, a few raisins, some walnuts and some left-over apple sauce. Bananas, dried apricots or pineapple are good too if I have them. In fact, it's always good and never the same twice. Would Dr Bircher-Benner from Zurich recognise it? I wondered.

On the way to the office, I detoured so as to look at Hammersmith Pier. Being so close to it, I'd seen it countless times but I wanted to have another look at the place where thousands of lamprey had been washed up dead. One lamprey is a frightening sight — almost prehistoric in appearance. Thousands must have been terrifying — the crowds would have been enormous.

From the "Unfinished Business" file, I plucked the letter from Dunsingham Castle and jotted down a few ideas as a start towards a proper reply.

One recommendation I wanted to make was that "Egurdouce" should be on the menu. This is kid — young goat — and a very ancient dish. The roast kid of the Holy Land perfumes the pages of the Bible with its appetising aroma. It is the roast of patriarchs and kings and retained its popularity into the Middle Ages. The meat is browned then cooked with ginger, raisins, onions and red wine.

Swan deserved some consideration if Dunsingham Castle really wanted to present authentic mediaeval food but it would take an expert chef to reduce the oiliness of the flesh which gives the swan its resistance to the water in which it spends its life. The texture can be leathery too though marinating could take care of that. The castle might have to prepare itself for a siege as the conservationists would probably storm the walls. Still, that could be a bonus — a real-life spectacle.

A wild boar's head would be very impressive but dressing it is a long and expensive business. Other dishes, more orthodox, could be included and would be safer in appealing to the general taste. Steak and kidney pudding, leg of lamb with dumplings and thin sirloin steak covered with oysters would be good choices. Desserts should be no problem as many of the mediaeval desserts are similar to those of today — Madeira cake, rum gateau and many fruit dishes. A nice touch would be trays of jellies and blancmanges, carved or moulded into the shapes of animals, birds, crowns and miniature castles.

I re-assembled my notes on the wines suitable for a barbecue at Graceworthy Manor and prepared them for typing. Then I turned to the mail. It contained one letter which promptly intrigued me.

It was from a woman who said she was compiling a book of famous meals. She had heard of a dinner given by the Man Who Broke the Bank at Monte Carlo to celebrate his unique feat. Could I provide details? She offered a small fee. I'm a sucker for bizarre questions like that and I would enjoy this one. I recollected reading about the dinner to which the lady referred and believed it was in one of the books by that celebrated caviare taster (yes, as a profession), André Launay. I had a copy in the flat and would look it up.

There was an invitation to a testimonial dinner. I don't usually attend those and was about to throw it in the waste basket when I noticed that the dinner was for Per Larsson. I set it aside to read later.

Another letter introduced its writer as with a group seeking a ban on synthetic food colourings. It urged my support for this worthwhile cause on the grounds that these are "unnatural".

I would certainly send them some comments that might be helpful and perhaps correct some misapprehensions. For instance, when peas are canned, their natural green colour is destroyed and has to be replaced with an artificial colouring. Who would eat colourless peas? A great variety of natural food colouring substances is available but most of them are not used because they are unstable. Artificial colours are so much more stable. Stability is, of course, not the most important consideration but natural substances can be just as harmful as artificial ones. Spinach wouldn't be allowed on the market if it were a synthetic product. It contains as much as 1 per cent oxalic acid and one fifth of an ounce of oxalic acid can be fatal to humans. Altogether a very tricky subject, food colouring. It would be my public service for the day to give this group some pointers on where to go for further information.

There was the usual number of requests and invitations that I didn't want to accept and several offers that I couldn't refuse. I refused them. Mrs Shearer answered at once when I called and she said she would come down and collect my typing. Usually, she sent one of the girls but she was burning with curiosity about my new status.

She bustled in and I handed her the folder.

"Is everything going all right?" she asked, wide-eyed.

"It's a very perplexing affair," I said solemnly. "But have no fear — we'll get to the bottom of it."

"Not dangerous, is it?" she breathed.

"There are always risks involved in this kind of work."

As we went to the door, she asked in a hushed voice:

"Have you ever been shot?"

I regarded her briefly. "Do flesh wounds count?" I asked.

We went out and I locked the door and headed for the stairs, leaving her standing there with the folder in her hand and an awed expression.

I took the bus to Streatham and walked to Bookery Cooks. It was mid-morning and too early for the pretty and enthusiastic young cooks to be offering any food but they were at work, chopping and preparing. Michael took me into the office and called to Marita for a pot of coffee.

"How's the Great Detective today?"

I outlined what had happened so far. He pushed his glasses back up into place every time they slid down.

"Sounds like murder to me," he commented when I finished. "And probably tied up with all those other events," he said.

"I'm beginning to think so too. The Yard are at the point of conceding that such a high level of poison — and in IJ only — is not very likely."

Michael nodded agreement.

"An unpopular man — our TV star," he said. "Nobody liked him but who disliked him enough to kill him? And why?"

"You're not the first with that observation. If he was killed though — then the comments he made while affected by the botulin may have a direct bearing on something he had found out."

"Something which someone at that dinner wanted kept silent," added Michael. "But those other people absorbed some poison too. How does that fit in with IJ getting a deadly dose?"

I took out my diary. "There may — just may — be a clue or two here."

Michael glowed. "I say, Holmes, this is exciting!"

"Keep your smock on, doctor. Let's see what any of this might mean — we'll go through the Musgrave Ritual."

I copied from my diary on to a sheet of paper the inscriptions I had taken from the board at NTV studios. On further viewing, they didn't look that promising but Michael's ingenuity knows no limits and I watched as he studied the sheet.

"Where did you find these?" he asked.

I told him where and how. "So IJ did write them — we can be sure of that."

He read out the items, one by one.

"Dr F — BF CC. VDZH St Armand — 12, 9.30."

He read them out again, more slowly.

"One of the fellows at the studio — knew IJ a little — said the last one was probably a payment to one of IJ's informers."

"Whose initials are A.S.?"

"Possibly."

Michael moved his finger to the first item.

"Dr F? Who's he?"

"A mystery man so far. The doctor at the studios doesn't

have those initials nor does IJ's private doctor."

"H'm, not much to follow up there." Michael moved to the second item. "Maybe this is more promising."

"Go ahead, Mr Enigma, decipher."

"Nine thirty — sounds like a time. If it is, 12 may refer to a date." He pulled a desk calendar closer. "Four days before IJ died!"

"Good, Michael. And the rest? Is there a hospital called St Armand's? Maybe that's where our Dr F is!"

He was already reaching for a hefty volume from his shelves of reference books. He thumbed through it. "No," he said in disappointment. "No such hospital. It does sound like one though. Funny thing it seems vaguely familiar. Wonder where I've heard it?"

"Heard what?" asked Molly coming in to the office with an arm-load of new books.

"St Armand," said Michael and spelled it.

Molly shook her head. "No, I don't — wait a minute! That insurance company . . ."

"What insurance company?"

"That real expensive one. Wanted to sell us a policy covering all our book shipments."

Michael frowned. "They weren't called St Armand."

"They were on Armand Street."

Michael snapped his fingers. "You're right!" He turned to the reference book shelf again and took down an Inner London Street Register. After a moment of page turning, he chortled with glee. "Here it is! St Armand Street — let's see who's on it . . ." and when he yelled "Aha!"it was so loud that Dorothy came from the kitchen to see what catastrophe had befallen.

"Number 21!" Michael was beside himself with excitement. "VDZH Bank!" Before I could ask the obvious question, he was grabbing another mighty tome. "Here they are!" he announced triumphantly. "They're a financial institution rather than a bank. Dutch — originally founded by a Van Der Zwet and a Henningsen. They furnish venture capital, offer investment advice to corporations and arrange mergers and acquisitions." He looked up and his glasses slid all the way down his nose. "And — and they specialise in the food and drink industry!"

"Well done!" I congratulated him.

He scribbled down the address and phone number and handed them to me. I looked at the paper. "No time like the present," I said. "May I use your phone?"

A polite but distant female voice: "VDZH."

I gave my name. There was a frost-edged silence which said very plainly that she'd never heard of me.

"I want to make an appointment with Mr Van Der Zwet or Mr Henningsen," I told her.

"That won't be possible," she said flatly.

"In that case, who can I make an appointment with?"

There was another silence but I could hear far-away clicks. When she came back, it was "May I ask what this is in connection with?"

"Investment or possibly venture capital."

I hoped that was enough. I could add merger or acquisition if I was pushed.

"Mr Broodman could see you a week from Monday —"

"This is VDZH, isn't it?" I asked, sounding incredulous.

"Yes —"

"This is an urgent matter. It won't wait till a week from Monday."

"I'm afraid we don't —"

"Oh, I see. Maybe this is bigger than you wish to handle — well, that's okay. Could you recommend a larger organisation? This really is too hot to wait."

Michael was grinning, listening to every word.

"Just a moment," said the girl and returned in seconds.

"Mr Broodman could spare you a little time tomorrow afternoon."

I knew that one. She meant that if what I had to offer was worthwhile, I could stay for hours but if it wasn't, the "little time" would be down to five minutes. Well, Mr Broodman wasn't going to be overjoyed when he learned the real reason for my visit but that was tomorrow's problem.

"Two o'clock," I suggested.

"Two thirty," said the girl, evidently used to having the last word.

Michael grinned widely as I hung up.

"And so, once again, our fearless investigator goes out into the world of petro-dollars and pro-forma invoices," he said in his best Pathe newsreel voice. Then he became serious. "I wonder what their angle is? They sound snobby enough to be genuine."

"That's what's puzzling me too," I admitted.

"Think they'll tell you anything? Banking people don't top the list when it comes to being informative."

"I don't know but I'm going to give it a try." I mentioned the request for data on the dinner given by The Man Who Broke the Bank at Monte Carlo and told him I would be grateful for anything he had. I also asked him to keep working on the snail project.

"At a hare's pace," he assured me.

As we reached the door, he had another thought.

"The mysterious Dr F couldn't be one of the guests at the Circle of Careme dinner by any chance, could he?"

I hadn't considered that but I told Michael I would check the guest list.

"There are some people who have a doctorate but don't use the title especially if it's not a medical degree," he reminded me.

"I'll look into that," I promised and headed for Raymond's and lunch with Paula Jardine.

The restaurant was almost full when I arrived. A table for two had been squeezed in though the neighbouring tables had been cleverly re-arranged to avoid crowding.

The waiter brought me a Punt e Mes after I had declined offers of something stronger. More diners were coming in and the place was full when Paula joined me.

She looked ravishing in a cream-coloured linen suit with chocolate piping at the collar and cuffs and it fitted her tall shapely figure perfectly. Three bangles that looked like antique gold clattered on one wrist but she wore no rings.

"Sorry to keep you waiting. Problems in the kitchen."

"Nothing serious, I hope?" I said.

"No, no. Some late deliveries but everything's fine now."

Her lustrous coppery-red hair shone and the warm brown eyes were inviting. The waiter put down a glass of what appeared to be sherry. She raised it and looked at me over the rim.

"Nice to have this opportunity to get to know you," she said softly.

"Delighted to be here," I said and we clinked glasses.

"I told Louis — Louis Deneuve, our head chef — what to bring us." She flashed me a dazzling smile. "I hope that's all right?"

"Certainly," I said. She was obviously a bossy lady but she would have to be to hold down such a responsible job at one of London's finest restaurants.

"Some men object to a woman ordering for them."

"Not me," I told her. "Not when it's a woman who knows the restaurant business as well as you obviously do."

"I've learned most of it from Raymond."

"An excellent teacher, I'm sure," I said. "You didn't have ambitions to follow him as a chef though?"

She sipped her sherry appreciatively.

"I graduated in Business Administration," she said. "The business that interested me most was eating. Have you ever thought — it's the one enjoyable activity that you can do three times a day?"

"Well, perhaps there are others that —"

"Every day?" she asked with a tiny smile.

I drank some Punt e Mes. "You're right."

"So food and drink had to be the business I wanted to go into. Think about it — growing in proportion with the population, getting more sophisticated and more demanding. Prodded by merchandising, expanded by the media, aided and abetted by technology. What a wonderful business!"

"I like your enthusiasm," I said. "So you joined your uncle . . ."

"No. I wanted to get started on my own — no nepotism. I worked for Branford Bakeries in sales and marketing then went on to restaurant administration. Raymond offered me a job as assistant general manager and when the general manager retired, I took his place."

"And you like the job," I said. "That's clear."

"Love it — but to come back to your question, it is strange

that there aren't more women chefs, don't you think?"

"I agree. Women are natural cooks — there should be more of them."

"Why do you think there aren't?" she asked me.

"Male prejudice," I suggested.

She tilted her head in a charming gesture of surprise.

"I didn't expect you to say that."

"Would you hire a woman chef?"

"Of course," she said.

"Would Raymond? Or Louis?"

She considered then said, "No, probably not."

The waiter came with the first course and terminated that discussion. It was one of the classic omelettes, Bourguignonne, with chopped snails, garlic and walnut. The wine waiter brought a glass of Meursault, not normally one of my favourite white wines. I find it occasionally thin and steely but this was a Domaine des Comtes Lafon, one of the best wines of the apellation. It was fresh and light but still assertively ripe and balanced. The garlic in the omelette was undetectable as a separate taste so there was no conflict with the wine.

I congratulated her and she smiled delightfully. "I'll tell Louis — he'll be pleased."

As we finished the omelette, I asked her casually, "Have you been bombarded with questions from reporters these last few days?"

She shook her head and the coppery hair shimmered. "We've had two or three but we haven't been bombarded, no." She regarded me seriously. "Why do you ask?"

"I would have suspected the press would be reviving those tales about the feud."

As our plates were taken away, Paula reached for a roll. She hadn't demonstrated any interest in bread until now and I wondered if it was to cover her hesitation in answering.

"Feud?" She paused but continued, "the feud between Raymond and François, you mean?"

"Yes. It's bound to be revived by the media. It makes such a good story. It always did but now especially with the focus on Le Trouquet d'Or and the death of Ivor Jenkinson — the press must be about to trot it out again."

She pulled the bread roll apart with long fingers and exquisitely manicured finger-nails in a hot pink colour. She didn't eat any though.

"Surely there are other aspects of that awful business that should interest the press more than that old story."

"They'll be digging out all they can. You can expect to have them here asking about it." I wasn't as convinced of that as I sounded but I was determined to get some details out of her.

"It was a long time ago . . ." she said.

"Some men have waited twenty years for revenge."

"Revenge!" Her brown eyes widened in alarm at the word. Then she shook her head and went on more calmly, "The media have their uses but if they try to develop a theory out of that, they're wasting their time."

"You don't believe François could be responsible for the incidents here?"

She shook her head again. "I don't think so. Why would he do such things?"

"Retaliation maybe?"

As soon as I had said it, I realised it was a mistake. I wasn't supposed to be privy to any knowledge of what was happening at Le Trouquet d'Or. The careless question put me in a position that was going to be difficult to defend. Even Columbo wouldn't have said that, dumb as he was.

"Retaliation?" Paula said. "Retaliation for what?"

I tried to look cool and calculating when all I was doing was searching for a good answer. Apparently it worked.

"Ah," said Paula, understanding. "The gossip about sloppiness at Le Trouquet d'Or."

"You know about it?" I changed my tone just in time from surprise to casual.

"Stories of that kind spread fast in the restaurant business." She eyed me carefully. "What have you heard?"

"Same as you probably," I said cheerfully. "So you think it's sloppy housekeeping?"

"Of course. All restaurants — even the very best — have to battle constantly to maintain standards. Why, even the —" She stopped and said gently, "you're actually suggesting that it wasn't sloppy housekeeping? Surely you don't think that Raymond would —" Her eyes almost flashed sparks. "That's absurd — I know him too well — he would never do anything like that!"

The timely arrival of the waiter with the main course defused the situation. Paula sat silent. The wine waiter came and reverently displayed a bottle. She glanced at the label and nodded abstractedly. He uncorked the bottle, poured, she tasted and nodded again.

By the time the waiters had departed, her mood had changed completely and she was her enchanting self again. She said brightly:

"Beef en croute. We don't often serve it but it's one of Louis' favourite creations. He loves to cook it."

"I can understand that. It's a challenge to any chef."

The waiter had carved it at the table. Paula put slices on my plate then on her own. A potato dish I didn't recognise was one which we served ourselves and there were tiny browned cèpes and baby carrots. The beef was succulent and fork-tender, the crust crisp but not too flakey. Layered pâté de foie gras and slivered truffles on top of the beef added to the exquisite flavour.

"More congratulations to Louis," I said. "He has set a new landmark in beef en croute."

Paula smiled. "I'll tell him. He loves compliments."

We ate in silence while the wine waiter poured a Romanee-Conti, one of the most brilliantly intense red wines of France. I strained to catch a glimpse of the label. It was a 1985, probably the best year of the decade.

We both savoured the food and we were on the last few mouthfuls when Paula returned to the unfinished topic.

"Raymond couldn't have had anything to do with it. It's ridiculous. You've met him — don't you agree?"

"From the little I know him, it's unlikely, yes. But then you know him better, he's your uncle."

"By marriage, as a matter of fact. But he's still my uncle," she said.

"Then if Raymond isn't responsible for the happenings at Le Trouquet d'Or — if the feud isn't being carried to those lengths — who's responsible for your cancelled order of tenderloin, the switching of the labels and the disappearance of the reservations book?"

Her attention was being diverted even before I had finished. A few tables away, voices were being raised and a waiter appeared to be involved. Paula crumpled her napkin, threw it on the table and rose hurriedly.

"Excuse me — I'll be back in a moment."

It was too far away for me to hear the conversation, much as I tried. Paula's presence brought the voices down to normality anyway and from what I could see of the faces of the diners, a happy settlement was quickly reached.

Paula returned and gave me a satisfied smile.

"All's well."

"A complaint?" I asked.

"One of the diners thought he had ordered a different dish than the one he was served."

"An example of sloppy housekeeping?" I asked, ever the abrasive investigator.

It didn't ruffle her in the least. "Carl is one of our best waiters," she said. "He doesn't make that kind of mistake."

"How did you resolve it?"

"Carl apologised naturally and said he would correct his error at once. I told you he was one of our best waiters."

We finished the wine and a simple but carefully selected fruit compote completed the meal. As the coffee arrived, I decided to try a shot in the dark.

"You know Roger St Leger?"

She inclined her head. "A little. I hear he's taking over IJ's progamme."

She knew more than I did but I wasn't going to let it show. I wondered if she knew more than St Leger did.

"And Sally Aldridge?"

"She was here recently, I heard. I didn't talk to her, she likes to talk to Raymond." She sipped coffee. "Are you going to her book-signing tomorrow?"

"Is she having one?" I asked then I remembered. "I did get an invitation now that you mention it. I didn't make a note of the date — I seldom go to them. Too many words about food and not enough food. Are you going?"

Paula laughed. "I don't think so. I ought not to encourage her radical ideas — they're bad for the restaurant trade. What was that last title of hers — *Any Gourmet Meal in Thirty*

Minutes? We don't want many people reading that — could put us out of business." Her laugh died away and the import of her words hung in the air. She tried to go on as if it meant nothing. "What's tomorrow's title?"

"I forget," I said. "But I'm sure it will be just as controversial. Maybe I'd better go along and find out. She is a busy girl though, isn't she?"

"Is she?" Paula's delicately traced eyebrows raised.

"She's already at work on yet another book — the one she came here to talk to Raymond about."

"Is that why she came? Raymond didn't say. Another disturbing title?"

"Probably."

The waiter placed a slip of paper before her. It could hardly be the bill so I supposed some vital matter had arisen. I rose too.

"Thanks for a magnificent meal. You probably have things to attend to."

She led me to the door and took my hand, not in a handshake but in a soft warm clasp.

"I've enjoyed it too. I feel we got to know each other a little better, don't you?"

I nodded.

"We must do it again — very soon."

"Nothing I'd like better," I told her.

CHAPTER TWENTY

It was time for some serious thinking. I took the tube to Waterloo, the bridge over York Road and walked past Festival Hall and the National Film Theatre. I passed the outdoor bookstalls which normally delay me but today there were sterner things on my mind.

Walking on, it was quiet with only the distant hum of traffic and the occasional lap of water from a barge or a pleasure boat. It's one of my favourite places for walking and the weather was ideal, cool but a clear blue sky and a sun which shone as if it did it every day. "Rain? Me?" it seemed to be saying. "Never."

I reflected on the chat at lunch. Raymond was lucky to have such an efficient general manager. He was lucky to have such a niece. He was also lucky to have someone defend him so vehemently for I realised that was why she had invited me.

She had heard about the events at Le Trouquet d'Or and she was astute enough to connect them with the famous feud and know that Raymond must be a suspect. She felt it necessary to protect him and I admired her for it. But what she had done inadvertently was to reinforce the growing conviction I had that Raymond was more deeply involved in this entire affair than he had appeared to be.

I had told Winnie I was "getting close" to having a suspect. Now I was more sure of it — oh, he didn't look like a villain. I had been fooled there. The thought that I had to face up to now was a nasty one — was he also a murderer?

A helicopter clattered overhead but it didn't break my train of thinking. I tried to piece it all together . . . Raymond and François were continuing — or perhaps renewing? — their feud. I had unwittingly co-operated in it by unmasking the secret of Oiseau Royal. Raymond had arranged the sabotage at Le Trouquet d'Or — I felt that "arranged" was the best word, he could hardly have done it all himself. François had begun retaliating.

In poisoning the lamprey served at the Circle of Careme dinner, Raymond had over-reached. The words that had been among IJ's last came to me, "Two of them are in it together. . ." IJ, while investigating restaurant scandals, had discovered that Raymond was using an accomplice.

The death of IJ? The Yard had concluded that it must be murder, which meant that IJ was uncovering Raymond's scoundrelly plot and he had over-dosed him with the botulism. Out of character? Well, all the famous poisoners had had unblemished reputations — the doctors, vicars and cabinet ministers. Why not a restaurateur?

It wasn't a perfect re-construction — after all, I wasn't Miss Marple. But it wasn't bad and Scotland Yard could fill in the gaps.

The sky had clouded and a cold breeze swept across the Thames. Drops of rain were falling. The weather was as deceptive as people.

I had come this far, I might as well go on. I hurried over Blackfriars Bridge towards the station, wishing I had a raincoat even one as ancient as Columbo's. He might be dumb but he knew enough not to go out without one even in Los Angeles.

Back at the office, there was a message from Nelda Darvey, asking me to call her. Before doing so, I pulled out the guest list for the Circle of Careme dinner. There was no Dr F. There was only one person with the last initial "F" and I knew him slightly. He was not a doctor of anything.

I called Nelda and her strong voice echoed on the line.

"How's the gourmet detection going? Found a good cure for a hangover yet?"

"I haven't had much time to work on that —"

"So I hear —"

"What have you heard?" I asked.

"Meet me for a drink and we'll talk about it."

"Fine. When?"

"I'm just going into a meeting with the editor. After that,

I'll be dying for some reviving fluid. Say about six?"

"The Bishop's Mitre?"

"Where else?" she said.

The pub is at the Ludgate Circus end of Fleet Street and one of the hang-outs for columnists and name journalists. The prices are kept high so as to force the lower echelons — the mere reporters and computer operators — to patronise the better-known Red Lion, the George and the Cheshire Cheese.

I enjoyed walking in this area, once the larder of London. The names were evocative of raucous Cockney voices, piercing smells and bartering and selling — Bread Street, Milk Street, Honey Lane, Poultry and even Cornhill. Meat was sold on flesh days and fish on lean days and when the sunset bell rang, the frantic scramble to pack and leave began, for penalties were severe for those not complying.

Nelda was only ten minutes late. The demanding pressures of Fleet Street probably enforce punctuality until it becomes a habit.

"God, I need a drink!" she gasped. "I swear I'm going to strangle that bloody editor. I'd pull her blonde hair out by its black roots except it's grey —"

"Please, Nelda," I said. "Don't be so conventional. Every journalist I've ever known has hated their editor."

"She's a bitch," said Nelda passionately.

"You don't like her. It's just a guess but —"

Given suitable provocation — and quite often without it — Nelda could be as foul-mouthed as a professional tennis player but she was on her good behaviour today. She must be after a story.

"My editor," said Nelda, "has a great personality — but not for a human being."

"I admire your restraint," I told her. I also admired her appearance. She was wearing a yellow silky sort of suit with a flared skirt and several loops of pearls. She had one of those large bold faces in which every feature was large and bold — from the flashing eyes to the prominent nose and the wide slash of a red mouth. Her gestures and body language were as uninhibited as the rest of her, making Nelda a stand-out in any crowd. She was also tough, shrewd and every inch as good a columnist as she claimed.

"Thanks Brian," she said as the waiter put a drink before her. "You're a mind-reader."

"Since when did you drink anything but double Famous Grouse?" he asked. He looked inquiringly at me.

I shook my head. "Not at the moment." I had ordered a vodka and tonic on arriving.

Nelda looked at me curiously.

"What's this? Cutting down on earthly pleasures now that you're coming up in the world?"

"Am I? Coming up in the world, I mean?"

"That's the way I hear it. Assisting Scotland Yard in their inquiries, special advisor to the Food Squad —"

"Where did you hear that?" I asked, alarmed.

She patted my hand, the one reaching for the vodka and tonic.

"Don't worry. Only a newspaperwoman with my unerring instincts and unparalleled resources would know about it." Her pat turned to a squeeze. "Now tell me — what's the real story?"

I disengaged my hand but only long enough to take a sip.

"Nelda, I think there are lots of stories. More than enough to keep you going for a while — or at least until the next ten day sensation comes along."

Nelda shook her head. "They don't last even that long any more. Goddam television! You may be right about lots of stories though and the big one at the moment is IJ. Tell me now — did he fall or was he pushed?"

"Your delicacy does you great credit, Nelda. Must derive from your early days on the *Mile End Courier*."

"Don't side-track me," said Nelda firmly. "What did happen to IJ — I mean, really?"

"Really, I don't know for sure. In fact, I don't think I know much more than you — or anyone else who was there at the time."

"I don't know anything from being there," said Nelda. "I learn things from asking questions — like I'm asking right now."

She finished the Scotch in one swallow and waved a long arm at the waiter. Then she swung it in my direction and pointed a finger.

"But you — you are in a position to know all the inside goodies," she said.

"Not at the moment," I said. "I may soon."

"And when you do — you are going to remember all the wonderful times we have had together and out of gratitude, you will —"

"Give you an exclusive so that you can stop the presses and splash the story all across the front page of the early edition, thereby scooping all Fleet Street and most of Wapping too."

"Your terminology is decades out of date but what else can you expect from those trashy crime novels you read?"

The waiter arrived with another double Scotch and Nelda drank half of it before he had left the table.

I was still trying to avoid dropping any clues which might be in tomorrow's paper. I admired Nelda's professionalism — maybe it was because I had such a healthy regard for it that I was being so cautious. But it was not the right time to print anything and certainly not anything attributable to me.

Mainly to divert her, I said:

"You may be in a better position to know something than me."

Nelda raised her strong dark eyebrows.

"How is that?"

"If a dastardly deed was done at the Circle of Careme, it may have been one of the members who was responsible."

She studied me for a moment.

"I had considered that. What a story, eh! And by the woman who was there."

"If it is a story," I said, "you'll be remembering all manner of things you didn't know you knew."

She chose to disregard that.

"Why do you say I'm in a better position to know something than you?"

"You're a champion digger of dirt, a rattler of skeletons in closets, the Queen of Gossip —"

"I never repeat gossip," said Nelda.

My mouth opened and Nelda chuckled. It sounded like a boiler about to overflow. "I don't need to," she said, "I'm always the one who starts it."

She laughed out loud and drained her Scotch. The waiter

evidently knew her drinking frequency for he came over and looked at me, not bothering to ask Nelda.

"All right," I agreed.

"I know I'm a great columnist," said Nelda. "But I wish you'd get to the point. What do you think I know and about who?"

Her large shining eyes were fixed on me and her breasts jutted out audaciously beneath the silky suit as she leaned in my direction. Nelda was all woman.

"We've already raised the possibility of the members of the Circle being suspects," I said. "Which of them seem suspicious and why? You always know who's doing what and to whom. Anybody stand out?"

The waiter brought the drinks. Nelda dived into her purse and came out with a pack of king-sized cigarettes, a long ivory holder and a gold-plated lighter. When Nelda smoked, there was nothing surreptitious about it.

She lit up, puffed furiously for a while, took a big gulp of Scotch and said:

"There's that bastard Tarquin Warrington. I'd believe him capable of anything."

"Specifically though?"

Nelda puffed hard, drank some more whisky.

"Businesses he's busted, people he's humiliated and bankrupted. . . I know of at least one suicide."

"The Warrington chain is that active in the market?"

"Sure," she said. "Buying up competitors left and right."

"Is that the truth?"

Nelda smiled. "I never tell a lie. I don't have to — I can always do more damage with the truth."

"Who else does your evil eye rest on?"

"There's Roger St Leger. Since he lost his TV show, he's been all over town like a blue-arsed fly trying to get another. The Beeb said no and ITV weren't interested. Sky talked to him — or rather let him talk to them. Result — zilch. He's getting desperate."

I looked at her sharply.

"How desperate?" I asked.

She caught my look.

"Ah . . . maybe not that desperate. . ."

"Trapped in a web of events?" I suggested. I was just fishing but Nelda was a good source — one of the best. If there were things to know, she knew them.

"He's been keeping some very strange company and, of course, it's well-known that he's been brown-nosing IJ."

"Who couldn't help him?"

"Wouldn't, more likely. IJ wouldn't hand you a glass of water if your house was on fire."

"There's a rumour going around that St Leger has latched on to a programme," I said.

Nelda exhaled a cloud of smoke from a magnificent pair of lungs. "What kind of a programme?"

"IJ's."

She drank some Scotch. "H'm, haven't heard that . . . who told you?"

"Nelda, do you reveal sources?"

She chuckled.

"Do you think he can do IJ's programme?" I asked her.

"He's not the ruthless son-of-a-bitch that IJ was, that's for sure. St Leger could do a programme, but it would never be IJ's or anything remotely resembling." She drank more Scotch, inhaled strongly and added, "Nor can I see him killing IJ to get the chance."

"I understand he's quite a drinker. What about if he were under the influence?"

"St Leger?" Nelda looked surprised. "He's not a drinker."

"That's not what my information says."

"Malicious chatter," Nelda chuckled. "You know how I detest it."

"Any other candidates?"

She took a studied look at her now-empty glass.

"Well, there's one of your old girl-friends."

I signalled to the waiter this time. It also gave me a chance to assimilate her remark.

"Oh, really? Which one?"

Nelda smiled, enjoying herself. She took her time to answer.

"Sally Aldridge," she said.

I was surprised. I must have looked it for Nelda smiled wider.

"What's suspicious about Sally? It's true she writes books which upset a few people but —"

"*Any Gourmet Meal in Thirty Minutes?*" Nelda pulled a face and there was a lot of it to pull. "That's like a carving knife to the heart for real food-lovers!"

"At least she was smart enough to get accepted by the Circle of Careme before she came out with any of those outrageous titles," I said.

Nelda shrugged. "Would have made no difference. The Circle's too powerful to bother about gnat-bites. What's this new book she's coming out with next? Signing's tomorrow, isn't it?"

"I'm sure you know the title, Nelda. You took up half a column in blasting the last one. You'll no doubt do the same to this."

Nelda smiled again, looking like a cat that has just swallowed a very large canary, stuffing, gravy and all.

"The new one's called *Why Eat Out?*" I reminded her.

"Oh, yes," Nelda nodded as if she had just recalled it. "Sub-titled 'How to Cook Any Restaurant Meal at Home'. The restaurant trade will love it."

"If you're tossing suspicion around, Nelda, it won't wash. Sally may be getting herself detested in the business but that's no motive for her to take any action against them."

"Supposing," said Nelda, "the restaurants put pressure on her publisher. Then he might want to dump her. Might that not make her furious?"

"A cute theory," I said, "but I don't buy it. Any other ideas?"

"There's the company she keeps." Nelda tried to be coy but it was not a success.

"What about it?" I prodded though I knew she was dying to tell me.

"Well, you know Sally. Girl has an impediment in her speech — she can't say 'no'."

"She can. I've heard her say it."

"Must have had a hell of a headache," said Nelda. "Where are those bloody drinks?"

The waiter came with them and was in time to hear Nelda's question.

"Sorry, Miss Darvey," he said. 'Martin Ranicar's over there with six blokes."

"You mean he gets priority over me!" Nelda was furious. "I'll take my business elsewhere."

"Hope not, Miss Darvey. We'd miss your cheerful, friendly chatter, your pleasant —"

"Go away, Brian. Go kneel before Sir Martin."

He left, chuckling.

"You were telling me about the company Sally keeps."

"Well," said Nelda, "there's that crummy photographer for a start. Sells his work to any sleazy rag that'll buy it."

"So maybe he's not a regular in *Vanity Fair*. There are worse occupations."

"There's also the company Scarponi keeps."

A bell rang inside my head.

"Scarponi? Do you know his first name?"

"Alessandro, I think." She glanced up. "Why? Know him?"

The initials AS on the board at NTV studios. One of IJ's informants according to Joel Freedman.

"I don't think so. What's wrong with the company he keeps?"

"Mixed up with some unsavoury characters in Soho, they say."

"Some good Chinese restaurants there," I said to keep her talking.

Nelda shuddered. Her whole magnificent frame shuddered with her.

"I know. I ate in one last week. I think the head waiter was a former war-lord. Place was full of Eastern promise — and that's all they were — promises."

She fortified herself with Scotch and lit another cigarette although I could still just see her through the pall of smoke.

"Then there's Le Trouquet d'Or."

My interest quickened. I sipped my vodka and tonic slowly, trying not to look too concerned.

"What's happening there?"

Nelda flashed me one of her withering looks.

"Don't tell me you haven't heard. Carelessness in the kitchen, negligence in book-keeping, slack management. Poisoned fish was only the latest incident."

"Has any of this appeared in your column?"

"Don't you read it?" Nelda was shocked.

"Ordinarily, I never miss it," I said with pardonable exaggeration. "I've been busy lately and haven't seen many papers."

"I haven't printed any of it yet," Nelda said. "I'm holding out for the bigger story."

"IJ?" I guessed.

She nodded.

"You think it's all connected?" I asked.

"I don't believe in coincidence," Nelda said. "Neither is it coincidence that Miss Best Selling Aldridge has been at Le Trouquet d'Or and that photographer of hers has been seen hanging around too."

"What do you make of that?" I asked.

"You're asking an awful lot of questions," said Nelda, "and not giving me any answers."

"Shows how little I know."

Nelda pursed her lips. "Maybe — but more likely, maybe not. Anyway, if you do learn anything you think I ought to know, give me a call, will you?"

"You promise anonymity?"

Nelda gathered up her purse and leaned forward.

"You know me. Never promise anything — and if I do, you don't have to believe it — unless of course, it's in print."

She stood, all five feet ten or so of her. "Glad we had this chat. Keep in touch."

"I will," I said.

Nelda was already looking around. "Brian — put it on my tab, will you?" She turned to me. "Got to rush, meeting an unimpeachable source."

"Aren't they all," I said to her back as she left.

At home, the first thing I did was phone Winnie at the Yard. As I had expected, she had left but when I identified myself, the Yard operator gave me her home phone number.

"Hello," she answered warmly, "something new?"

"There's a photographer, a freelance, he may know something. IJ used him occasionally and —"

"You mean Alessandro Scarponi?"

"Oh," I said, deflated. "You know about him."

"One of our handwriting experts went through the photographs of the board at NTV and matched up IJ's entries. The computer ran through AS's and picked up Scarponi. Our Squad which handles blackmail talked to him last year concerning some photos he'd taken — they were very incriminating. They couldn't make anything stick but they filed him."

I was disappointed the Yard had beaten me to it but I had demonstrated my co-operation. That couldn't hurt.

"Have you talked to him?" I asked Winnie.

"Not yet. Can't find him. He's an elusive character."

I wondered whether to mention that his name had been linked with Sally Aldridge's. I decided against it.

"Anything else?"

I had held out — but only a little — on Sally. I'd better come clean on one other item if I wanted to stay in the best books of Sergeant Winnie.

"That other entry on the board — VDZH," I said.

"Yes?" she prompted.

"Know what it means?"

"It's a bank."

"Confound it!" I said. "How does Scotland Yard know all these things?"

She giggled and it sounded so delightful that I wished I could have been able to see her doing it.

"We have our ways. That one was easy though. We simply circulated it to all quarters and the Banking Squad came back with the answer immediately."

"Have you talked to them?" I asked.

"Inspector Hemingway went himself. He was almost grumpy when he came back. They wouldn't tell him a thing."

"I wonder why," I said.

"There may not be anything sinister but the inspector has applied for a court order. He can force them to open their files to him if he wishes."

"Any objections if I try?" I held my breath.

"If the inspector couldn't get anywhere —" Winnie began.

"I might try a different approach."

"All right. Why not?"

"I'll tell you what I find out," I promised.

"Your suspect?" Winnie reminded me. "Want to tell me about it?"

"I'm nearly ready."

"I'm here," said Winnie, "whenever."

After I had hung up, I reflected on that. I was sure I was right in my suspicions of Raymond though some of the details might be fuzzy. But it was not the kind of thing to discuss over the phone — and a personal meeting would be so much more pleasurable anyway.

The lunch with Paula and the three vodkas with Nelda had left me with little appetite. I worked on the Man Who Broke the Bank at Monte Carlo query.

Charles Deville Wells parlayed £400 into £40,000 over a period of three days. He put even money bets on red and black but it was the red which won repeatedly until Wells had exceeded the 100,000 franc "bank" limit allocated to each table.

Returning to London, Wells gave a dinner for 36 of his intimate friends at the Savoy Hotel. The press referred to it as "The Red Dinner" for everything was red. The ceiling was painted red and the carpets were red. The waiters wore red costumes even to shirts, ties and gloves. Red flowers were everywhere and the lights were red.

The dinner was served on a huge roulette table and was composed of Prawns, Queues de Langouste, Crème Portugaise, Saumon à la Nantua, Mousse au Jambon, Filet de Boeuf (rare, of course), Tomates Farcies, Choux Rouges braises, Poularde à la Cardinale, Canard Sauvage au Sang, Salade de Betterave and Mousse au Fraises — everything red. It was said that Wells' bank account was a similar colour when the evening had been paid for.

Reading that menu made me hungry when I had thought I wasn't. I raided the larder, found some turkey and some cheese and made a couple of Monte Cristo sandwiches, one of California's great contributions to cuisine. A half bottle of California Chardonnay seemed like an appropriate accompaniment and rounded off the day.

CHAPTER TWENTY-ONE

Fictional detectives have such an easy time. True, they get beaten up, punched in the face, coshed, slugged or half-drowned (with either water or bourbon) now and then but as far as the actual detection goes, coincidence, luck, chance and good fortune are all in their favour.

When our detective finds the first body, there's a chopstick alongside it which is inscribed "The Celestial Palace". While eating the Fried Noodles with Spiced Beef there (detectives are never gourmets), an exotic Chinese waitress tells him that the victim used to come in every day from The Happy Feet Massage Parlour. Prone on a couch in that establishment, our hero is threatened by a 30 stone bruiser who is about to let slip a vital clue when he collapses with a knife in his back.

The knife has a price sticker from Sam's Hardware and there the detective learns from the terrified wife of the proprietor that Max Nicht, the gambling boss at the Spinning Wheel Casino . . . well, that's the way the plot goes. Every place or person leads to the next person or place in a rigged game of Snakes and Ladders.

Would that it were so. All I was able to do was wallow around like a crouton in a thick soup of suspects. There was no continuity — I might as well play eeny-meeny-miny-mo.

I had a little time in the office before going to Sally's book signing so I tackled the post. The first letter caught my attention at once.

"We understand," it read, "that there is a tenth-century Chinese cookbook written by a Madame Wu. Can you suggest where we might be able to obtain a copy?"

That was definitely a question I would have to pass on to Michael. The semi-legendary volume that the correspondent mentioned was very difficult to find in a reliable translation.

The next letter stated:

"We are opening a restaurant to be called The Duck Press. We plan to feature Caneton à la Presse as a special. Where can we obtain a genuine duck press?"

That was an intriguing one. The traditional recipe called for roasting the duckling and sending it directly to the table. There, the legs were removed and discarded and the rest of the bird was carved. The carcass was chopped and put into the duck press with some red wine and a little brandy.

Duck presses must be rare today for they are made of pure silver so as not to affect the taste. A few restaurants by that name might remain — I recalled an outstanding one some years ago in Los Angeles, on the wrong side of the railroad tracks. More work for Michael.

I wrote it all out for Mrs Shearer, dropped the package off with one of her girls and headed for Chelsea.

The bookshop near Sloane Square was packed with more people than you could squeeze into Stamford Bridge football stadium. Sally had certainly had some great publicity but in fairness, her previous books had all been best-sellers so it was not surprising that there was a huge turnout here.

The babble of voices wasn't quite as deafening as the cheer going up at Stamford Bridge when Chelsea scored the winning goal two minutes from time but it was deafening. I fought my way through the doorway where the crowd was already spilling out on to the pavement. Most had glasses in their hands and the others were battling their way inside.

A tray of hors d'oeuvres came sailing through the air held high by a skinny uniformed wrist with no visible means of support. The tray was emptied within seconds and another appeared behind it. The clatter of conversation was pierced by barks of laughter and shrill cries of recognition as old friends, enemies, rivals and competitors greeted each other. An occasional argument erupted and reminiscences filled the air like locusts.

Several faces looked familiar but in the pressure of the noisy crowd, a nod, a wave or a verbal greeting that was swept away into oblivion were all that could be accomplished. I found myself shoulder to shoulder with an attractive woman with orange hair, a very low-cut lacy kind of dress and an uninhibited expression.

"Aren't you with the *Spectator*?" she asked.

"Funny," I said. "I thought you were."

"God, no. I just come to these things for the drinks — and the men," she added with an appraising stare. I could see her mind making ticks in "for" and "against" columns.

"Ever get hold of any?"

"Men?" she asked eagerly.

"No, drinks — ah, there they are, excuse me —" I forced my way through the throng and whisked a glass of sparkling liquid from a passing tray.

"Neatly done," said an elderly man with grizzled grey hair and a weatherbeaten face. "Survival of the fittest here, isn't it?"

"No matter how many waiters they have, seems like you still have to forage for your own."

"I didn't mean that," the man said. "I was referring to your escape from Ursula. You did that very smoothly."

"She a writer?"

"Works in the Hanson empire somewhere."

"Is he in publishing too?"

The man laughed. "Might be. He's in everything else — but then so is Ursula."

I examined the man's face again. "You look familiar," I said. "Excuse my lack of originality. With women, I try to do better than that."

The man looked rueful. "I took off across the South Atlantic in my thirty-footer when I found that too many people were recognising me. Now I may have to go again."

"Not on my account," I grinned. "You're Rollo Sterling, the single-handed yachtsman. I've read a couple of your books. Great stuff — I could feel the spray."

"Thanks. Rather sail than write but unfortunately it's necessary to do one in order to do the other."

"You know Sally?" I asked him.

"Sally?" A surge of the crowd pulled him away but he came back.

"Sally Aldridge — the Queen for the Day."

"Oh, her up there signing? Seems to love it — used to hate it myself. No, I don't know her, we have the same publisher that's all and he twists my arm to show up at these functions."

"Sally does lap it up," I agreed.

"Know her well, do you?"

"Pretty well."

"Well as I know Ursula?"

"How well is that?" I parried.

"Married to her once. In fact, she insists that she should get credit for my first round-the-world voyage. She may be right too. It was about that time I was ready to do anything to get away from her."

A hand pulled at his arm and as he turned, his expression lit up with recognition. He gave me a wave and was gone.

I took another sip. It wasn't bad, not vintage but that could hardly be expected with this many people. Someone jogged my elbow and I spilled the rest.

"Sorry," said a voice. "My fault — let me get you another."

I laughed. "Optimist!" but before I could turn, my benefactor had done exactly that and a full glass was in his hand.

He was balding, heavily-built but active looking.

"You must have pull to do that," I said.

"You're lucky I was around. We're cutting the drinks off in ten minutes. Too many freeloaders coming in."

"When what you want is bookbuyers."

"That's what I want." He stuck out a hand. "Don Stone."

I identified myself. I recognised his name. "Sally's publisher."

"One of the partners, yes." He studied me. "Which are you — a freeloader or a book buyer?"

"Neither. Just an old friend of Sally's."

He nodded.

"You've got a hot property there," I told him.

"Yes, she's one of our best meal tickets."

"Long may she reign."

"It's a precarious business," he said. "You a writer?"

"No, no."

"Publishing?"

"Certainly not. You really know how to hurt a person, don't you?"

He laughed. "Didn't think you could be or I'd know you." He went on in a more serious voice. "Don't mind me. I'm having a suspicious day today."

"Suspicious of what?"

"Everybody. Some outfit's trying to lure Sally away from us. Could be some bastard here — might have been you."

"I can assure you it isn't. But didn't she sign a new contract with you recently?"

"Publishers and their writers are like husbands and wives — they all want somebody else's."

"Interesting," I said. "Because I was talking to a person the other day who suggested the opposite."

"Opposite how?"

"They thought it was you wanting to get rid of Sally."

He said nothing but kept looking at me. I decided to go a step further.

"Restaurants can put that much pressure on, can they?"

He shook his head. "Don't know what you mean." His expression didn't change though. "Enjoyed talking to you." He was still looking at me as he moved away.

I squeezed past a good-looking woman in a sequinned black dress. She was saying, "I didn't really want to come here today but I would have been furious if I hadn't been asked." She turned and smiled as if she would have liked me to squeeze past her again but the human tide had me and I floated by.

Then I saw it — an oasis. I pushed through the gibbering, gesticulating natives and came upon it, a haven of peace and tranquillity.

It was really just a small clearing in that jungle of noise and motion. It consisted of a table piled high with books, all the same one, and a diminutive figure seated, scribbling her name time after time.

I worked my way behind her and said, "Personally, I only read library books. After all, when you've read a book, what can you do with it?"

"You can throw it at somebody," said Sally without moving her head or stopping signing.

"And your aim is good as I recall."

Sally dashed off two more signatures. The line of requestors was temporaily vanquished. She swivelled in her seat to look at me.

"I don't see any scars. I should have used heavier books."

"At least you're writing heavier books. How many pages do you have here? 500?"

"Only 469." Her face crinkled in a welcoming smile. "Nice of you to come. Not your kind of thing, is it?"

I gave her a hug and a kiss on the cheek. "Always support worthy causes."

"Liar. You didn't support me."

"That was because you always made more money than I did. Sally, you look great."

"You're lying again but I like it."

She did look good. Her dark hair had an untamed appearance that was probably the result of hours in the beauty shop. Her small face had an elfin charm, just enough little girl in it to persuade you that she was sweet and innocent. Not at all obvious was the steely resolve to do whatever she set out to do and do it supremely well.

"You seem to have another hit," I said, indicating the stacks of books.

"Coming out in the States next month, simultaneously in hardback and paperback. Should do well there." She examined me more carefully. "What about you? Still gourmet detecting? You look well. Must be taking care of yourself. Under-nourishment is never going to be a problem to you, is it?"

"I'm fine. I seem to be getting enough to eat."

Her expression changed. "I didn't get the chance to talk to you at the Circle of Careme. Wasn't that an awful business?"

"Horrifying. I've never seen a man die once before — let alone twice."

"I wonder what the police have found out." Her eyes searched my face.

"Not too much as far as I know."

"You've talked to them of course."

"They've talked to me might be a better way to put it," I said.

"And they're not making much progress?"

"Last I heard," I said casually, "was that they're looking for some fellow called Alessandro Scarponi."

I didn't need to be Mike Hammer to spot the reaction to that. She gasped, turned pale under her make-up and bit her lip.

"Know him, do you?"

She nodded. "I did. I used him for some photographic work

— he's a freelance and a very good photographer. We became friends — went out together a few times.''

"Seen him lately?"

She shook her head.

"Know where he lives?"

"No. He used to live near King's Cross but I know he moved."

"You know who else he worked for, don't you?" I asked.

"Who?"

"Ivor Jenkinson."

She nodded, regaining her composure quickly.

"Sandro told me. Why are the police looking for him?"

I shrugged. "Just his connection with IJ. They're checking everybody known to have had any contact with him."

"Oh." It seemed to satisfy her.

"What about all these rumours concerning you?"

She was quite her normal self again.

"Which rumours?"

"Changing publishers."

She frowned. "Where did you hear that?"

"A friend in the trade."

Her face darkened. "Must be that nosy bitch Nelda. Is she using the present vindictive tense again?"

"Thought she was a friend of yours," I said mischievously.

"I'm glad she's not. She picks her friends — to pieces."

"Then she wouldn't tell any secrets about you?"

"With Nelda, secrets are always too good to keep."

"So you're not thinking of changing publishers?"

"I keep an open mind about the future."

"Even if it means breaking a contract?"

"They have lawyers to take care of that kind of thing."

"Publishers have lawyers too," I reminded her. "Aren't you afraid you might get dumped?"

Her eyes widened. "Listen," she said and her voice rose, "this book is going to be a best-seller in several continents and twenty countries. Think they're going to dump me? If that's what that boozy, overdressed lesbian is saying about me, just let her put in in her column — I'll sue her so —"

Sally became aware that a small group was gathering around, whether to hear the rest of this fascinating diatribe or wanting to have books signed wasn't clear.

A wispy little man came bustling up and said in a surprisingly deep voice, "If you will all get into line, Miss Aldridge will be delighted to write a personal inscription in each book. Now please, will you —"

"Bye, Sally," I said but she didn't hear me. She was turning on her best beam for her admiring public. I struggled through the mob and went in search of lunch.

CHAPTER TWENTY-TWO

I had received a request a short time ago from a new Mexican restaurant just open in Hampstead. They wanted to know where to get quinoa, the protein-rich seeds of a high-altitude plant native to the Andes but used primarily in Mexican cooking. It resembles couscous but is much more nutty. I had to admit defeat in finding a European source but did manage to put them in touch with an old friend in Chile who could arrange direct shipment.

Ever since that episode, I had wanted to try their food and as I had time before my VDZH appointment — now was the opportunity.

The partners greeted me cordially. One was Mexican and the other his brother-in-law was English. The former was the chef and the Englishman ran the restaurant. It was a delightful place. The dining areas were on three levels and the walls and richly detailed ceilings were painted cream with a blue trim. Strikingly colourful wall hangings of Mexican tapestry decorated the walls and agaves stood in the corners.

I explained that I wanted a meal of several small courses so as to sample as many different dishes as possible.

"We call it Mod-Mex," said Daniel. "Enrique prepares the basic food and I modify it wherever I think it necessary to suit the English palate. Not too much though."

They began with a dark brown mushroom soup. The darker colour than usual was due to the cèpes in it and the taste owed something to the chiles serranos, while the floating croutes were sprinkled with salty anejo cheese.

Next came masa cakes — like tostados and made by frying balls of fresh corn-meal and stuffing them with chorizo sausage and chopped peanuts. The principal course was Lamb Picadillo, chunks of lamb stewed with almonds, currants and red chillies. It was not a true picadillo, more like a spicy lamb hash but still delicious.

Dessert was an empanada — like a flan — filled with blueberries and apple slices. Several French wines were on the list but to stay in the spirit of the place, I had a bottle of a quite passable Mexican table wine, the Santo Tomas.

They apologised for not being able to serve Quinoa as it was still on its long journey from the Andes. I promised to return when it arrived. I walked to Hampstead Station and took the tube to King's Cross where I changed to the Piccadilly line and alighted at Hyde Park Corner.

St Armand Street was in the heart of Belgravia. It was not an obvious address for a financial institution but if the intent was to convey near-unlimited wealth in one of the world's highest rent districts, it succeeded admirably.

I examined the plate outside. It was brass and not gold. I touched the button and a voice answered — not distant and scratchy as with so many such devices but clear, loud and very authoritative.

There was a pause after I gave my name. Then there was a faint click and a tiny buzz. Looking up, I saw a movement of black metal as a video camera scanned me. "Please come in," said the voice and the door opened smoothly when I pushed.

The hall was panelled in a light-grained wood and there were Persian carpets on the wood-tiled floor. What looked like a Klee was on one wall and a Hockney pool on the other. They weren't copies. An exquisite side-table in some rare wood had a silver ash-tray and an elaborate silver lamp. An umbrella stand with a silver base stood alongside it.

Again I heard the soft buzz of a video camera. I couldn't spot it but it presumably liked what it saw for a door opened and in came a pencil-slim girl with varnished blonde hair and a light grey suit which must have been a Valentino exclusive.

She murmured my name and I nodded.

"Follow me," she invited. She led me past an alcove containing an antique bronze head, round a corner past a wall with a Utrillo and knocked gently at a door. A voice from within said something unintelligible.

"Mr Broodman will see you," smiled the girl as if she were

granting me an audience with the Pope.

The office was furnished in the same style as the rest of VDZH, lush, plush, expenditure without crass consideration of money, the ultimate in wealth and power.

Mr Broodman was a big, burly man in his early sixties. He had one of those faces like a hairless bull terrier. His ears were large and protruding and he had short, scrubby grey hair. He didn't greet me, just pointed to a chair.

I sat and pulled it nearer to his large polished desk so that I could place my card on it. He examined it as if it were in Sanskrit. As there was nothing on it to tell him my business, he didn't seem too interested in it. He put it down before it could contaminate him.

"Yes?" he said.

Evidently the treatment of visitors didn't match up to the decor or maybe he was an expert at sizing up people and had ruled me out as a client already. I thought I would shake him up a bit for openers.

"I had expected to talk to Mr Van Der Zwet or Mr Henningsen," I said, pleasant but disappointed.

"You can talk to me."

"They're not available? Oh well, perhaps I should come back . . ." I rose to leave.

"You can't see them. Not ever."

"They're not active in the business?"

"Not active, no. They're dead."

That certainly explained why they weren't active. Broodman's English was flawless and there was only the merest trace of an accent.

"Perhaps I can talk to you then?"

He nodded. His head only moved an inch but it was a nod.

I sat down and studied him doubtfully.

"This is a very confidential matter," I said.

I was beginning to penetrate. There was a noticeable impatience in his voice as he said, "All the matters we deal with here are confidential."

He was probably right there. They might be so confidential that I would get nothing out of him. Still, I was here and it was worth a try.

"You deal in venture capital," I told him. "Mainly in

businesses related to food and drink."

"Only in such businesses," he corrected me stiffly.

"Your clients are major companies and corporations —"

He said nothing.

"— or organisations such as . . . well, such as restaurants, for instance."

He blinked but as far as I could tell he gave no other reaction.

"You say the matters you handle are confidential. Undoubtedly, your clients like to keep it that way."

"Is there some reason for your visit, Mr — er," he looked again at my card. He had forgotten my name already.

"Do you watch television, Mr Broodman?"

This time his head jerked.

"Really! If you are here for some reason, be so good as to tell me what it is."

"If you watch television, Mr Broodman, you will know who Ivor Jenkinson is. You will also know that he died under mysterious circumstances. Now, Mr Broodman, if your clients are so confidential and you treat them as such — why did Ivor Jenkinson plan to use the name of VDZH in a forthcoming television programme?"

It wasn't the blockbuster approach I would have wished but it was the nearest I could get. Perry Mason usually did it with more flair and Horace Rumpole did it with more aplomb but I was quite pleased with my version. It had some effect.

Mr Broodman's Adam's apple moved up and down twice. His eyes moved from my face and back to my card. He was thinking of several responses in turn and discarding them one by one. He wasn't going to give away anything easily though, I was sure of that. He probably faced tougher situations than this every day of the week and with millions involved.

He decided on the hard man approach.

"Scotland Yard have been here already," he said in a brittle voice. "I can call them and say that you are here asking me questions and you have no authority."

I breathed a sigh of relief for having told Winnie.

To Broodman I said: "Call them. Talk to the officer who was here — Inspector Hemingway."

That took him aback. He had thought he could get rid of me

by threatening to call the police. Now he had to find another approach.

"I'm only concerned with the matter which brought Ivor Jenkinson here at 9.30 on the morning of the 12th," I told him, hoping that the detail might be impressive. "I am not concerned with his death and I am not investigating it."

He digested this.

"What business is it of yours?" he asked.

"Perhaps one of the principals in the matter is worried about all this publicity. They might want to pull out. They certainly don't like the prospect of it all appearing in the media."

"That is hardly our fault," Broodman said curtly.

"They do expect confidentiality," I said, rubbing it in.

I felt that the balance had tilted in my favour. He wasn't quite as overbearing now and he was uneasily trying to find out how much I knew. One chilling thought followed though — IJ might have died because of how much he knew. Did I want Broodman and VDZH to think I knew as much as IJ?

Don't be silly, I told myself. Banks don't kill people. Well, all right, maybe in Robert Ludlum they do but not in Belgravia.

Broodman had been watching me as he worked out his next move. When he spoke, there was a disquieting echo of my thoughts:

"And how do you know this?"

"I was with IJ when he died," I said.

He considered that with all its implications and I had tried to manoeuvre my statements so that they bristled with them. I was getting myself in deep, I knew that but I couldn't back out now.

"It is true that publicity could damage the success of this project," he said slowly.

I waited for him to say more but he stopped there. I had fired nearly all of my big guns and I would soon be out of ammunition. I pulled the trigger on what was left.

"Publicity is especially damaging to the restaurant business," I said. "It's very volatile."

He might have nodded or I might have imagined it.

"You were working with Jenkinson?" he asked.

"He had a large and very active network," I said truthfully.

"What will happen now to the information he had gathered?"

"We won't know that for some time."

His gaze moved back to my card on his desk.

"Why does a principal send you?"

"A low profile would seem advisable after an unexplained death, wouldn't you say?"

"Who else knows about this?" His voice seemed to grate but perhaps it was because this was a question I hadn't wanted to hear.

"Ivor Jenkinson was not a man to take others into his confidence — very few," I added quickly. Turnabout was fair play, I thought and I asked him: "Who knows on your side?"

A lifetime of buttoned-lip banking regimentation stood firm and he sidestepped the question.

"I may talk with the principals and see if they wish to consider an alternate strategy."

I clung on desperately. "Why should they? The death of Jenkinson makes no difference to their plans."

He didn't deny or confirm it. He repeated:

"I may talk with them."

I made a last ditch effort.

"Perhaps you should talk to the decision maker, you know . . . maybe it could be kept out of the media. When I report back . . . who will you speak to first?"

It didn't work. He picked up my card.

"Yes," he said. "Maybe it can be kept out of the media. Let us hope so." He gave me a nod of dismissal. "Thank you for your visit."

The glossy blonde appeared in response to some hidden signal and conducted me out.

CHAPTER TWENTY-THREE

There was a message waiting for me when I returned to the office. It was the kind Mrs Shearer liked to bring me in person as it said "Call Scotland Yard". When she handed it to me, she gave me a look which showed she thought they couldn't get along without me.

"I was thinking," said Winnie when I got through to her, "about that suspect of yours . . ."

"Good," I said. "I counted on feminine curiosity."

"You're mistaken," she said crisply. "It's police curiosity."

"Whichever. I still want to tell you about it — and I was at VDZH this afternoon."

"Any luck?" she asked.

"I learned a little."

"Then you did better than the inspector. We'd better talk about it. Look, I can't get away just now and I'm going to be on duty tonight. Can we meet for coffee at about six?"

"You can't get away for longer?" I asked, disappointed.

"Afraid not." She sounded sincere.

"Where do you have in mind?"

She named a coffee shop near Victoria Station and we agreed on six o'clock.

Winnie was not only prompt but she looked adorable in her neat uniform. Her blue eyes shone and a happy smile curved her lips as she sat down. The place wasn't much but it was clean and quiet. I had been early so as to choose a secluded corner but it hadn't been necessary. They were all secluded.

Pleasantries were out of the way quickly — Winnie was obviously anxious to hear of my investigations. First, I told her of my suspicions of Raymond. She listened without interrupting until I had given her the full picture as I had pieced it together walking along the Thames bankside.

When I finished, she drank some coffee and said:

"You think the poison was introduced deliberately? It wasn't an accidental overdose? Why?"

"Too many other items to need explaining. They all point to a wider scenario than just an accident caused by a careless kitchen."

She nodded. "That sounds reasonable. But Raymond —?" she paused.

"I know. He seems unlikely but he isn't innocent simply because he's a well-known restaurateur. What about Count von Bulow, Professor John Webster of Harvard, Thomas Neill Cream, Doctor Crippen, the Earl of —"

Winnie held up a restraining hand. "I concede. Fame isn't proof of innocence."

"There's another aspect to this which you'll find a bit of a paradox."

"Tell me," invited Winnie. "We already have several puzzles. We might as well have a paradox too."

"I talked to Raymond's niece."

Winnie looked interested. "Paula Jardine. What did you make of her?"

"She seems like a very efficient manager."

"Very attractive too," Winnie said. "Didn't you think so?"

"Yes, I suppose she is . . ." I said. "I was thinking only of the investigation when I was talking to her."

"When we have robot police, they will be able to do that," said Winnie. "Until then, humans are human."

There was a twinkle in her eye and I nodded.

"Can't fool you. You're right. She is very attractive."

"So back to the paradox —"

"Well, she was very strong in her defence of Raymond. Very insistent that he couldn't be mixed up in anything underhanded."

"Loyal — to Raymond or the restaurant?"

"Both. Fiercely loyal."

"So where's the paradox?" Winnie wanted to know.

"I'm not sure. Maybe it was just that — like the character in Shakespeare and I can't remember who — she did protest too much."

"Making you think she was shielding him?"

"Something like that."

Amusement showed in her face. "Interrogation isn't that easy, is it?"

"I'm finding that out. You must long for lie-detectors."

"In the meantime, it's just hard work."

"You must have had background checks carried out on both Raymond and François," I said. "Did you find out anything about the feud?"

"The Paris police sent us all they had but there's not a word about the cause of the feud or its nature. Of course, the police had no reason to be suspicious of either of them so we couldn't expect them to have much in their files."

"You don't accept Raymond as a villain though?"

She looked prettily pensive for a moment.

"I don't think he's THE villain," she said finally.

"Inspector Hemingway? What does he think?"

"He hasn't suggested any likely candidates to me."

"Time's running out for him," I reminded her.

"He knows it. He has something up his sleeve but I'm not clear what it is. Should know today or tomorrow." She put her elbows on the table. "Now — tell me about VDZH."

Again she listened attentively, not speaking until I had finished.

"You have a good memory," she commented.

"Archie Goodwin could remember a long interview almost word for word. He never made a mistake and never forgot a thing."

"Archie —? Oh, yes, Nero Wolfe's assistant. I've only read one of the books. So you got the impression from Mr Broodman that VDZH are contemplating furnishing venture capital to a restaurant or restaurants? And Ivor Jenkinson had talked to him because he had some reason to suspect that it was illegal in some way — and was going to expose it on one of his programmes?"

"An admirable summary."

The waitress came by with a pot of coffee and we both had refills.

"So Broodman was left with the impression that you were acting for one of the principals?"

"I said nothing to suggest that — he jumped to that conclusion," I told her quickly.

She smiled. "You're clever at that. NTV probably still think you're from the Yard."

"Honest," I said. "I haven't told —"

"It's all right," Winnie said. "I believe you."

"But on the subject of VDZH —"

"Yes?"

"Well, if there is a vast amount of money involved and if there is some plot afoot —"

"Go on."

I took a deep breath and blurted it out.

"Am I in as much danger as IJ?"

"Are you asking for police protection?"

"Only if you can provide it personally," I told her.

The smile came back. "Then you're not that worried. Good."

"I am serious," I said. "About the personal protection of course . . . but can you see VDZH rubbing anybody out?"

Winnie's smile widened. "Rubbing out! What a lovely euphemism! Has it been used since Edgar Wallace?"

"Seriously —"

"I don't think there's any risk — really." Her eyes searched my face. "I'd tell you if I thought otherwise. I'll mention it to the inspector though and we'll get more run-down on VDZH — we'll see if the Banking Squad have picked up any rumours about them."

"You told me to be careful, remember? Any reason?"

She shook her head. "No. Just in general."

"Thanks," I said. "I'm relieved. Now how about Scarponi? Found him yet?"

"Not yet but we're close."

"The sinister Dr F?"

Winnie shook her head. "We're further behind there. Don't have any ideas about him at all. You?"

"Nothing. I have another question though."

"Go on," she said.

"If it was deliberate poisoning, how was it done?"

Winnie nodded, pleased to be able to report some progress.

"We've been working on that. The poison in the lamprey is

in glands in its mouth. This breaks down the muscle tissue of the fish it eats — and that includes shark. It's possible to culture the poison quite easily —"

"Easily?" I asked in alarm.

"We're keeping that information from the media and want to continue to do so. We don't want any copycat crimes — but yes, it's very easy."

"But wouldn't someone need lots of lamprey to provide that much of the botulin?"

"We've been working on that too. We've checked every fishmonger in Greater London. A sale was made of 50 lbs of lamprey a week before the Circle dinner. That's enough to provide poison to kill several people."

"How long does it take to culture it?"

"A few days."

"You investigated the sale naturally?"

"Yes," Winnie said. "Cash. No record."

"You've also checked, I'm sure, on the lamprey that was bought for the dinner. Could the botulin have developed through careless handling? Keeping it too warm . . . in unhygienic conditions . . .?"

"Yes. It was ordered 48 hours in advance as the preparation is quite lengthy."

"So it is possible that it was just carelessness? And the other sale of lamprey was unconnected?"

Winnie shrugged. "About one chance in a thousand, the experts say. And Inspector Hemingway doesn't believe in those odds any more than he does in coincidence."

"So where do you stand now?" I asked.

"We're making a detailed study of every person connected with both Raymond's and François' restaurants and everyone who's worked there in the past five years. We're making a similar study of every member of the Circle of Careme." She made a wry face. "That's why I have to work tonight."

"In that case," I said, "my invitation to dinner is extended to tomorrow night."

"M'm," she murmured, considering. "I'll accept — but you'll have to understand that there may be a break in the case between now and then and I won't be able to get away."

I nodded. "Otherwise — it's on?"

"Yes. Where?"

"I, er — have a modest reputation as a cook. I'd like to prepare a meal for you."

Her eyebrows rose a fraction. She considered again.

She smiled. "All right. We'll view this discussion as strategic. Tomorrow, we can discuss tactics."

"Any food dislikes? I gathered from our meal at La Bordighera that you like almost everything."

"Anything," she assured me. "There's one other question I must ask though — where are your investigations taking you next?"

"Oh, I'm not forgetting my duty to my client," I said virtuously. "I'm going to stop by Le Trouquet d'Or tonight."

"Just routine?"

"Yes. I may spend a half hour at Raymond's too. Nothing in particular."

"You're not giving up on your suspicion of Raymond, are you?"

"Not yet," I said.

"Well, good luck. I must get back. What time tomorrow?"

"About eight?"

She flashed a smile. "Fine. See you then."

During the tube ride back to Hammersmith, I made a list of the items I wanted for tomorrow night. I knew the markets which would still be open at this time although it meant several scattered visits.

I put some of the symphonic tone poems of Villa-Lobos on the CD as appropriate music to cook by. Originality was the quality of primary importance to Villa-Lobos when he wrote these and this makes them a good combination of music to listen to and music to hear — two different things.

At a suitable break-point, I drank a kir while stir-frying the scallops I had bought with some garlic and ginger. I ate these with some rice. Then I went back to preparation for tomorrow.

I had checked on the times for last orders at the places I was going to — 11.30 at Raymond's and 12.00 at Le Trouquet d'Or. I wanted to arrive just after these had been taken, reasoning that anyone I talked to would be relaxed because the working day was almost over but also tired from a long day. In other words — vulnerable to questions.

So much for theory. Travis McGee never bothered with such niceties — he just went. But then he didn't take tube trains. At almost twelve o'clock, I was still sitting in the Gloucester Road station. The station announcer had said that there was an electrical fault on the line and it would be repaired in a short time. After fifteen minutes had dragged by, I left the train and found an official who knew nothing. I went out and took a taxi.

It was almost a quarter to one when we stopped at the corner by Raymond's restaurant. Two taxis were loading in front and my driver could get no nearer. From the corner, I could look down at the back door of the restaurant. In the narrow alley, a bulky figure was shuffling towards a waiting cab. The figure was so bulky that I couldn't be mistaken. It was Raymond. Something about his furtive manner and the back door exit seized my curiosity.

There cannot exist a single reader of fiction who has not wished that he could, just once, shout to a taxi driver "Follow that cab!" Readers of detective stories drool over the possibility, guzzlers of mystery fiction would forego the next six issues of the Sudden Death of the Month Club for the chance and all other readers from Barbara Cartland to Anthony Trollope and Armistead Maupin to Thomas Hardy must secretly wish it could happen to them.

Here was my opportunity. In fiction, they never had it so good as me. They had to look around frantically for a cab to appear as if by magic — I was already in one. I watched Raymond's cab pull away. My driver turned to see why I wasn't getting out. I pointed, took a deep breath and said it.

"Follow that cab."

"Right, sir," said the cabbie as if it happened to him several times a day. He reversed and turned down the alley, ruining the whole effect. I thought of asking him if he didn't find the request at least a little unusual but instead I just sat back, disappointed.

It was a short ride. Barely five minutes later, the lights of the cab ahead glowed.

"He's stopping, chief," said my cabbie matter-of-factly.

"Stop here," I told him.

Raymond climbed out of the cab. With his size, it was an effort. He handed the driver money then turned and went down the alley off James Street. I knew he wouldn't walk far but then I also knew where he must be going. I paid my cabbie and gave him an extra three pounds. He took it as if it were routine.

I watched Raymond as he stopped before a door. It was too dark to see any detail but it opened and he disappeared into Le Trouquet d'Or.

CHAPTER TWENTY-FOUR

I pondered this strange development. It didn't help and I was trying to decide if I should make a decision when I remembered that the key François had given me was still in my pocket.

A light drizzle had started and the alley was quiet. I took out the key and turned it in the lock. Inside, all was quiet. I went first to the restaurant areas. They were dark. A small night light enabled me to find my way to the kitchens.

They were dark too except for a yellowish light which filtered in through an alley window. It reflected off some highly polished stainless steel pans creating hulking shadows and bottomless pools of darkness. I edged my way slowly so as to make no noise. It's easy to make noise in a kitchen — everything clinks or clanks, tinkles or rattles, everything is metal or pot or glass.

I found my way over to the side of the big kitchen where the ovens were located. I thought there was a light switch there. I had an almost uncontrollable urge to turn it on and make sure that the shadows didn't contain other, more dangerous shadows which could — I was getting edgy. I forced myself to calm down then my fingers found the switch.

The kitchen sprang into normality. It looked just as it should. The shadows fled and I breathed normally again. There was no one here and nothing out of the ordinary — except. . .

I was standing before a large rack of knives. The bright light glistened on their shiny blades. What was strange about that? I wondered. "Nothing" seemed to be the answer and I was about to turn out the light when it struck me. I looked once more.

The last knife was missing. Judging from the others, it had a ten inch blade and my breath caught in my throat. Two deadly rivals, one prowling in the other's restaurant after hours — and one missing knife. I looked around more carefully and a lot more nervously. Still there was nothing. With an effort of will, I snapped off the switch. Only the offices were left and I made for François'.

The heavy door didn't permit any eavesdropping. I pressed my ear tightly against it but I wasn't sure if what I could hear was the murmur of voices or the blood pounding in my head. I didn't know what to do next. A knife missing — which of them had it? I examined the door — could I kick it down? No, the whole Liverpool football team couldn't do that if they kicked all day.

I was still pondering my next move when the door swung silently open.

It swung wide and gave me a view of Raymond, sprawled comfortably on one of the large couches and managing to occupy most of it. The table was spread with trays of food. An opened bottle of champagne stood there with two part-filled flute glasses. Raymond was regarding me but there was no surprise on his face.

François stepped into view from behind the door. He smiled gently, his battered boxer's features creased into good-humoured contours as he said:

"Come in, my dear fellow. Come in and join us in a glass of champagne."

There was no ten inch knife in his hand or anywhere else that I could see. What was I to do? I went in.

The door closed behind me with a double click. I looked over my shoulder in time to see François turn the key in the lock and drop the key into his pocket. He went over to the wall where a red lamp glowed. He snapped a switch and it went out.

"There's a beam outside," he explained. He motioned to one of the couches around the table.

"Sit down, sit down," he invited. He went to the cabinet and took out another fluted glass which he brought to the table. I sat on the couch facing Raymond. François took the one between us and filled my glass from the champagne bottle. It was Louis Roederer Cristal, Cuvée de Prestige.

Raymond picked up his glass.

"Your very good health," he toasted.

François did likewise.

"Long may it continue," he murmured.

It was all very civilised — but macabre.

Even under those circumstances, I couldn't pass up the chance to drink one of the great champagnes though.

"Try one of these," said François, pushing one of the trays towards me. It was piled with small delicate sandwiches of thin brown bread, slices of smoked salmon and heaped with caviare. I took one. It was delicious. The room was silent.

"You two seem to be getting along well," I said as breezily as I was able. There was another silence then Raymond said:

"You probably think we've misled you — François and I."

"Oh, not much," I said, being as sarcastic as I could. "You're obviously two deadly rivals." I waved a hand to the champagne, the trays of food and the mellow ambiance of the room.

François reached for another tray containing tiny open tarts of what looked like avacado and bacon. He took one, bit into it daintily and nudged the tray in my direction.

"Please," he said. "Help yourself. These are very good."

He settled back in the couch, wriggled to get comfortable and started to talk.

"Raymond and I worked together as apprentices in Paris. We were friends — not close — but we went out in the same groups and got to know each other. When the time came for us to get jobs, our apprenticeship over, I heard about one in a good Paris restaurant. I confided to Raymond that I was going to apply for it the next day. When I arrived, Raymond was already there in line ahead of me."

Raymond did not look in the least perturbed. He sighed heavily and changed his position a little. He poured more champagne for all of us.

"I heard about the job from someone else after François had told me he was going for it," Raymond said. "There was no reason why I should not apply too. There was only one vacancy in any case. The restaurant would hire who they wanted."

"That's not so," said François hotly. "You broke my confidence after I had told you about the job."

"Nonsense," scoffed Raymond. "Jean-Claude told me about the job so I would have applied anyway."

They glared at each other and the expression "daggers drawn" came into my mind. I looked around again but couldn't see the knife. Then Raymond chuckled and François joined in.

"Besides," Raymond continued, "what about Le Calvet?"

"That was different," François countered immediately. He glanced at me. "All right, here's what happened. Neither of us got the job we were talking about. We went our separate ways then — some, oh, two years later, I was working as sous-chef at Le Calvet on the Boulevard Saint Germain. I had developed a special dish that was very popular — Filets of Sole with Coquilles, Ginger and Garlic. It's very tricky for the garlic and ginger can overwhelm.

"One day, I heard that Chez Gramond, not far away in the sixth arrondisement, was serving the identical dish. I hurried over there and found Raymond. He was claiming credit for it! Can you believe that?"

"And why not?" asked Raymond, waving his hands energetically. "No dish is completely original. I took the basic ingredients of your dish — ordinary as it was — and made a culinary success out of it."

"You stole it!" shouted François.

"I made of it a real dish — not an everyday fish fry!"

"You did not — you —"

Once again they glowered at each other and I was glad there was no knife in sight, ten inch or any other size.

Then they burst out laughing simultaneously.

"This happened several times after that," Raymond said. "He took my finest creations and tried to copy them."

"Me!" snorted François. "You — you stole from me!"

"I never stole," said Raymond. "The most I ever did was simplify. Your extravagant dishes always needed simplification so customers could enjoy them."

François shook his head firmly. "It was your peasant tastes that always cried out for a more imaginative touch."

They both chuckled. François went to the cabinet and came back with another bottle of champagne. While he was opening it, Raymond pointed to the other tray. I took one of the tempting nibbles on it — chicken liver pâté with paper-thin slices of pepperoni sausage.

François poured. "When we were both full chefs," he went on, "we continued our rivalry. When I came to London, Raymond followed me."

"Nothing of the kind. I had contracted to come here before you even thought about it. I had to work out my contract. At least, I chose to — you would probably have just broken yours."

François kept talking. "As chefs working in competitive restaurants, we kept up our rivalry. We criticised each other whenever an opportunity occurred and when a journalist came looking for a good story, I blew it up bigger than a balloon."

"That appeared in a major magazine and was re-printed in others," said Raymond. "Just after that, I was on television and added more fuel. The media were full of stories about these two combatants in cookery, bitter enemies since some mysterious incident in the past."

"It was great for business," said François. "Customers wanted to know what was our latest dish as if it were some new weapon in a tournament."

Raymond's massive frame quivered and his usually doleful features eased into a smile.

I drank some more champagne.

"And Oiseau Royal was part of the duel," I said, musing.

François looked startled.

"Oiseau Royal? What about it?"

I looked invitingly at Raymond. He was avoiding my eye by reaching for another slice of smoked salmon and caviare. He ate it and then reached for his champagne glass. I suddenly realised that François didn't know that his famous recipe could be duplicated — and by Raymond. I had put my foot in the ragout.

François was eyeing Raymond suspiciously.

"What about Oiseau Royal?" he demanded.

Raymond put down his glass with a slow studied movement. He gave me a steely glance which meant "Keep your mouth shut".

"I told our Gourmet Detective friend here that I could cook Oiseau Royal," he said. "If I wished," he added carelessly.

"Ha!" barked François. "You couldn't even come close!"

"If I wanted," said Raymond, "I could cook it better than you."

François was sitting bolt upright.

"Tell me," he challenged.

"Well," said Raymond thoughtfully, "I'd use ortolans and I'd . . ." He was clever. He was a brilliant chef and as he talked, I could see his mind picking out the important parts of the preparation and the cooking. At the same time, he was skilfully discarding the items that he couldn't possibly have learned without my information, items like the honey from Crete and the rocambole from Valencia.

While Raymond expounded, François gradually relaxed, happy in the knowledge that his secret was secure. Some aspects of the cooking could be guessed by a good chef, he was thinking, but not even Raymond could reproduce authentic Oiseau Royal.

When Raymond had finished, François shrugged.

"I wouldn't order a dish like that myself," he said. "It would be terrible."

"Don't worry," said Raymond. "I would never cook it for you."

Their stares clashed like rapiers. Then they began to laugh.

François reached to refill the three glasses. We watched the foam effervesce to the tops and subside.

"Tell me about IJ," I said brutally.

François drank then took another of the tiny tarts.

"It was one of the worst days of my life," he said. He ate the tart, flicking away some crumbs. "The next worst was when I realised I was going to go out of business. There will be one more," he added sadly. "That will be when I have to walk away from here."

"That's not what I meant," I said. I would start to feel sorry for him if I let him get away with this. "IJ's dead — probably murdered. What's the connection between his death and you losing your restaurant?"

"Murdered!" said François in a low voice.

"You're surprised?" I asked.

"It couldn't have been the lamprey. We were careful — we're always careful," François said, half to himself.

"If it wasn't an accident or carelessness then it had to be murder," I insisted. I looked from one to the other. "Who and why?"

François shook his head, said nothing.

I turned to Raymond.

"Then you must know about it."

Raymond looked more melancholy than ever.

"Me?" he said, puzzled. "I know nothing. I have problems in my restaurant too." He sighed and drank more champagne.

"A fine pair, you two," I said, my voice rising. "You're both being put out of business — you say. A man's murdered by poisoned fish and you too are guzzling champagne and eating caviare. What are you celebrating?"

"We do this once a month," François said.

"François told me when he hired you," said Raymond. "I admit I was surprised —" He gave me a warning look. I didn't doubt he was surprised — he probably thought as I did at the time, that François had found out about my investigation into the preparation of Oiseau Royal.

Raymond was continuing "— but then when similar incidents started occurring in my restaurant, well, that's when I asked you to look into the matter for me."

"Raymond told you that?" I asked François quickly.

François nodded. "Oh, yes, he told me."

It was further confirmation that the two of them really were on good terms but did I need any more confirmation after the food, the champagne and the laughter?

They didn't tell each other everything though — François didn't know that Raymond had secured his secret recipe.

"What progress have you made?" Raymond asked me.

I could hardly tell him that I had cleverly figured out that he was the number one suspect.

"I expect it all to be cleared up in the next few days," I said, trying to sound confident.

François' head jerked in my direction. Raymond didn't move a muscle.

"Really?" said François. "I hadn't expected to hear that."

Raymond murmured something in agreement then leaned forward to ask me:

"Is there any information you can give us now?"

"No," I said firmly. "In fact, I must be going, I've got to get on with the investigation. . ."

"At this time of night?" said François.

"Crime never sleeps." Dashiell Hammett had said that once.

"Where are you going now?" Raymond asked curiously.

"We'll all know everything very soon," I said evasively.

I rose. François and Raymond remained seated. I walked to the locked door.

"By the way," I said, being as off-hand as I could. "There's a knife missing from the rack in the kitchen."

There was silence.

"A knife?" François sounded perplexed.

"Yes."

"Oh." François' brow cleared. "Yes, it was broken yesterday."

Raymond didn't look interested.

I stood there. François got up, came and unlocked the door.

"I can find my own way out," I said, anxious to do so. "Thanks for the hospitality."

CHAPTER TWENTY-FIVE

In the peace and quiet of the office next morning, I started to list all the reasons why Raymond was still suspect no. 1. There weren't enough to even convince me. I tried François on the same basis. I had to acquit him too.

They couldn't be sabotaging each other's restaurants in a continuing feud because the feud didn't exist. Could each be sabotaging his own restaurant? I was getting so far out in my theorising, I considered even that but it was too absurd.

And if Raymond and François were not sabotaging each other's restaurant then there appeared to be no connection with IJ that could have led to murder.

I needed a new suspect.

Roger St Leger moved to the head of the list.

He had a clear motive. He wanted IJ's programme and if the current rumours were correct, he was about to get it. Could he have poisoned the lamprey? He had visited the restaurant. True, he looked clean-cut and innocent but I was disregarding that.

The only other clues I had were the furtive way he handed that envelope to IJ at the Circle dinner and his denial of any knowledge as to what the envelope contained. I had also found him dead drunk and thought he was dead but I couldn't really hold that against him.

A fresh viewpoint was what I wanted. I read the post, tossed it all in the waste basket and went to Bookery Cooks.

An enticing smell of baking was in the air.

"Coffee cake with chopped apricots," Molly said, greeting me. "Beats anything from Vienna. I'll bring you a slice with your coffee."

Michael was on his knees. He had cleared a whole shelf corner and was re-stocking it.

"Throwing out all the diet books?" I asked.

"Good Lor' no — they sell too well. No, we're starting a new section of food for pets."

"Putting them on the bottom shelf where the pets can see them?"

"Lots of new books coming out on feeding pets. They need vitamins and minerals the same as we do but sometimes they're different ones."

He was placing books in alphabetical order on the shelves. He handed one to me. It was *The K-9 Cook Book*. It was full of good advice and I wondered if animals could become gourmets too.

In Michael's office, he listened attentively while I brought him up to date on Paula, Sally, Nelda, St Leger, Scarponi and finally last night's encounter with Raymond and François.

"What an exciting life you're leading!" he said admiringly. "Better than tracking down a new source for Birds' Nest Soup!"

I pointed to the cork board over his desk. On it, on three separate sheets, were the three inscriptions I had found on the board at NTV studios. Red lines ran through two of them. The inscription remaining read: "Dr F B4 CC".

"Any luck?" I asked Michael.

He shook his head. "No — although just a minute ago, something struck a chord . . . it was just as you came in." He paused in thought. "Just a minute." He hurried out of the office.

He came back in with *The K-9 Cook Book*.

"What about it?" I asked.

"I don't know. Something . . . ah, yes — K-9 and B4. Do they seem to have anything in common?"

"Identification numbers?"

"Not only that. Both are abbreviations. K-9 means 'canine' so could B4 mean 'before'?"

"I suppose but —"

Michael was excited now. "What could CC mean that is relevant? What else but Circle of Careme!"

"It's possible. And Dr F? He doesn't seem to fit. We can't find any trace of any Dr F."

"Because he doesn't exist? Maybe there is no Dr F — maybe it means something completely different."

I was getting into the codebreaking spirit now. "You mean Dr might not mean Doctor?"

"Exactly! So what else could it mean?"

"Well, if the two don't go together — what about 'F'? That could stand for François —"

"And Dr in that case . . . — something François before the Circle of Careme."

Michael snapped his fingers. "Drinks? 'Drinks with François before the Circle of Careme'?"

"Makes more sense than whatever else we've got." I looked at the wall clock. It was 11.30. Molly came in with a slice of an airy looking cake still steaming slightly and with a cup of coffee. I tasted the cake. "Fantastic." I reached for the phone and called François.

"Before the Circle of Careme dinner . . ."

"Yes?"

"Where were you?"

"Where was I?" François sounded incredulous. "In the kitchen, of course, where else?"

"You went to your office?"

"No, I told you. The kitchen."

"The whole time?"

"Certainly. An occasion like that! I had to be in the kitchen all day."

"Did you entertain anyone there?"

"Of course not. I was much too busy."

"Did you entertain anyone in the dining room before the dinner?"

François was getting exasperated. "Entertain! One of the most important dinners I have ever put on — how would I be entertaining?"

"Thanks." I hung up.

"Perhaps we're on the wrong track," I said to Michael.

"M'm," he said. "Or François is not telling the truth."

I enjoyed the cake and the coffee, declined seconds on both. We discussed the case further but nothing useful emerged. Michael kept coming back to last night, unwilling to accept that the famous feud didn't exist.

"Maybe your suspicion was right — but you had the wrong

man. Maybe you should be suspecting François and not Raymond."

"You mean François hired me to find out who was sabotaging his restaurant when he was doing it himself?"

Michael grinned. "Didn't they often do that in your private eye stories?"

"I believed it then. I don't now."

"Fact is stranger than fiction."

"If it's maxim time, I'm going."

I did. I went back to the office and spent most of the afternoon in non-productive speculation. I went home early to make preparations for receiving Winnie.

One of the most important things was to avoid clichés. No peanuts, no crisps, no pâté, no bits of quiche or pizza and no pretzels. Other no-no's were champagne, kir and sherry. All of these have their place and time but not here or now.

On the CD, I discarded Claire de Lune, Scheherazade and Richard Clayderman. I chose Le Coq d'Or to start. It's romantically Oriental but not cloying. Rimsky-Korsakov used the lyrics as a criticism of petty bureaucracy but that doesn't show in the music.

When Winnie arrived, she was avoiding clichés too. She wore a simple but stunning black two-piece suit with a thin gold necklace.

I brought her a glass of Lillet, the wine-based aperitif from Bordeaux. It is light and dry and its herb content perks up the appetite like few other drinks.

"Business first," I said after we had toasted and sipped.

Her blue eyes sparkled. "More progress?"

"You may not think so after I've told you." I related last night's excitement and when I had finished, she put down her glass.

"Scary at the time," she admitted. "You don't carry a gun, I suppose?"

"Certainly not!" I said indignantly. "Like I keep saying, I'm not really a —"

She laughed and waved a hand. "I know you insist you're

not a real private eye. But go on."

"That's all there is. François let me out — and it was a relief to get out of there, I can tell you."

"So what does that do to your theory about Raymond?"

"It would seem to blow it out of the window. I thought about François as a replacement but I don't see how he could be guilty either. By the way," I added, "what did your experts make of the inscription on the board at NTV — 'Dr F B4 CC'?"

"Nothing so far."

I told her of Michael's construction without mentioning him.

She thought for a moment. "Plausible. But you say François denied it?"

"Yes."

She nodded. "At least that fits in with what he told us. He said he was in the kitchen the whole day before the Circle dinner."

"Speaking of dinner," I said. "I must check."

I did so quickly. One of the tricky things about entertaining a charming lady is that you want to spend the minimum time in the kitchen. On the other hand, you want the meal to be memorable. Pre-preparation is vital but it can't be allowed to affect the quality of the meal.

"I have some news too," said Winnie. "We've found Scarponi."

"That's great! What did you get out of him?"

"He wasn't really hiding out, he says. He was doing a photographic assignment at the docks at Ipswich. I think he saw the news about IJ and took the first opportunity to duck so that he wouldn't be mixed up in it."

"Does he have anything to hide?"

Winnie sipped the Lillet. "This is delicious. Less lethal than a Martini, more original than gin and tonic. . . Scarponi admitted he worked occasionally for IJ. Says he was hired to take pictures of staff going in and out of Le Trouquet d'Or."

That surprised me. "Staff? Going in and out?"

"That's all he'll admit to."

"Sounds as if IJ had some strong suspicion of someone there."

Winnie nodded and her blonde curls danced gently.

"We're interrogating him again. We'll try for more this time."

"Thumb-screws and the rack?"

She smiled. "You know better than that. The inspector'll get something, don't worry."

I refilled her glass.

"Did you find anything in IJ's possessions that might correspond to any photos Scarponi could have taken?"

"No," Winnie said. "But I want to ask you a question. What did you think was in IJ's pocket when he was supposed to be dead?"

I drank some Lillet to cover my confusion. She was watching me carefully and laughed gently.

"The inspector knows too, of course. He never misses a thing like that. You couldn't have known there was nothing in IJ's pocket except by feeling in it — and you were the only person near him when he came back to life."

I explained what I had seen earlier. "It was the satisfied look on IJ's face that convinced me it was something important. Until then, he hadn't shown much emotion."

"St Leger denies knowing what it was too," said Winnie. "Says he merely handed it over. The interesting point is that Scarponi was the man who handed the envelope to St Leger."

"Then Scarponi knows what was in it!"

"He says it was photos of the staff of Le Trouquet d'Or."

"All of them?" I was astonished.

"So he says. But he must be lying if it was important enough for someone to beat you to it and take it out of IJ's pocket."

"I learned a lesson," I told Winnie. "Never try to hide anything from the police."

She pouted prettily. "Very wise," she said and smiled.

The CD player moved on to Saint-Saëns' Sonatas for Cello and Piano and the two instruments blended beautifully. I had taken the centre section out of the table to make it a suitable size for two. I lit the candles but left the lights on — still avoiding clichés. Continuing in the same vein, I pulled the cork on a bottle of Sancerre, the Millet Frères, a complex blending of tastes both dry and rich but still crisp.

With Winnie seated at the table, I brought out a bubbling sizzling tray of oysters. Her eyes widened.

"Are those Oysters Rockefeller?"

"They certainly are."

Her face glowed with anticipation. "Wonderful! Tell me, is it true about the original recipe being such a closely guarded secret?"

As we ate, I told her that the dish had originated at Antoine's in New Orleans. It had been made with snails then but as Antoine Alciatore, the owner, became aware of the fine Gulf oysters available locally, he began to use them instead. It was said there were 18 ingredients in the sauce.

"And it must have been John D. Rockefeller's favourite dish."

"Actually, no. John D. Rockefeller was at that time the richest man in the U.S.A. and the dish was named in his honour because it was so rich."

"Pity," said Winnie in between oysters. "He couldn't have done other than find it wonderful if it was anything like this. It must be a lot of work."

"A few of the ingredients are hard to find and I had to substitute," I told her. "Herbsaint — a cordial containing anise — is difficult to get, for instance."

"Presumably they used absinthe back in Alciatore's day."

"Right."

I poured more of the Sancerre which was perhaps a touch fruitier than I would have preferred. Maybe a dry Chilean Riesling would have been better . . .

As we sat savouring the wine — which maybe was a good choice after all, being formidable enough not to be over-whelmed by the chervil, Tabasco and shallots in the oyster sauce — Winnie said:

"I forgot. There is one more question. You must answer it as you were there. How long elapsed between eating the fish and IJ's collapse?"

I thought. Finally I said: "Fifteen to twenty minutes."

"H'm." Winnie looked pensive.

"Why? Has something come up?"

"Well," said Winnie, "the inspector has spent more time with the poisons experts in Forensic. The quantity of the botulin that IJ received has now been estimated to take at least an hour to cause death.''

"That doesn't make sense. Do the experts have a margin for error?"

"Yes, it's a considered opinion, no more. The files are not that full of lamprey poisoning cases.''

She smiled. "Anyway, back to eating. Enough of poisons!''

I rose and took the oyster trays.

"Next course coming right away.''

I had bought boned squabs from the butcher and had him halve them. I had cooked some bacon in butter and then put in the squabs, browned and removed them. I cooked onions, shallots and carrots and removed them too. I sprinkled in some flour, added white wine and boiled till thick. Then I added chicken stock, Madeira, fennel, thyme, basil, oregano and marjoram. I simmered this, added the squabs and the vegetables and cooked till it thickened.

I had boiled olives and sautéed some mushrooms in butter. I had removed the squabs, strained the sauce and added the mushroom liquid.

Tonight, all I had to do was heat the sauce, add the squabs, the bacon, the olives and the mushroom liquid. It was slightly thick so I added some more Madeira. I served it with lemon slices and a couple of tiny potato pancakes.

It was a huge success. With it, we had a bottle of Pomerol.

"Not a very common wine,'' commented Winnie.

"It's still a subject of debate. It's the best of the Bordeaux reds but does that have anything to do with the fact that Pomerol is the smallest district in Bordeaux? Disagreement continues.''

"But not about the wine itself. It's marvellous.''

The CD player moved on to Scarlatti. Played on ancient instruments, his music is tender and affectionate. The strawberries with kirsch went well with it. I did the flambé work in the kitchen — still avoiding clichés. Michael refers to all flambéed dishes as "food you can read by".

I sat beside Winnie on the couch as we drank coffee. The food and wine had brought the faintest of flushes to her cheeks and her eyes were merry. I put down my coffee cup. Our hands touched.

The phone rang.

"I should have pulled the plug," I said.

It continued to ring.

"Maybe they'll go away," said Winnie.

It rang and rang.

Winnie sighed. "They can sound so insistent, can't they?"

I picked it up.

I couldn't understand a word at first. The voice was husky and rasping. I could hear breathing.

"Who is this?" I asked impatiently.

"This is Larry Leopold."

I wouldn't have recognised his voice at all.

"Are you all right? You sound strange," I said. "This is a dreadful line."

"Listen carefully. I don't have much time." It wasn't the line, it was him. He sounded terrible.

"I couldn't go on any longer. Those were awful things I did. It all went wrong — I didn't mean for IJ to die but he — anyway I've ended it all now."

"What do you mean, you've ended it?"

I caught the look of alarm on Winnie's face as she heard my words.

"I've killed myself. It was the only thing to do."

There was a throaty noise and a click as the connection was severed.

CHAPTER TWENTY-SIX

W innie had her hand on the phone before I had finished telling her of the conversation. While she was being put through to Inspector Hemingway, I was looking through the phone book for Larry Leopold's address. It was a mews house behind the Victoria and Albert Museum. Winnie relayed it to the inspector.

"He'll meet us there," she said. "I came here by taxi. Can we —"

"I'll call Gupta," I said and did so. "He runs a 24 hour service," I explained to Winnie. "Often does emergency runs for me. He'll have a car downstairs by the time we get there."

The driver was one of Gupta's best. He dodged around the late night traffic at Hammersmith Broadway and raced through Brook Green. He slipped over to Cromwell Road and we shuddered to a stop at the entrance to Brompton Mews.

A constable was standing in front of a mews house down the narrow cobbled thoroughfare.

"The inspector had the nearest man on the beat come over here," said Winnie and even as she spoke, an unmarked car pulled up behind us and Inspector Hemingway jumped out.

The constable was a fresh-faced young man with a West Country accent. He saluted Hemingway smartly.

"Arrived here four minutes after your call, sir," he reported. "Door was unlocked. I went in. Body of a man. Dead, sir. Constable MacAvoy arrived five minutes later. He's been covering the back door and I've remained here ever since."

"Right, constable." Hemingway was crisp and efficient — though I'd not seen him any other way. "Stay here. We're going inside."

The inside of the mews house was a surprise after the old, cobbled road outside. Deep brown leather couches flanked an enormous glass coffee table with mechanisms of ancient clocks embedded in the thick glass. The hard-wood floor was waxed to a mellow sheen and a large fireplace was set in a stone wall, between deep bookcases.

A heavy table of hewn wood had been converted from one-time kitchen duty to serve as a desk and had a typewriter and papers and books strewn over it. Close by were two deep armchairs in the same deep brown leather as the couches. Larry Leopold sat in one of them.

His face was chalky-white but otherwise he looked the same in death as in life. His reddish beard stuck out at a jaunty angle and I stayed out of range of his hands. I hadn't forgotten my terror when Ivor Jenkinson had reached out from beyond death and grabbed my wrist.

Inspector Hemingway was checking Leopold cautiously too but his caution was professional. Winnie, meanwhile, was prowling around the room, looking at everything but touching nothing.

"Is he really dead?" I asked. I was a little hoarse.

"You haven't forgotten IJ, have you?" Hemingway said. "Well, we'll have a more extensive examination very soon but as far as I can tell — yes, he's dead."

"So was IJ," I said, not taking my eyes off Leopold.

Hemingway straightened up and his glance swept across the room.

"Anything, sergeant?" he asked Winnie.

"There's a message in the typewriter," she said.

The inspector and I read it.

> I can't go on. I must end it. I didn't plan it this way. It started with a dream and it would have worked — it would have been the most powerful organisation on the British food scene.
>
> I had promises of financing but I needed seed capital. François had said that he would give me first option on buying Le Trouquet d'Or but he loved the business too much to give it up.
>
> I did all those things to get him discredited so that he would sell out to me. Then Jenkinson started probing the food business and caught on to me.

I cultured the botulin. I decided that making guests ill at the Circle dinner would be the last straw. IJ came early, told me what he had planned for his programme.

I panicked, put the extra botulin in his drink.

Now I've put it in mine.

We read it again. Near the typewriter was a glass, empty but used. The inspector sniffed it cautiously and looked inquiringly at Winnie. She nodded.

"The botulin has little odour but I think it was in there with the Scotch."

The two of them continued to prowl through the room. I tried to do the same thing but I didn't know what I was looking for.

There was a knock at the door and the young constable admitted two men in plain-clothes who were evidently known to Inspector Hemingway. While they were talking, there was another knock and a few minutes later another.

I tried to count but they were all moving round too much. I did establish that there were three ambulance attendants, two technicians from the Mobile Crime Squad, a woman from the Photo Unit, a man and a woman from Forensic, a poisons specialist, an officer from the Metropolitan Police, one from the Records Department and two more constables. The dazzle of electronic flashes, the interchanges of unintelligibly technical conversation and the scurrying to and fro were making me dizzy.

I sought out the inspector.

"You've probably got more experts coming," I said. "If I leave, it will make a little more room for them."

He nodded. "You can go. Be in my office at two o'clock this afternoon. We'll run through the whole scene to date."

I waved to Winnie and battled through the crowd.

In the Middle Ages, students took lemon balm to help them in exams. Ergot, a fungus growing on rye, is the basis of a new miracle drug that improves intelligence and learning ability. Lecithin and choline have similar effects and rosemary has recommended by many including Shakespeare for improving the memory.

I could have used all of them when I prepared breakfast the next morning but instead I made some Mexican eggs. The green peppers and the chilli powder stimulated my taste buds but I didn't notice any sharpening of my mental faculties. I was still baffled.

Baffled and disappointed. Larry Leopold of all people! He had certainly seemed a dynamic and ambitious individual but I wouldn't have thought he would stoop to the dirty tricks with which he had tried to damage the reputation of Le Trouquet d'Or.

Ivor Jenkinson had certainly lived up to his reputation as master investigator but his professional skills had then proved to be the death of him.

The questions remaining were — what had been happening at Raymond's and who was the other person? I still placed a lot of store in IJ's dying remark that "The two of them are in it together". My money was still on Roger St Leger.

I went to the office but couldn't concentrate. Sage was supposed to help that. One of these days, I would have to look into this subject in depth.

I went to Bookery Cooks where Michael and Molly were agog to hear the story so far.

"So it's over," said Molly. "What a relief for you."

"Scotland Yard will soon find the accomplice — if there was one," Michael said.

"If the events that happened at Raymond's were deliberate," I said, "then there was one."

Michael looked thoughtful. "Even the best restaurants have lapses —"

"True," I agreed. "But there was the statement by IJ that two of them were in it."

"IJ was under the influence of a powerful toxin," said Michael. "Why did anything he said have to make sense?"

I had to agree that sounded reasonable.

"And," Michael went on, "if there was another involved, it seems to me more likely that it's someone outside the restaurant business."

"That leaves several choices," put in Molly. "The book

business, the frozen food business, the market business, the banking business and the television business."

"A busy lot of businesses," commented Michael.

"Well, thanks for the ideas," I said. I sniffed. "That smells good? What is it?"

"Very well, Mr Gourmet Detective," said Molly. "What does it smell like?"

I sniffed again. The aromas coming from the kitchen were not at all strong so I presumed that Marita and Dorothy were cooking dishes traditionally more delicately flavoured.

I could just detect soya sauce and certainly there was a smell of frying scallions and vinegar.

"I'll guess at Japanese or Korean," I said.

Dorothy heard me and nodded and her pony-tail bounced up and down.

"It's Japanese today. A lot of dishes are the same though."

There was Sashimi — cooked so as to convert even the most sceptical eater of uncooked fish; Nori Maki, rice rolls in seaweed; Kushi Dango, meatballs in soya sauce and ginger; tender strips of Teriyaki chicken; and specially tasty sardines, marinated and barbecued.

I sampled all and complimented Dorothy and Marita. I declined sake so they poured me some Campo de Borja, a recent DO wine from Aragon and an excellent and inexpensive white deserving wider distribution.

The sardines were so good that I had two more. Molly was on the phone arguing with a transport company and Michael was trying to find a book on the herbal value of garlic that a professor from the University of Michigan wanted. I waved goodbye to both of them and walked up Kensington Park Road towards Notting Hill Gate tube station and my rendezvous at Scotland Yard.

Inspector Hemingway closed the file he was studying. He looked as dapper and competent as ever. His small moustache was trimmed to the last hair and his eyes penetrated me like sharpened skewers. He leaned back in his chair.

Winnie had brought me in from the lobby but we had exchanged only pleasantries on the way. She sat now in the

same seat as before, demure in a way that contrasted delightfully with her severe uniform.

"You know," Hemingway said, "you're beginning to
resemble the albatross at the feast."

"Daniel Webster, the University of Oxford and the Smith-
sonian Library would all dispute the existence of such a
metaphor," I told him. I felt more comfortable in his presence
now. Well, somewhat more comfortable anyway. "Nevertheless, " I said, "I can sympathise with your view."

Hemingway nodded. "I'm glad. You understand then that I
see you in the form of a sort of lightning-conductor, attracting
bizarre events though not responsible for them."

"If you didn't know me this well, you'd be suspicious of
me, you mean?"

"Exactly. Here you are, a gourmet detective, a fan of lurid
and far-fetched crime stories and somehow or other you're
involved in a real case involving a famous man who dies in
mysterious circumstances of a very unusual poison, comes
back to life and dies again. As if that's not enough, you receive
a phone call from a man who says he murdered the first man
and has now killed himself."

"I can see your next question," I said. "I've been wondering
too. Why did he call *me* to tell me he was committing suicide?"

"That's not the question," said Hemingway flatly.

"We believe we know the answer to that one," put in
Winnie.

I was deflated. "You do. What is it?"

Winnie was off-hand. "We can come to it later."

"There's another question?" I asked Hemingway.

His features were non-committal as usual.

"A more important one," he assured me.

"What is it?" I asked, interested.

"We can come to it later too," said Hemingway. "Along
with the other finalising details."

He patted the file before him.

"So it's all sewed up," I said. Someone had to keep the
conversation going and neither of these two was very forthcoming.

There was no reply. "And you're satisfied," I added.

Winnie darted a glance at the inspector. He caught it.

"We have the Forensic report on Leopold. As they knew what they were looking for, it didn't take them long. It was the same botulin and about four times the lethal dose," he said.

"And traces of the botulin have been found in his garage. It's very virulent and nearly impossible to eradicate completely," added Winnie. "He was a graduate in Food Science. It would have been easy for him to culture it and there's no doubt that's where he did so."

"There are a few loose ends that need tying up," said Hemingway. "The Forensic people are going through Leopold's place with a fine toothcomb, checking the drinking glass, the typewriter, the kitchen . . . we'll have their report tomorrow."

"Oh," he went on, "we have persuaded Scarponi to tell us what was in the envelope you saw St Leger hand to Jenkinson."

"Really!" I was excited. "What was in it?"

"Photos he had taken of staff of Le Trouquet d'Or," said Hemingway.

"Do you have them?"

"No." It was Winnie who answered. "It was news of Leopold's suicide that prompted Scarponi to tell us what he knows. Leopold is in several of the photos. Oh, Scarponi photographed others too but he got scared when he heard about Leopold."

"That's all?" I asked. I was disappointed.

"Almost all. Scarponi insists he didn't keep prints. He told us where he has his photos processed though." Winnie went on. "I'm going there this afternoon."

They were both taking the closing of this case very casually, it seemed to me. Then they probably did this kind of thing every day of the week whereas it was still new and exciting to me.

"Then there remains the matter of Leopold's accomplice," I said.

"Accomplice." Hemingway wasn't really asking a question. His tone was steady.

"I still remember IJ's words," I told them. "The two of them are in it together."

"Do you have any suggestions?" asked Hemingway.

"St Leger. I still think he knows a lot he's not telling."

Hemingway leaned back and regarded me. "We've talked to him further. He insists he know nothing more."

I looked from Hemingway to Winnie. She turned her guileless blue-eyed gaze on me, enchanting but uncommunicative.

"You believe him? He has a strong motive."

"You mean his own show on TV?" asked Winnie.

"IJ's show — an even stronger motive," I said.

"You think that's motive enough?" asked Hemingway.

"Not for a murderer perhaps but surely for an accomplice."

Hemingway didn't answer. Winnie said nothing.

"Is there something else?" I asked.

Hemingway looked negligent, as if he were trying to remember something. He didn't look the forgetful type.

"Oh, just one thing . . ." he murmured.

Was I right? Was he just a shade too casual?"

"The day after tomorrow, there's a special commemorative dinner for Per Larsson — acknowledging his exceptional services to the food and drink industry."

I nodded. "I think I heard something about it."

"I want you to be there," said Hemingway.

My astonishment must have shown in my face. Hemingway went on smoothly.

"I said there were a few loose ends and they are all details that Circle of Careme members will be able to clarify. Sergeant Fletcher and her team have made sure that they will be present the day after tomorrow at the Lanchester Palace Hotel."

"All of them?"

"All except for half a dozen overseas guests who were at Le Trouquet d'Or — yes, all of them. We have cleared those six, we'll ask a few questions of the others as soon as the dinner is over."

My suspicions were justified.

"You're up to something, aren't you?"

Hemingway's eyebrows went up half a millimetre. Winnie's lips puckered in a half smile that disappeared just before Hemingway looked over at her.

"You're pulling a Nero Wolfe," I challenged him. "Get all the suspects in one room —"

"No, no," he said mildly. "Nothing like that."

"Charlie Chan then. He was an Inspector of the Honolulu Police. A comparison with an official detective is better, isn't it?"

Hemingway seemed more suave and urbane than ever. He said:

"If I were 'pulling anything' — as you put it — I would rather it be considered a Ronald Hemingway."

"And just what are you going to do?"

"Get some answers. Clarify some unclear issues."

"Uncover an accomplice?"

Hemingway shrugged.

"But the case is closed?" I persisted.

He pushed the file on his desk away from him in a dismissive gesture.

"As of this moment, the case is closed with Larry Leopold's suicide. I won't be working on it any more after Monday. I want it all to be neat and tidy when I hand this report in to the Commissioner."

He gave me, what was for him, almost a smile.

"I'll see you on Monday at the Lanchester Palace. The sergeant will show you out."

In the lift, I turned to Winnie.

"What's the cunning old fox up to?"

Winnie smiled.

"You're using that smile in place of answers," I told her.

She chuckled. "I'm sorry our evening was disturbed. We'll have to make up for it."

"Nothing would please me more. We'll do that. Now — what's he up to?"

We reached the lobby. It was quiet today except for four Africans who were engaged in an incomprehensible discussion.

"He doesn't tell me all," said Winnie.

"But you can guess at the rest."

She shook her head. "He's a very, very clever inspector.

Besides, a lot depends on the forensic report he gets tomorrow."

"You'll be there on Monday?"

"Of course." She smiled again. "Wouldn't miss it for all the coffee in Brazil."

CHAPTER TWENTY-SEVEN

The Great Room at the Lanchester Palace had the reputation of being the biggest in Europe. Its original capacity was two thousand guests but in recent years the demand for such enormous functions had lessened. This led to the ingenious installation of removable partitions so that the room was divisible into three, each with all its own facilities and access to the kitchens.

For this occasion, the Circle of Careme had one of these rooms and already, it was nearly full. A hundred feet overhead, vaulted ceilings curved into ornate friezes while magnificent chandeliers illuminated the scene of splendour below. The panelled walls lent an old-world air which still blended with the crisp, modern efficiency of one of the world's finest restaurants. The Lanchester Palace had newer neighbours on Park Lane but none more prestigious.

I recognised many faces from the previous Circle of Careme occasion. At that time though, I had no way of knowing what a gruesome end the evening would have or I would have been much more alert to every face. I saw one character who must have been at the previous dinner but I hadn't noticed him. His laugh was as memorable as his face.

Eric Saunders owned a chain of shops known as "The Pastry Chef" and it was equally popular with caterers and with the retail public. Each of the shops operated as a small personal home-cooking unit but there were over twenty of them and Eric ran them with a firm hand.

Many attributed Eric's success to his knack of selecting the right people to run them. Perhaps that was true for Eric's own personality startled most of those meeting him for the first time. "Eric the Joker" was what many called him as his sense of humour was, to say the least, well-developed.

He hailed Gus Stapleton, whose seafood restaurant had an enviable reputation.

"Hey, Gus, still serving the Plankton Thermidor?"

Gus was difficult to ruffle. He grinned amiably.

"Haven't considered it yet. Still wondering about cod and chips."

"Let me know when you do," Eric called loudly. "If it's not better than your turbot, I won't be a customer."

"You don't like our turbot?" asked Gus who should have known better. "When did you eat it last?"

"1968," guffawed Eric and moved on in search of another victim.

Benjamin Breakspear was there, never one to miss a good opportunity to eat. He was regaling a small group as usual.

"Rabbit pie," he was saying and the famous jowls quivered with salivatory reminiscence. "Rabbit pie — that's what I miss most from my childhood. Rich, savoury, nourishing — there's never been a dish to touch it."

"Goulash," said Mike Spitalny of The Bohemian Girl restaurant and always fond of an argument. "The greatest food in the world. I wish my restaurant could make it half as good as my mother used to."

"Eat up, master Benjamin." Breakspear's decades of film experience had taught him never to be up-staged. He went on as if Mad Mike were not there. "Eat up, my nanny used to say. Eat every mouthful, there's a good boy. And I was a good boy — as far as eating goes anyway. Seldom left a morsel. I got tapioca pudding if I promised to wash behind my ears. I had the fullest stomach and the cleanest ears in the country."

I resumed my patrol. Hemingway had not contacted me further and I knew nothing more than he had told me in his office. I decided that all I could do was keep my eyes and ears open. Of course, I had done that on the previous occasion of the Circle dinner and the results of my vigilance were not happy ones. Still, without further instructions from the inspector, I didn't know what else to do.

The next group was getting profound. A man with a shock of white hair was saying, "The greatest villainies of history have been perpetrated by sober men — usually teetotallers. On the other hand, all the finest creations of man from the Song of

Songs to Beethoven's Symphonies to the plays of Shakespeare to Crêpes Suzette and champagne have been given to humanity by men who recognised the value of alcohol."

Sally Aldridge was just joining the group and a statement like that was all the stimulant she needed.

"Men and women," she corrected loudly. "A woman was responsible for Crêpes Suzette and Madame Pol Roger was more influential in making champagne famous than that monk. If it had been left to him, it would never have been seen outside the cloisters."

"Still claiming equality, Sally?" laughed another man.

"Certainly not," said Sally. "Equality is a myth. Women are superior."

"Ah," said the man, "if only Adam had been able to control his urge for a bite of that apple."

There were titters at that.

"Some theologians" said the man, "think that God is a woman."

"Nonsense," retorted Sally swiftly. "That's not possible. If she were, she would never have created man."

"Have you seen that woman with that new wine programme on television?" someone was asking nearby.

"Oh, the one with the name — what is it —?"

"Francesca Amelia Waddesdon-Sandringham," supplied another. "By the time they've finished introducing her, you can hear the fade-out music starting."

Not far away, Eric Saunders was taunting Frankie Orlando.

"Still hiring the singing waiters, Frankie?"

"Ask Eric if he's still doing the catering for Lord Greystoke," whispered a trouble-maker.

I strolled on through the thickening crowds. Everything was normal and jolly. If there were memories of the last Circle dinner, all the guests were pushing them to the back of their minds.

Maggie McNulty came up to me, resplendent in a blue gown of a wrong colour and uncertain fit. Fashion was not Maggie's thing.

"It's all solved then!" she said breathlessly. The gown was tight in the wrong places.

"So I believe," I said.

"I saw it on TV just before I came here."

"Ah," I said, still giving nothing away.

"I'm glad it's all settled," said Maggie. "Tonight would have been under a cloud otherwise."

"True."

"Are the drinks over here?" asked Maggie, getting back to essentials.

I pointed. As she left, I caught a snatch of conversation from a vociferous group. I moved that way to listen.

Ted Wells, the distinguished general manager of Stapleton's Seafood Restaurant, was engaged in defending himself. His attackers were led by Milton Marston, an occasional food-writer for *Private Eye* and renowned arguer. Also in the ring around him were Louis Deneuve, the head chef of Raymond's who gave me a nod of recognition and Tarquin Warrington who looked at me as if he thought I should be outside emptying the garbage.

"So why aren't you serving Orange Roughy?" demanded Tarquin Warrington.

"It's a designer fish. Quite out of keeping with the quality standards we have always maintained," said Ted stoutly.

"Why do you say that?" asked another in the group.

"Every once in a while, some new fish comes along. If it didn't, someone would invent one. There was the monkfish, then there was St Pierre then Hoki — and now it's Orange Roughy."

"You should jump at it," said Marston. "It's all things to all diners. You can bake it, boil it, fry it, poach it, barbecue it —"

"But that's exactly what we don't want!" Ted Wells' voice rose half an octave. "Those attributes are fine for the home cook but they're not attractive to the restaurant. People eating out want to order dishes they can't get at home."

"Awful looking thing too," said a lady with bluish hair and very large glasses. "All those nasty teeth and those orange scales."

Tarquin Warrington came back into the discussion.

"It doesn't bother people to see scorpion fish — we sell tons of them in our markets. Call them by other names, of course."

"Why do you call it new?" asked the lady. "How can a fish be new?"

"It comes from New Zealand," explained Ted Wells. "It was introduced into California and became very popular then it spread through the rest of the States. It's always existed but the marketing people in New Zealand didn't start to push it until recently."

"You could sell it as bass," suggested Tarquin Warrington. "It tastes like it and it's cheaper."

Ted Wells turned a withering look in his direction.

"We have a reputation to uphold."

"Tastes more like cod to me," said Marston. "But then, like I said, it's all things to all diners."

Across the room, I espied François. I made my way through the throng towards him.

His face was grim but he was putting on a good front.

"I can't believe it," he said. "I would never have thought that Larry would betray me like that. Such treachery . . . ah ambition is a terrible force, is it not?"

"What about Le Trouquet d'Or?" I wanted to know. "You were concerned about being driven out of business but now the threat has been removed with Leopold's suicide. You must feel great relief — you can carry on."

François gave a Gallic shrug.

"I don't know. This has all been so shocking. I am drained. Do I really want to go on in this business, I ask myself?"

"You shouldn't be influenced by what's happened," I told him. "You have a fine restaurant, a strong following —"

"Alas, no longer so strong."

"You can get it back."

"Perhaps, I don't know. Anyway, we will see. Now then, you and I have a financial matter to settle . . ."

"Why don't we talk about it in a day or two?" I was even more uncertain about the outcome of tonight's proceedings than François was about his future.

He managed a weak smile and shook my hand.

A few of the Circle members, the upper circle so to speak, were unobtrusively shepherding the assembly towards seats. I found my nameplate — I was between Klaus Klingermann and a restaurateur from New Orleans, Sam Beauregard. Opposite were Leila Garrison from the Ministry of Agriculture, Food and Fisheries, popularly known as MAFF; Vito Volcanini, the owner of Trevi and Nelda Darvey off to my right.

At a distant table, I could see Paula Jardine's coppery-red hair shimmering in the light of the chandeliers. I had caught a glimpse of Roger St Leger approaching a table not far away but I couldn't see him now. Craning my neck, I noticed Raymond — the saddest countenance in the room. Benjamin Breakspear's unmistakeable baritone was regaling his neighbours with a tale of eating strange foods while on location for one of his films made in Africa. I couldn't see him for he was somewhere behind me but from the scraps of his conversation, he was not improving their appetite.

The first course was arriving so I had no time to see who else I could identify. The table arrangements were completely different from the previous Circle of Careme dinner, a good decision by someone to divorce the two meals in every regard and avoid the unpleasant memories of the former meal.

We were served Asparagus Vinaigrette Mimosa. It was a clever way to start and the seasoning was faultless. Klaus Klingermann applauded it as one professional appreciating another.

"It is rare today to get a perfectly seasoned salad," said Klaus. "That is evident when salt always has to be on the table. Oh, tastes differ certainly but a top-rank chef should be able to season so that the food and the seasoning are so carefully matched that no one even thinks of adding to it."

The lady from MAFF wanted to know why it was called Mimosa and Klaus explained that it was the name of the method of preparing the hard-boiled eggs.

"You will notice too," said Klaus, "that the vinaigrette is so delicate that it will not sully the palate for the wine that is now being poured." Klaus went on, speaking of the vinegar used in dressing. "It must *always* be the mildest you can find. That way, if you put in a few drops extra it doesn't make the dressing more acid."

The wine was a light-bodied red, labelled Sukhindol Gamza from Bulgaria. Klaus sipped and approved and even Vito Volcanini who was not easy to please, grudgingly admitted that it was very palatable.

The next course was small fillets of red mullet. Vito said that they had been pan-grilled for less than one minute on each side. They were served on a bed of sauce which Klaus and Vito identified between them as containing shallots, rosemary, double cream and white wine. Both gave it a high rating.

Sam Beauregard from New Orleans was engaging Nelda in conversation. It seemed they had a common acquaintance in the restaurant business and that person — whose name I did not catch — was not receiving any commendations from either of them.

"He's not a cook — he's an arsonist," said Sam vigorously.

Nelda nodded agreement. "His idea of seasoning is to keep adding garlic till the paint starts to peel off the walls."

Leila Garrison from MAFF, joined in with a comment. She was a tall, bony lady with silvery hair and patrician features. I had not met her before but she was pleasant and knowledgeable.

"You should be more critical of restaurants, Nelda," she admonished.

Nelda's eyebrows rose. She was used to criticism for her forthright — some said vitriolic — manner but was probably the first time she had been urged to be more critical.

"Oh, I don't mean the food," Leila went on. "I mean the ambience and the service. Too many restaurants today are show-biz, not food. They are owned by film stars and people go to them to ogle, not to eat."

"If a place becomes fashionable, the names go there," said Nelda. "Then the no-names go there to stare at the names."

"But when the food standards slip, people need warning that they may be spending fifty pounds or more for a meal that isn't worth half of that." Leila turned to Sam Beauregard. "At least that's the way it is in London. What about New Orleans?"

"The same," said Sam. "Of course, it's more of a problem in New York and Los Angeles but we get the same kind of thing too. Can't criticise the food here though — it's great."

Vito pointed to Sam's plate. "That won't need washing."

He was right. It was clean as if it had just come out of the washer.

"So's the wine," said Sam and everyone agreed.

"A daring choice of wines," said Leila, "serving reds all through the meal."

"Starting with a very light one and then progressing to heavier and heavier with each course," said Nelda. "Maybe we can learn from this." She looked meaningfully at Klaus, Sam and Vito, the three restaurateurs in the group.

The conversation had split into several directions by the time the main course arrived soon afterwards. It was Mignons de Veau, given an unusual warmth and sharpness by the addition of grated orange peel, Grand Marnier and green peppercorns.

With the veal came a magnificent Côte Rotie which succeeded in being defiantly independent and not trying to be a claret. Nelda commented on this and the others agreed.

"The service is excellent too," remarked Sam Beauregard.

"Unfortunately," said Leila, "the art of waiting is rapidly being lost."

"Oh, I don't know about that," retorted Nelda, always ready to be argumentative. "There are dozens of restaurants in London where you have to wait."

Leila smiled. "True, Nelda. But don't you agree that the art of being a waiter is dying?"

"What makes a good waiter?" I asked.

Klaus was the first to answer.

"A good waiter never walks past his tables empty-handed without scanning each one to see whether anything is needed or should be cleared away."

"More than that," said Vito. "A good waiter can memorise the meal orders from half a dozen tables. A good waiter knows what every diner has ordered. He does not have to stand and ask 'Whose is the rare steak?'"

"A lot more than that," said Nelda. "A good waiter must be able to describe every dish on the menu and tell the diner what it contains and how it is prepared."

"You're all absolutely right," Sam Beauregard said. "Compared to Europe, maybe our American waiters try too hard."

"They certainly do," Nelda said. "They sing, they tell jokes, they are funds of information on politics and economics. They should stick to being good waiters."

"Good waiters work in good restaurants," said Leila. "Their profession is being a waiter. Too many of the staff of restaurants today are ballet-dancers or actors or chorus boys in between jobs."

There were murmurs of agreement at this. During this episode, the next red wine had been poured — a Gevrey-Chambertin, Clos de Beze. Its intense, plummy richness rounded off the main part of the meal admirably and everyone was smiling and relaxed.

I looked around the room where the occupants of the other tables appeared equally satisfied. Was one or more of them in for a big surprise? Inspector Hemingway had denied that he was "up to something". Or had he? Now that I thought about it, he had not denied it at all. He had said that he was going to get some answers and clarify some issues. Then too — what further forensic information was he waiting for?

St Leger's fair hair could be seen. He was deep in conversation with Johnny Chang. Milton Marston was getting a little red in the face but whether it was the wine or the proximity of Benjamin Breakspear was hard to say.

Leila caught the direction of my attention and smiled.

"Those two are having a real battle, aren't they? I wonder what it's about?"

"Worthy opponents anyway," I said.

Leila smiled again.

"When I first came in, I ran into Benjamin — spent an hour talking to him for a few minutes."

Cheese was served. It was Chevrotin de Moulins, small pyramid shapes of strong goat cheese from the Auvergne.

"A real challenge to serve a meal this good to so many people," said Leila. All agreed and Nelda, in a rare moment of praise, said:

"It's a challenge to run a really good restaurant at all."

"Amen to that," laughed Sam Beauregard.

"How *do* you run a really good restaurant?" asked Leila, looking around the table.

"All you need," said Klaus, "is the dynamism of Michel Guerard, the boldness of Alain Chapel, the simplicity of Alastair Little —" he paused, thinking. Vito finished for him.

"— plus the brashness of Marco Pierre White and the originality of Peter Langan."

"You could answer that another way," Nelda said. "The integrity of Prue Leith, the showmanship of Julia Child, the ingenuity of Simca Beck —"

There were laughs from the men, acknowledging Nelda's well-aimed shaft. Further contributions to the lists were cut short by the arrival of the dessert.

This was Nougatine Glacée au Café according to the menu card. The nougatine was heavenly in texture, very slightly chewy but melting in the mouth. It was filled with hazelnuts, walnuts and almonds and served at precisely the right temperature, not frozen and burning the tongue but not yet thawing either. A spoonful of melted bitter chocolate over it was delicately flavoured with coffee. It was a perfect example of the difficult and exacting made simple.

I was certainly eating better than any of the private eyes of fiction, I reflected. Philo Vance enjoyed beluga caviare on occasion but Miss Marple seldom seemed to be observed being served anything but tea and scones and Mike Hammer was so busy with women's bodies — dead or alive — that he had no time for food except the infrequent cheeseburger. I excluded Nero Wolfe of course. Reaching 320 lbs meant he ate a lot in addition to eating well.

The coffee came and I felt relief. At least we had progressed beyond the stage of the ill-fated earlier Circle of Careme dinner. Brandy and liqueurs came but I declined. I didn't know exactly what was to come but I wanted to understand it to the fullest. Nelda raised an eyebrow at my abstinence and was about to make a pointed comment but Sam Beauregard asked a question comparing British and American press techniques and Nelda's professionalism prevailed.

We were called to order and the speeches began. First Ted Wells thanked us for our attendance and made only fleeting reference to the previous dinner. He spoke of Per Larsson's great service to the food industry in Britain and suggested that he be made an honorary member of the Circle. I gathered that this was a rarity.

A cabinet minister spoke briefly, decrying his own expertise in the matter but commending Per Larsson in the highest terms. Benjamin Breakspear rose to his feet and there were one or two carefully suppressed groans but he had evidently been carefully briefed because that is what he was — brief, however uncharacteristic.

Ellsburg Warrington, presumably one of the elder states-men of the Circle, paid a short tribute and so did Leila Garrison, representing MAFF. Ted Wells wisely cut off one or two other attempts at speech-making and invited Per Larsson to say a few words.

He was gracious and highly appreciative of the honour paid him by such a circle of luminaries, he said. He continued, pointing out the tremendous strides made in recent years by British hoteliers and restaurateurs but acknowledging the support given by publishers, writers and food critics, inspect-ors, wholesalers and retailers, wine merchants . . . The list was long but he was careful to give credit to all. There was an echoing round of applause and Ted Wells smilingly said that if this were a musical concert there would be a dozen encores.

He thanked the assembly for its presence and then, just as the evening was about to break up, Ted made his almost casual announcement.

Would all those who had not been present at the previous Circle of Careme dinner at François' restaurant, he asked, please adjourn to the next room where coffee and after dinner drinks would continue to be served.

All those who had been present were asked to remain seated for a few moments. There was renewed activity by the staff who were bringing more coffee and this effectively stifled any objections to the arrangements. Other staff herded those going to the next room so discreetly and swiftly that all the move-ments were completed as Inspector Ronald Hemingway and Sergeant Winifred Fletcher walked in.

The inspector looked neat and dapper in a dark suit and bow tie. Winnie looked demure but alluring in a linen suit of a dark burgundy colour with a white silk blouse. Her shoes matched the suit and her hair was blonde and alive.

All the staff disappeared. Ted Wells had moved those guests at the head table to adjoining tables, leaving the head table free. The inspector and Winnie took their places at it, standing alone and all eyes were upon them. One or two faint murmurs arose but died instantly as the doors were slammed one by one with an ominous finality.

CHAPTER TWENTY-EIGHT

"I won't keep you long," Hemingway said briskly. "There are just a few points to clear up."

"Why?" called out Mike Spitalny loudly. "You have a confession."

"Which covers the whole case," agreed Hemingway. He paused for just the briefest part of a second before adding "— except for one or two things."

"But why are you keeping *us* here?" asked Frankie Orlando. "What can *we* tell you?"

Inspector Hemingway's expression was placating, almost benevolent. I knew he was at his most dangerous.

"That's precisely the reason, Mr Orlando. You can tell me something —" he waved away the immediate protestation. "Perhaps not you specifically but several people in the room know some details. They may not be aware of their importance."

From one side of the room came the carefully enunciated words of Johnny Chang.

"Inspector, you have talked to each one of us. We have told you all we know. How can we do more?"

There were murmurs of support for this but again the inspector calmed the objectors.

"If you'll all just bear with me for a short time, we'll have this over very quickly and you can all leave."

I wondered if anyone else in the room beside Sergeant Fletcher was taking that assurance with a large pinch of salt.

"Mr St Leger," called out the inspector and heads swivelled in that direction.

"Yes, Inspector?" He looked slightly nonplussed but answered readily enough.

"Would you tell the assembly how it all started as far as you are concerned?"

St Leger glanced around. He was silent for a moment then he said:

"I received a phone call. A man said that Le Trouquet d'Or was being run in a very sloppy way. He said it typified a deplorable decline in London restaurant standards."

"This man did not identify himself?"

"No."

A murmur ran around the room. Every member of the Circle felt themselves affected.

"What else did the man say?"

"He described mice being found in the kitchen, failure to order supplies properly, not keeping records . . ."

The murmurs grew louder.

"What did you do, Mr St Leger?" The inspector's sharp tone reduced the murmurs to silence.

"I asked why the person was calling me. He said the public should know they were being taken advantage of — he said they should be made aware of unreasonable profits, unsanitary kitchens, callous practices. He said he had always admired my television programmes and thought I was the right person to do something about it."

"And what did you do?"

St Leger rubbed his chin in what would have been embarrassment if he hadn't been a television performer.

"I — er, talked to one or two people at the studio but they said that scheduling pressures meant they couldn't give me another show just then."

"So what did you do?" prompted Hemingway.

"I talked to IJ. It sounded like the kind of thing he might be interested in developing."

"Was he interested?"

"He said he had programmes lined up for six months — suggested I talk to him again then."

"You accepted that?"

"I said that the story might be in other hands by that time. This was an immediate issue."

"His reply?"

"He said there was nothing he could do."

"And then?"

"The next thing I knew was that he was asking questions

about the restaurant business, hiring people — freelances, to dig around."

"You approached him again?"

"Yes. He said he'd changed his mind, was going to give it a top priority. From what he said, I was sure that the same man had phoned him — he seemed to know even more than I did."

Over to my left, François half-rose to his feet then changed his mind and sat down again. Hemingway's strategy was clear — he wanted to get the opinions of all in the room on the statements they had all made to the police. Which of them would be in a position to contradict?

"What happened then?"

"He asked me if I wanted to help him."

St Leger was clearly having a difficult time explaining what most of the room knew — that NTV wouldn't give him a programme of his own and he was forced to accept a demeaning and probably subservient role to the demanding IJ.

To his credit, the inspector didn't pursue the point. He switched his line of questioning.

"You agreed?"

Relieved, St Leger hurried to answer. "It was a good opportunity for me to get into the investigative side of television journalism."

"So that you might eventually have the opportunity of replacing IJ?"

Aha, I thought. Now he's zero'ing in.

"Yes." St Leger's relief tapered off as he realised the implications of what he was saying. "No, I didn't mean that . . . all my recent experience has been in TV, naturally I wanted to explore other styles —"

"Quite so." The inspector was urbane. "You were also looking into other career opportunities, I believe?"

"Well, yes." St Leger was less buoyant now. He sounded reluctant to go on but the inspector's silence was projected at him like a pressurising beam.

"I was approached by Larry Leopold —" St Leger's mention of the name seized everyone's attention immediately. "— it was concerning a chain of cooking schools. I had taught cooking on TV and Leopold said Le Trouquet d'Or wanted to sponsor a chain of schools all over the world, Europe, the U.S.A., Japan, Australia —"

François was really on his feet this time, shouting.

"I know nothing of this! I have never even considered cooking schools. This is not true!"

"It *is* true," insisted St Leger.

"Then Leopold was acting entirely without my authority," snapped François. "What proof do you have of this? A proposal? A contract? A business plan?"

"It — it was all verbal," said St Leger weakly.

François sat down with a "I rest my case" gesture.

The inspector continued smoothly as if there had been no interruption.

"You had no suspicion at any time that Leopold was your anonymous caller?"

"No," said St Leger defiantly. "None at all."

"Thank you," said the inspector. "You have been very helpful."

I was disappointed. He was letting St Leger off the hook for the time being. But he was cunning — he would be back at him, I felt sure.

Benjamin Breakspear stood, his portly figure pushing his chair back.

"Inspector, is this getting us anywhere? You said you only had a few points to clear up. I trust that you have almost done so?"

"Almost," nodded Hemingway. "Almost, Mr Breakspear."

I would have bet a six course meal that he didn't think so at all. He went on, smooth as double cream.

"Mr Ellsburg Warrington. Can you help us now?"

A rumble of surprise. Heads turned.

The very tall, very lean figure rose and the grey head towered as he faced Hemingway.

"What can I tell you, Inspector?" Surprise showed in his voice.

"Sergeant Fletcher —" Hemingway called and Winsome Winnie rose, delectable as chocolate fudge cake with Chantilly cream.

"I have a statement here," she said in a clear, almost girlish voice, "which, summarised, states that an agreement was prepared whereby Le Trouquet d'Or would supply an extensive range of gourmet foods to the Warrington chain of supermarkets."

She sat demurely.

"Absurd!" boomed Ellsburg Warrington. He might be old but there was nothing aged about his voice. It reverberated through the room. "Absolutely absurd! We have agreed no such thing."

A few rows from him, François was on his feet too.

"Inspector, this is nonsense! I know nothing about any such plan either!"

Both were ready to go on. Both were glaring at each other but the inspector calmed them down.

"Please, gentlemen . . . we're making excellent progress here. May I ask you both to sit down so that we can conclude?"

The two glowered at each other a moment longer then they both sat reluctantly.

"Thank you," said the inspector politely. "Perhaps Mr Tarquin Warrington can clear up this question?"

A few sharp intakes of breath punctuated the quiet of the banquet room. Heads turned to look at Tarquin Warrington, sitting some distance from his father. The quiet persisted, an uneasy interval which awaited the first voice to break it.

"We had a couple of casual conversations." The words seemed squeezed out of him. His voice was hoarse. He drank some water, didn't stand up. "There appeared to be some advantages in such an idea that we wanted to assess before going further —"

François was on his feet again. "I didn't take part in any such talks! I know nothing about such a plan!"

"Mr Warrington —?" The inspector's silky voice was inviting but had a needle point to it.

"The talks were with Larry Leopold," Tarquin Warrington said.

"Without my knowledge!" snapped François.

"I didn't know that," Warrington insisted.

"It's easy to blame a dead man," retorted François.

"Now that we've clarified that matter," went on Hemingway, "we can move on."

No wonder he was almost cheerful. He was getting all kinds of help, even if much of it was unwilling. He looked around the room. Who was he going to settle on?

"Miss Sally Aldridge," he called out. "How can you help our investigation?"

Sally remained seated. She toyed with her wine glass. She looked up at Hemingway then back at her wine glass.

"You were approached too, weren't you, Miss Aldridge?"

She glanced up at him finally.

"This may affect my work in a way that —"

The inspector didn't let her finish.

"I don't believe so. If it did happen, I would regret it. Nevertheless, I still intend to follow up this point. Let me remind you that two men are dead, both under abnormal circumstances —" his tone was hardening "— and I intend to continue this investigation until we have a full explanation."

He eased up, playing the game like an expert fisherman.

"Now please tell us what happened."

Sally gave a small sigh of resignation. "I began a book which I planned on calling *Secrets of the Great London Chefs.*" She glanced in the direction of Nelda Darvey. "Then I heard that a certain female journalist was preparing a newspaper series on the same subject —"

"Nothing of the kind!" called Nelda loudly. "Besides, my work isn't so flimsy that it's that easily affected."

A few chuckles sounded. Many knew of the vendetta between the two of them.

Nelda was continuing. "— And my series is quite different. It's on London's Great Restaurants." She turned an accusing stare on Sally. "I thought that was your title too."

"I don't believe it" blurted Sally. "You were —"

"Ladies!" There were a few titters at the mild reproof in Hemingway's voice, especially as he neatly avoided any hint of sarcasm. "At least we've accomplished one worthwhile objective today. We've sorted out the misunderstanding between you. Would you continue, Miss Aldridge?"

Sally tossed another blistering glare in Nelda's direction for face-saving purposes and went on.

"I talked to Raymond and François and got some information from both of them. After a conversation with François, Larry Leopold took me aside and asked me various questions about printing, publishing and so on. We chatted and then he invited me to lunch. He proposed the idea of a writing and publishing group as part of an expanded organisation, financed by Le Trouquet d'Or. He wanted me to direct such a group."

Up popped François again. "I know nothing of this either!" he protested furiously. "Inspector, this is going too far! I must ask you —"

Hemingway held up a placating hand.

"Mr Duquesne, I agree. This has gone far enough. What have we learned so far?" He lifted his head to take in the rest of the great room.

"Combining Larry Leopold's confession with the statements we have heard, we know that he was trying to put Le Trouquet d'Or out of business so that he could then buy it. He intended to use it as leverage so that he could set up a vast food empire — a world-wide chain of cooking schools, a line of gourmet foods for sale in supermarkets, a printer and publisher of books on food, possibly others we have not yet uncovered."

He had everyone's full attention now and he continued, slick as golden syrup.

"We have established that Larry Leopold was acting without Mr Duquesne's authority in all this for obvious reasons.

"We have also established that IJ became interested in an exposé of Le Trouquet d'Or — and possibly other restaurants — but then he realised he had a much more explosive story, the illegal establishment of a vast food empire."

He stopped, looked around the room. I knew him just well enough to know that he was spinning a web and waiting for someone to step into it. There was a barely audible gasp of expectation from several mouths.

"Well, go on, Inspector," urged Ted Wells. "Leopold killed IJ. Is that what you're saying? The lamprey was poisoned — we know several others got minor doses. But why did IJ die?"

Inspector Hemingway had got the reaction he wanted for continuing.

"He arranged to have drinks before the Circle of Careme dinner. He confronted Leopold with evidence that established his guilt. Leopold had already put small amounts of the botulin in some of the lamprey — just enough to look like carelessness in preparation. Alarmed at finding that IJ was about to expose him, he put an additional dose into IJ's drink. He hoped it would look as if several people had got small doses and IJ an extra dose. Determined to be sure that it would be lethal, he overdid it."

Maggie McNulty raised a hand. "But surely it was reckless of IJ to tell Leopold what he knew? Dangerous, even."

"Mr St Leger has given me his opinion on that," said the Inspector.

"I probably knew IJ as much as anyone did," admitted St Leger. "He didn't need proof as much as the police would. His technique was to accuse — then let the accused defend themselves. It made a much better programme that way. He was a journalist first and an investigator second. With him, there was no searching for truth or justice — he was simply putting on a TV show."

"How could you tell that some of the botulin was in the lamprey and some in a drink?" asked Nelda, scribbling furiously.

"It was the timing. The botulin takes at least an hour to kill. Less than thirty minutes elapsed from the start of the meal to the serving of the lamprey. At any time before the meal started, Leopold would have been having drinks with IJ in François' office."

There was a lengthy pause. Hemingway didn't seem anxious to go on. There were one or two buzzes of low-level conversation then Raymond spoke up.

"Inspector, as you know there were some similar incidents at my restaurant . . . you haven't mentioned these."

Hemingway addressed him with a nod.

"Thank you, Mr Lefebvre. There are just a couple more items and then we have all the answers we need. The point you make is one of them —" he paused. This casual manner of his was likely to have a juggernaut following close behind.

"Larry Leopold must have had an accomplice. We believe that Leopold was not satisfied with taking over control of Le Trouquet d'Or but he wanted to take over Raymond's Restaurant too."

More gasps sounded. The air trembled with expectation. So did I — Hemingway was going to expose St Leger, I was sure of it.

Raymond stood up. He was bulkier even than Benjamin Breakspear and his expansive face had that perpetual irritable look.

"You know who this accomplice is?" he asked.

"I said there were a couple of items . . ." Hemingway said. "The other concerns the typewriter on which Leopold typed his suicide note."

Raymond was still standing.

"The typewriter?" he asked perplexed. "Why is that important?"

"Typewriters have plastic keys today," said Hemingway as if imparting information of great wisdom.

Everyone hung on his words but it was Benjamin Breakspear who interrupted. He had once played in a James Bond movie, I remembered, and he didn't intend to let anyone forget how much the role had taught him about police work.

"Fingerprints, eh, Inspector?" he said with a knowing smile.

Hemingway regarded him innocently.

"The fingerprints on the keys are those of Leopold and no one else."

Deflated, Benjamin looked back sullenly.

"A great deal of progress has been made in recent years in the forensic identification of body fluids," Hemingway continued. "They are present in the skin and can readily be transferred to other surfaces — especially absorbent surfaces such as typewriter keys. The body fluids that our forensic people picked up on those keys are definitely those of Leopold only but —"

The inspector paused and looked around the room. He must have studied acting at the Sahara Desert School of Dramatic Art.

"But those body fluids were transferred to the keys after Leopold had already died from botulin poisoning."

There was a stunned silence. Even speculation was frozen.

Finally, Vito Volcanini could contain his impatience no longer.

"What are you saying, Inspector?"

"I'm saying," said Hemingway, "that the suicide note was typed by a dead man."

CHAPTER TWENTY-NINE

A faint rattle of pans could be heard from the kitchens. They were some distance away but the Great Room at the Lanchester Palace was so still that the shelling of a peanut would have reverberated like thunder.

Hemingway paused, perhaps awaiting comments or questions but there were none. He resumed speaking.

"Our first thought was that Larry Leopold had recovered consciousness after taking the botulin in the same way that Ivor Jenkinson had revived briefly. Psychologically, it seemed unlikely — if he wanted to write a suicide note he would have done so before drinking the botulin. Scientifically, it was even more unlikely. The forensic lab ran further tests — they had no doubt whatever that Leopold was dead — thoroughly dead — when he typed the note."

Hemingway paused then added: "Or perhaps I should say 'when his body fluids were transferred to the typewriter keys'."

"Transferred?" The word floated out of the assembly from an uncertain source.

Hemingway nodded. "There is only one explanation. The note was typed using gloves then Leopold's fingers were pressed on the keys."

There was another silence but this time it was broken more quickly. It was François who called out in an unsteady voice:

"Then Larry did not write that note?"

"He did not."

"Did he — did he commit suicide?"

"No, he did not. He was murdered."

No silence this time but incredulous gasps and then a babble of outraged comments.

Maggie McNulty's voice was the first to cut through the forest of sound.

"Then it's not solved at all!" she cried. "Now you've got two murders to solve!"

The rising hubbub would have unnerved many a lion-tamer or prime minister but Inspector Hemingway looked cool and efficient. Unless I was mistaken, he was more — he was confident. He waited until the bedlam died down.

"I referred earlier to an accomplice. Ivor Jenkinson used several freelance helpers in his investigations. One of them was a photographer — a real paparazzo — who knew all the tricks. He took a lot of photographs including, as we now know, some that were in the envelope that you handed to Ivor Jenkinson just before the dinner. Mr St Leger —"

The inspector turned in his direction. "You have continually maintained that you did not know what was in that envelope."

"I didn't. I collected it from Scarponi and brought it to IJ as he told me to do. I didn't open it."

"We have been to the laboratory where Scarponi had his work processed. They said that Scarponi always took the negatives. He knew all the tricks, as I said."

"Then why don't you ask Scarponi what was on the photographs?" asked St Leger.

"He says they were shots he had taken of Leopold. Some had other people on them but no one he recognised."

"From the way IJ looked at them," said St Leger slowly, "*he* did."

"Can we come back to you now, Miss Aldridge?" asked Hemingway unexpectedly.

Sally looked back at him. From where I was sitting, I could only see her profile. She looked tense.

"You were a close friend of Alessandro Scarponi, weren't you?"

Sally nodded.

"Friend!" muttered Nelda.

"I have no intention of prying into your private life, Miss Aldridge, but as you were living with Scarponi for a time, he must have shown you many of these photographs."

"Why should he?" asked Sally carelessly.

"Because, as he told us, he didn't recognise everyone on them. What more obvious than to ask you? You knew every face in the restaurant and food business."

Hemingway went on, speaking directly to Sally now.

"With Larry Leopold's death, it was obvious that he had been the one sabotaging Le Trouquet d'Or. Who then was doing the same thing at Raymond's?"

Heads turned in Raymond's direction, including mine. He sat immobile.

"Miss Aldridge," asked the inspector, "in the photographs which showed Larry Leopold, did you recognise anyone who was associated with Raymond's?"

"Yes," said Sally quietly.

"Did you identify this person to Scarponi?"

"Of course not," said Sally, regaining some of her usual spirit.

"Why 'of course not'?"

"He was in the business too — I didn't want him taking my story. If he didn't use it himself, he would have sold it to the highest bidder."

"And what was that story?"

"It would have shown the feud between Raymond and François in a new light."

"Miss Aldridge," said Hemingway, his tone hardening, "in our discussions with you, you have never mentioned this person to us. Why not?"

"I was still holding on to the story so I could use it. It was good gossip. Besides, it has nothing to do with the police."

"It has everything to do with us," said Hemingway sternly. "Now please point out this person."

Opposite me, Klaus was holding his breath. Even Nelda was wide-eyed. There couldn't have been a person in the room who wasn't one or the other.

Sally stood, reluctantly.

Her finger reached out and she pointed to Paula Jardine.

I couldn't see Paula well, only her lustrous red hair.

"What did you conclude from the photographs, Miss Aldridge?" The inspector was inexorable.

"That Paula and Larry were — well, very good friends. There were several pictures of them together. Alessandro is an expert in his line of work."

Sally sat abruptly, clearly unwilling to say more.

"Well, Miss Jardine?"

I couldn't believe it. Nor it seemed could anyone else.

When Paula answered, her voice was cool.

"Very well, Inspector. I suppose I have to admit our relationship. Larry and I have been lovers for some time. We didn't want it publicly known because it might affect the image of two duelling restaurants that Raymond and François have worked so hard to build up."

"H'm." Hemingway's comment was dismissive. "Lovers, you say. Not partners?"

"Certainly not," said Paula, still cool as ice. "Oh, I knew Larry was ambitious and wanted to achieve so much more. I knew he was laying plans of some kind but he didn't tell me what they were. He wouldn't, of course. Our restaurants were in competition with one another."

"And you were not his accomplice?" Hemingway persisted.

"That's ridiculous." Contempt for the idea spiked Paula's answer.

She might be cool but Hemingway's temperature was comparable.

"I believe you," he said.

I don't know who else gasped but I did.

"I believe you," he repeated. "You were not Leopold's accomplice — he was yours. You were the instigator, the prime mover, the planner. You were the Lady Macbeth. I don't know which of you put the botulin in Ivor Jenkinson's drink before the Circle of Careme dinner but it was you who put it in Leopold's. Was he getting cold feet? You probably hadn't intended to kill IJ at first but then you found he knew too much. So it was very convenient to get Leopold out of the way and plant the entire guilt on him. That way, you could go through with the original plan alone."

Paula was on her feet now. She looked splendid as with flashing brown eyes and heaving breasts she protested her innocence.

"This is absurd! I don't know who his accomplice was but it's preposterous to accuse me!"

Another person was standing now. It was Roger St Leger and he was angry.

"So that's why you came to my house that day! To get me

drunk! All those questions! It wasn't me at all, was it? You wanted to find out if I'd seen those photos before I gave them to IJ. I hadn't but you didn't believe me at first. You probably had some of that poison with you in case I suspected you!"

Hemingway's plan was working. This was just the kind of corroboration he wanted and it was clear that the whole room knew it. The look that Paula flashed him said all too plainly that St Leger had had a lucky escape. She carried it off beautifully though. The look was gone in a second and she was herself again, all charm and outraged innocence.

But I knew and reluctantly I began adding up the other corroborating factors that I could supply.

Apparently protective of her uncle, she had cleverly hinted that "accidents could happen — even in the best restaurants", and leaving him to be suspected of either inefficient and unsanitary operation or involvement in the sabotage at Le Trouquet d'Or. She had continued to toss suspicion in all directions — at St Leger "I hear he may take over IJ's programme" — and at Sally "her radical ideas — bad for the restaurant trade — may put us all out of business".

And me! She had used me just as she had used St Leger — to find out what I knew. My vanity was bruised even worse than his for I realised why she had telephoned me from Larry Leopold's house rather than the police — if there were any clues to be trampled then an amateur like me was more likely to do it. She had even disputed the concept of a feud because she wanted to maintain the image of two sloppily-run restaurants.

She was magnificent though. I had to admit it even now as she faced Hemingway, spreading out her hands in a supplicant gesture of unfair accusation.

"If you are going to arrest me, Inspector, you will be making a very grave mistake."

"Arrest you!" Hemingway looked appalled at the suggestion. "Miss Jardine, I am Food Squad. I can't even arrest people for selling broccoli with too much Vitamin K in it! I couldn't arrest you — not if you were spraying oranges with DDE!"

For the first time, Paula looked taken aback. She had not expected this but she rallied instantly.

"In that case, I can sue you and Scotland Yard for making

false and malicious accusations!"

"I am not making any accusations of any kind," said Hemingway suavely. His "would I do such a horrible thing" look was very convincing.

"I have closed the case as far as the Food Squad is concerned. I sent the file to the Department of Public Prosecutions yesterday and I will be forwarding today's additions in the morning."

"You haven't heard the last of this!" stormed Paula. She was about to rage on but the inspector stopped her with a raised hand.

"You haven't heard the last of it either. There is one more request that will be made of you."

"Request?" said Paula uncertainly.

"Yes. I have recommended that you be invited to a test for Tintilinum botulinum exposure."

She said nothing, her body rigid.

"As most people know today, a simple test of a hand will determine if it has fired a gun within recent weeks — the gunpowder blowback remains in the skin. Similarly, anyone who has handled a botulin as virulent as Tintilinum retains traces of the bacteria for a similar length of time."

Paula gave out a sound like a sob then quick as a flash, she kicked away her chair and ran for the nearest door. Winnie and the inspector started in her direction then stopped as she put a hand into her purse and came out with a small glass bottle.

"Keep back!" she shouted. She pulled out the stopper then fumbled behind her for the door handle. She wrenched the door open and slipped through it — only to re-emerge with the arm of a burly police constable around her waist.

She was still not finished. She turned her head aside and flung the contents of the bottle full in the policeman's face. There were shrieks and cries as the policeman staggered back, releasing his grip. Paula disappeared.

The inspector and Winnie came running to the policeman's side and I followed. He was clawing at the wall, unable to see and Hemingway pulled him away gently. Winnie's reaction seemed strange. She stood sniffing then she bent and picked up the bottle that Paula had dropped. She sniffed it and held it out.

"The cunning bitch," she said in tones befitting a sergeant

but not a well brought-up young lady. "It's Chanel Number 5."

A second constable hurried in and Hemingway addressed him hurriedly. "See that this man gets attention. Let no one out." To Winnie and me, he snapped, "Come on!"

We went pelting along the corridor and it led directly to one of the kitchens. We poured in through the swinging doors and there was no need to ask any questions. A young kitchen helper sat on the floor, bewildered. The liquid contents of a large pan were all over the floor.

The young man looked up at us in comic surprise.

"Which way did she go?" Hemingway growled.

The young man pointed and we raced out in that direction. It was another kitchen, empty this time. Hemingway pushed through the nearest door but Winnie stopped him.

"No. That only goes out into the back street. She's more likely to head for the front where she can get a taxi."

Winnie had evidently done her homework on the geography of the Lanchester Palace. Hemingway digested this then nodded. We raced out of the other door. A corridor led to a carpeted floor in a long room with glass display cabinets. Clothes, jewellery, handbags, shoes filled the cabinets and Winnie panted:

"This is the way — goes out to the front lobby —"

It did and despite the lateness of the hour the lobby was busy. We got a few alarmed looks as we dashed through then we were out in Park Lane.

"There she is!" cried Winnie.

Paula was getting into a taxi at the head of the rank and the vehicle started to pull out. I had visions of yet another "Follow that cab!" episode though this time surely the name of Scotland Yard would get some reaction.

Instead, the cab stopped abruptly as an elderly lady in furs and with a tiny dog on a long leash walked out in front of it. In a few long strides I reached the taxi and jerked open the door. The cabbie looked round, mouth open to protest and by then Paula had pushed open the other door and jumped out.

She stood hesitant for a couple of seconds, undecided whether to try for another cab or run. It was a fatal hesitation.

Hemingway came for her, she turned — and ran straight at Winnie.

The blonde sergeant had paid full attention to her tutors in unarmed combat instruction. The grip she put on Paula's arm looked casual enough but Paula was unable to move and her face contorted with pain.

Back in the Great Room, Inspector Hemingway was assuring the guests that the case had been concluded satisfactorily and they could all leave. They were drifting out in small groups, excitedly discussing the events of the evening.

The guests continued to stream through the doors, all of them relieved that the case was over and that London's eating scene could return to normal. But not quite all . . .

Two dejected figures shambled out together, one — a big bear of a man with a long sad countenance that looked as if it would never know happiness again, the other — once athletic and spry, now weary and prematurely aged, the battered boxer's features creased and lined. They had each lost someone they loved and trusted. The picture of them going out of the door, the two deadly rivals with an arm around each other was one that I knew would stay with me for ever.

As the last guests left, the inspector and Winnie approached.

"So ends your first murder case," said Hemingway.

"And my last," I assured him. "I've had enough of murder. I'm sticking to mangoes and marjoram from now on."

"You were very helpful," said Hemingway.

"As a guesser of guilty parties, I was hopeless," I admitted.

"It must be because you're such a good gourmet detective," said Winnie. "You can't resist a red herring."

"You were magnificent," I told the inspector. "I underestimated you when I compared you with Charlie Chan. You were as impressive as Sir John Appleby in his finest hour."

"Praise indeed."

"Pity you're such a good detective," I said. "You would have made a great counsel for the prosecution. You'd have outdone Perry Mason and overcome Horace Rumpole."

"One thing I want to ask, Inspector," said Winnie. "I didn't know that Tintilinum botulinum could be detected in the skin of anyone who'd handled it?"

Did I see the faintest twinkle in the inspector's eye? Possibly not, though I thought I caught the trace of an admonishing smile on Winnie's lips. Maybe I was mistaken on both counts but I had a question of my own.

"And as Food Squad, you really can't arrest anyone?"

"I have to go and talk to the manager," said Hemingway. "Thanks again for your help." He strode off.

I looked at Winnie. "You really can't?"

She smiled that adorable smile.

"I shall need some more details from you so that I can complete my dossier. Is Wednesday night convenient?"

"Perfect," I said. "Scotland Yard?"

"Your apartment, I think."

"I'll take the phone off the hook this time. Dossiers should never be disturbed."

"About eight?" I nodded and watched as she walked away.

Definitely champagne, I thought — cliché or not. To start, a shrimp bisque with sherry then perhaps a slice of salmon with a nugget of lobster buried in it and covered with shreds of fresh-cut julienne vegetables. Now, for the main course . . .